The Yellow Doll

For our #1
electric MAN!

Thank you!

David Som
(AKA Wild Bill)

The Yellow Doll

DEADWOOD, HICKOK, AND OPIUM

A Historical Novel
by

DAVID A. SOMA

ISBN: 978-1-4269-6839-6 (sc)
ISBN: 978-1-4269-6840-2 (hc)
ISBN: 978-1-4269-6841-9 (e)

Library of Congress Control Number: 2011907048

Trafford rev. 05/05/2011

 www.trafford.com

North America & international
toll-free: 1 888 232 4444 (USA & Canada)
phone: 250 383 6864 ♦ fax: 812 355 4082

Introduction

General Crook's Proclamation, 1875
Ordering the Miners to Leave
the Black Hills

Proclamation

The president of the United States has directed that no miners or other unauthorized citizens shall be allowed to remain in the Indian reservation of the Black Hills or in the unceded territory to the West until some new treaty arrangements have been made with the Indians.

By the same authority, the undersigned is directed to occupy said reservation and territory with troops and to remove all miners or other unauthorized citizens who may be now or may hereafter come into this country in violation of the treaty obligations. Therefore, the undersigned hereby requires every miner or unauthorized citizen to leave the territory known as the Black Hills, the Powder River, and Bighorn Country by or before the fifteenth day of August next. He hopes that the good sense and law-abiding disposition of the miners will prompt them to obey this order without compelling a resort to force …

(SGD) George Crook
Brigadier General USA
Com'd'g Dept. of the Platte
Camp Crook DT
July 29, 1875

Chapter 1

June 28, 1876

The British can march around better than most, and on the hundredth anniversary of their colony's revolt, their parade was unrivaled by any grand march of the Army of the Potomac down Massachusetts Avenue. England's little toehold in America was a few acres of land where its legation house was located on the outskirts of the federal city. It was a chunk of land squeezed by a thicket of trees on the west—quite popular with local hunters—and on the east by a large vegetable garden that supplied most of Washington's flourishing eating establishments with its pick of the day.

Niles got himself so caught up watching the British celebrate the setting sun. He slipped the note that he found in the folds of his napkin into his vest pocket to read later, away from the crowd surrounding the parade ground. If the note were his instructions, he was not about to share them with anyone who might be tempted to sneak a peek over his shoulder—or worse yet, ask him outright what was on the paper, at which point, Niles Dewy would have to lie, which was something he would rather put off.

At the precise appointed hour near the end of the day when it was best to bow to the fading, golden light at His Majesty's outposts scattered across the empire, the flag was lowered to a flourish of military music, shouting of orders, and precise parade formations. These formations were executed by polished brigades of soldiers, who had been arriving in Washington from the far corners of the world all summer long in preparation for just this moment. For the English, all of this pomp was proof that the sun would never set on their empire and that British civility still existed, despite the Americans' declaration to the contrary. A summer sunset ruled the length of the Potomac River valley, displaying strips of orange and pink pinned to a humidity-washed blue sky.

It had been quite a spectacle.

Not until after the sun had set did the British Empire really get down to the business of impressing the great-grandchildren of those long-ago revolutionaries with the spoils of the empire. Besides bringing in a small army of soldiers for the parade, the English offered a buffet furnished by the British Royal Navy's supply line.

There were eggs the size of cannonballs from its Australian colony, along with roasts as big as a Buffalo hump of dark, rich meat from the birds that laid them.

There was a concoction of spices from India called curry, flavored beef strips, chicken pieces, and vegetables.

There were salted and dried fish of every size, color, and description from the oceans of the world.

There was roast lamb and mutton stews that were the pride of the Scottish highlands.

Wild geese, venison, and bear were provided by the Hudson Bay Company in Canada.

There were Scottish-sired eggs by the barrel.

There were plenty of drinks made with rum, limes, and sugar from the Caribbean, and there were bananas and other fruits with no names from far-flung island holdings.

There were also wild game dishes from their African colonies best left unknown by the evening's distinguished gathering of diners.

British navy vessels and dozens of British merchant ships had been arriving at the Bladensburg docks on the Maryland side of the District of Columbia, stoking the legation with all of the finest that the empire had to offer.

"Did you enjoy the ceremony, Mr. Dewy?" The waiter, wearing a stiff, high-necked white tunic, was a small person with dark, almond-shaped eyes and a long, black, braided queue. He offered a silver tray of rum and sugar-filled glasses.

Before answering, Niles looked around at the people nearest them, and then he leaned forward and whispered so that no one could easily hear, "I can't imagine the sort of party you all would have thrown if you'd beaten our revolutionary butts a hundred years ago."

"Ah," the waiter quietly replied, tucking a wide smile beneath a bow. "The British are not me, Mr. Dewy. Rubee is Chinese … I simply provide my services."

"And it is always a pleasure to be served by such a distinguished Chinese." Then, leaning even closer to the waiter, he said, "Thanks for the invitation." He bowed and smiled with appreciation.

"Pleasure is mine, Mr. Dewy," Rubee replied, bowing at the waist again before moving across the lawn to a group of ladies looking a bit wilted in the capital city's June swelter.

Niles wandered from the crowd, smiling over the little exchange he had just had with the waiter. He marveled at how so much could be said by saying so little. Like spring rains, winter snow, and falling leaves, summer was the time for Niles Dewy. And as far as he was concerned, summer was the best time to make pictures; it was the most profitable of all seasons.

Dewy was a name Rubee had devised. Really, it was Dui in Chinese, a word for the western point on the compass, a place where happiness was supposed to dwell. It was the name that Rubee used for signaling when they were about to embark on another journey. Using it tonight meant that they would soon be in pursuit of that happiness.

Niles Dewy had come to life once again.

When he was a comfortable distance away from the crowd, he stopped in a pocket of evening cool trapped under a giant oak. From there, he could watch the affair and Rubee moving among the guests, offering fresh beverages. Other than Niles's gaze, little attention was paid to the waiter. Most guests simply took their refreshments from Rubee's tray, ignoring the person offering it. Even from this distance, he could see that the smile on Rubee's face was one of humble pleasure. He suspected that Rubee's pleasure was found in some kind of anonymity. To be unseen was a quality of this Chinese, one he had come to appreciate. It was also one of the reasons why they had become partners.

Later, inside the legation in search of some of those fruits of the empire, he spotted his friend again. Rubee had traded the silver tray for a station at one of the buffet tables, flashing a set of carving knives over a glistening, roasted-to-perfection baron of beef.

Rubee handed him a small porcelain plate, holding a neat mound of thinly sliced beef and a fresh roll carefully tucked against the edge of the meat. The plate rested on a large linen napkin neatly pressed into a stiff square.

"Soon, Mr. Dewy," Rubee said, bowing again as Niles walk away.

"My wish also," Niles said, saluting a corner of the napkin against his brow. In doing so, he felt something inside the napkin. At first, he thought that it was some of the napkin's starch. No. There definitely was something in the folds of the napkin. Not until he was outside again and sitting alone on a stone wall at the edge of the parade ground did he unfold the linen and find the paper. Niles pulled the slip out and found the message from Rubee. The note, written in Rubee's careful penmanship, told him the date and time that a livery would pick up his baggage—July 6, two days after the nation's centennial celebration.

He had a week to prepare for a journey—one that it seemed he was always ready for. He had come to expect Rubee's annual summer engagements. They got him out of the federal city during the worst parts of summer and made him a rich man in the process. He had never backed out of one of the offers to travel, never giving a second thought to what was ahead.

And this trip would be no different. Rubee's annual engagements provided Niles Dewy with dozens of wet-plate photographs—frames of people, places, and events for which the East Coast tabloids were willing to pay. But Niles would never sell his work.

The profit from Rubee's endeavors made existence in the capital city a comfortable one.

"May I sit?"

The questioner this time was not the waiter. No. This time, the person doing the asking was a beautiful young woman. She did not wait for his answer before hoisting herself onto the stone wall next to him.

"Be my guest," Niles answered, sliding off the stones to stand.

"I've been watching you all evening, Mr. ...?" she asked, injecting a long pause and waiting for him to fill the silence.

"Dewy, madam." He said it slowly enough to allow himself enough time to look around to see if one of the gentlemen perhaps was searching for the lady he had arrived with. For now, it appeared that no one seemed to care.

"Dewy? Is that a first name?" she asked, looking him square in the eyes.

"Niles—"

"Miles," she interrupted. "Like in far away?"

"No. *N* like in *no*. Niles ... Niles Dewy."

"Well, Mr. Dewy, it is nice that you are someone who knows how to say no. It can be so difficult sometimes. And you are also a man who doesn't show how hot he really is in this horrid weather. You stay dry."

"It's not easy, believe me. I can't imagine how you must feel with all of those clothes on. Well, I mean ..." He felt the blush rise up his cheek.

The woman smiled, nodding her head. "It is hot."

"Excuse me, but have we met before?"

"No, I'm sure not. I go to many of these things. So, to amuse myself, I play a game. I pick someone out of the crowd and watch him or her all night. It's fun."

"Good. I think people should have fun."

"That's why you caught my eye. I've been watching you," she said, tilting a mischievous smile his way. In a low voice, leaning closer, she told him, "And so far, the only person I've seen you talk with, Mr. Dewy, is one of the waiters."

"I happen to know the waiter."

"Interesting. How would a man of your stature," she said, giving Niles a look from head to foot, "know a Chinaman?"

"I shot him once."

She was very good at not letting what he had just said break her composure. "What do you do, Mr. Dewy?"

"I'm a shooter."

"Oh my," she said, covering her mouth with her gloved hands. "Are you a gunfighter, Mr. Dewy?" she whispered.

"No, no, no, sorry," he apologized. "I'm a photographer. I shoot photographs, Miss …?"

"Sarah Culbert," she answered, offering her hand in introduction. "Well, I am glad to know that you are not mixed up with guns … such dreadful things. Don't you agree?"

"Well, they can be useful."

"That is a dangerous answer, Mr. Dewy."

"Sometimes it can get a bit dangerous making photographs."

"So, have you taken any pretty pictures lately?"

"I may have made a few, but I'm certain that none are as pretty as the picture you would make, Miss Culbert."

"You're full of it, aren't you, Mr. Dewy?"

"Yes, I am." This Sarah Culbert was asking too many questions, so he returned the favor, hoping that she would rather talk about herself instead of asking questions about him. "What is a Sarah Culbert?"

"Daughter of Congressman Culbert," she answered, still resting her eyes on his face. "She is bored and not fond of heat or Washington."

"Well, then, this would seem a fine place to be for one who is bored and overheated," he joked, waving at the many guests wandering about the legation's grounds.

"Why haven't I seen you before at one of these Washington affairs, Mr. Dewy?" Her smile certainly left the impression that she truly was disappointed that their paths had not crossed before.

"I apologize for such an oversight, Miss Culbert. This isn't exactly my usual circuit. And I often travel during the summer months. Perhaps that's why—"

"How exciting!" she interrupted. "Traveling. I'm going to do more of it myself," she declared, and then she leaned closer. "I want to see the frontier out west. Maybe as far as California."

"That's far from Washington. I haven't been that far. Not yet, anyway."

"We haven't made it yet, either. I'll let you in a little secret," she whispered, leaning close to Niles's ear. "Father comes to all of these embassy parties hoping to receive an invitation to tour their country and the continent someday," she whispered. "Have you ever been there, Mr. Dewy?"

"No, not the European continent. Only this one," he told her, rising off his seat on the stone wall. "Would you excuse me, Miss Culbert?"

"Maybe we will meet again, Mr. Dewy. Perhaps during next week's Independence Day celebration?"

"I don't think that will be possible," Niles told her, feeling a twinge of guilt when he caught another hint of disappointment in her eyes. He bowed his good-byes and began moving away.

"Such a shame, Mr. Dewy," she said, returning his smile. "Someday, I would like to see your photographs," she added as she slipped off the wall. "I could see them tonight if you allowed."

"It is getting late. Maybe some other time."

She watched Niles's face. "You give me one excuse. That is not good enough for Sarah Culbert. Come on," she said, taking a hold of his arm. "Do you have your own carriage, or will we have to hire a taxi?"

"Taxi."

With a firm grip on his hand, she guided them through the guests to the front of the legation, where they found lines of carriages in wait. A group of taxis had reined their horses directly across from where Niles and Sarah walked out.

"Taxi!"

Niles found it hard to speak. He was in shock over what had happened in the last twenty minutes. Here he was being taken by a woman to his townhouse to look at his work. Niles was one who seldom entertained guests. Nobody came to his home except for maybe a subject he had photographed earlier coming by to see how the plate had developed. It was a fact of life with which he was comfortable living. The night was humid, but that was not the reason Niles was sweating.

"Tell the driver your address," she told him as she was climbing into the cab.

Even in shock, Niles was still polite, holding her arm for support as she maneuvered the buggy's tiny step halfway between the ground and the carriage door. Niles did as she said and then set himself next to her on the small leather seat. "You certainly have an interesting way of getting things done."

"Interesting?" Miss Culbert asked.

Niles wished that he could study her features, but the dark shadows inside the cab prevented him from doing so. He decided that it was better to fill the darkness with conversation. "I hope my work is not disappointing. It's not organized. I make a lot of plates, and I don't really sell them. Most of the plates line the walls on the floor. I'd hang them from the ceiling if I could."

"It won't be disappointing, Mr. Dewy. I'm looking forward to this." It was a short ride from the legation to Niles's home, yet it was long enough for Niles to learn that Miss Culbert was from somewhere in the Carolinas and from some small town that he had never heard of. Her father had made it all the way from that Carolina hamlet to Washington, where he now lived with his daughter. That was the end of her story.

"So that it can't be said that you brought me here, I'll pay for the ride."

"Thank you. But I think I can handle any raised eyebrows we may cause."

"Please, I insist; it will make me feel better. That way, I know I am not being bought. Does that make you feel better?"

In the light of the streetlamps along his street, Niles could clearly see the look on her face. He felt that she was showing smugness, almost a power. Maybe it was just downright stubbornness. Whatever it was, Sarah Culbert had a definite way of controlling her circumstances.

From the first exposure she looked at, she seemed to be quite pleased with his work, almost overwhelmed with some of them. They quickly settled into a pattern, going through the hundreds of prints that filled the sitting room, dining room, and the vestibule where they had entered. There was one of the Chinese workmen all stopping their rail-laying work for that one instant to look at the cameraman, and there was another of a Negro boy, maybe twelve or thirteen years of age, sitting alone on wooden steps.

"Where did you find her?" she asked, picking out one of the plates on the floor leaning against a wall. It was a picture of a Negro woman who had stopped her work in a garden. With hoe in hand, she waited for the camera.

"Down by the Potomac. That's her garden. She grows vegetables for the restaurants downtown. I would venture a guess that you have eaten some."

Niles had been able to watch Miss Culbert while they looked at the pictures. She was not a tall woman, shorter than Niles's six feet. She had brown hair, which, for the evening, was pulled away from her face. He guessed her age to be in the late twenties.

Well past midnight, the two were still looking at sepia-tinted pictures of miners, Indians, Confederate soldiers missing arms and legs, bartenders in front of saloons, and a series of several plates showing buffalo skinners at work—all the sort of people that Niles found on his travels with Rubee. Sarah was particularly delighted over some photographs that he had taken at a Chinese New Year celebration of two Chinese women wearing beautiful, traditional gowns. But a short time later, they found one of a mortician standing beside his hearse, which made her cringe away. She used the opportunity to take a break from the viewing. She decided that the divan in the center of the room was a fine place to sit.

"You're very good, Mr. Dewy."

"That's very kind of you to say, Miss Culbert." His smile convinced her that he was serious.

"I think, if we are together in your home this late at night, it would be all right if you called me Sarah."

"Thank you, Sarah," he said, joining her on the divan on the end opposite from where she sat. "Please feel free to call me Niles."

"Is that really you?"

That question left him speechless. "It's close enough," he told her, realizing the moment he said it that it sounded as if he were revealing a deceit.

He must have appeared stunned. "All I meant was that you strike me as a gentleman with many identities, Niles. Artistic identities, understand?"

Niles stared at his guest, wondering what he had gotten himself into—and so near his departure. Quiet seemed appropriate. Watching her every move, he congratulated himself, though, on his ability to convince the woman of Niles Dewy's photographic career. That was the way it was supposed to work as long as his other professions remained unknown in the federal city.

Chapter 2

July 5, 1876

The headline across the top of every newspaper being read on the B&O station platform was the same: CUSTER MASSACRE.

News of the battle had just reached the East, putting a damper on the revelers returning from the centennial celebration that had taken place in Philadelphia two days before. Horses, steamboats, and telegraphs had taken twelve days to get the news of the disaster from the Montana Territory to the federal city. But it had only taken the crowd on the platform several hours to muster up a call for swift action.

"Hunt them down!"

"More cavalry!"

"Arrest the Indians!"

Niles could not help hearing the threats shouted all along the Connecticut Avenue station's platform. The steady chattering bottled up by the pressing crowd sounded like a swarm of birds, each singing a different tune so that only bits of a certain song could be heard at a time.

"Kill …"

"Hang them all …"

"Round them up ..."

But few individuals behind the voices seemed in any hurry to board the next train for the western frontier and stand behind their sword rattling. This crowd, returning to Washington from the Fourth of July festivities, was made up almost entirely of the political class—bureaucrats, politicians, lobbyists, foreign dignitaries—the people who made the government move. Most of these people *were* the government. They were the talking class. Their jobs were to talk. Silence seemed to make them nervous. Maybe quiet threatened their careers. Many of these people in the federal part of the city's life had created themselves to fit into the part of Washington where influence and money led to power. Washington's culture of the well known and self-promoted had proven to be an excellent place for Niles and Rubee to practice their own anonymity.

Niles was already familiar with the Montana Territory where Custer had fallen. Rubee had once taken them up the Missouri River into the Montana Territory. They traveled as far as Fort Benton, the end of the river for steamboats where they were all stopped by the Great Falls of the Missouri. There, the two had conducted business for a couple of months. Niles took photos of the trading post and its visitors, while Rubee conducted trade with the Chinese camp along the edge of the river, upstream from the post. Fort Benton had been the supply post for most of the Montana Territory east of the Rocky Mountains, north to the Milk River, and south to the Yellowstone River. The trading post provided what the prospectors, trappers, and river men needed when they returned to the Montana wilderness. Their selection included luxuries found back in the settlements—sugar, flour, molasses, salt, and dried fruit, as well as the necessities for survival, such as gunpowder, lead, knives, blankets, Indian women, and guns. But the biggest trade in gold and furs was for whiskey. Every drop of the liquor was smuggled hundreds of miles to Benton, which was located deep in the heart of Indian Territory. It was a very illegal and very dangerous endeavor. But it had been a pair of these Fort Benton whiskey peddlers who had allowed Niles to expose a series of photographic plates that could only be made at the end of a road.

Another one of those frontier roads had stranded Rubee and Niles at the end of the bankrupt Northern Pacific Railway, again in Dakota Territory. The company, as well as the tracks, both came to a sudden end. In Minneapolis, the railroad locked its doors, and its tracks stopped on the eastern bluffs of the Missouri River, near its big bend to the south where the channel aimed itself across the Dakota Territory's northern prairie. The river was an expanse of water not soon to be crossed by the railroad. Bankruptcy or not, the tracks would have ended there for some time, anyway. Yet a couple of dozen shacks, tents, sod buildings, and a few tar-papered structures had somehow taken hold near the end of the dead tracks. The only reason it was still able to hang on after the railroad shut down was because of the camp of Chinese coulees leftover from the track-laying construction crew. The settlement's fortune, though, was a couple of miles downriver, where the army had built Fort Abraham Lincoln, the headquarters for the US Army's Seventh Cavalry—George Armstrong Custer's Seventh.

Soldiers from the fort and river men passing up and down the Missouri found food better than their own cooking, plenty of watered-down whiskey, a few whores who got stranded when the railroad gave out, and frontier-wandering gamblers who made a habit of winning their wages. Niles knew that many want-to-be towns had survived on such a foundation. Many others, he could remember, had given up to the wind and loneliness.

The summer that Niles and Rubee found themselves stuck by the collapse of the Northern Pacific Railway was the same summer that a new commandant had taken over command of the fort—Custer himself. While Rubee continued to find a market for his trade, Niles had been invited by Custer to come out to Fort Lincoln with his camera equipment to make a photograph of the post's officers. By the time he and Rubee were on a steamboat leaving the captivity of the high plains, dozens of locals had shown up at their campsite wanting Niles to make their pictures. Some he had, but most were turned down because of the limited number of unexposed plates. Even though he could not take all of their pictures, he was certainly making more money from the ones he sold than the gamblers and whores made combined. But he was not making as much as Rubee, who, for the moment, was the most prosperous resident in the place. When they were back in Washington and Niles was able to take time with his new photographs, he discovered that he felt best about six particular pictures taken of individual army officers and enlisted men. Each had on the best uniforms that could be pieced together, and their hair and beards were freshly trimmed and combed. But it was the way they stood that had caught his eye. They stood erect. Proud. No slouching, no hint of regret that they had been assigned to another outpost at the end of some road.

Niles wondered how many of the men that he had photographed on that trip had been killed at Little Bighorn. "It was the end of your road," he had whispered to himself when he'd first heard of the massacre. Reading this latest dispatch from the Indian wars made him curious where exactly Rubee had planned to take them this year. All that he still knew for certain was what train they were ticketed on.

Niles had arrived early, happy to wait on the platform for Rubee to arrive with their luggage. Resting at Niles's feet were his personal valises and a long bag made of buffalo hide and fur. Rubee would bring the camera equipment, which had been picked up at Niles's home the day before. In addition to the polished wooden cases that carried the delicate photographic plates, chemicals, and black box, Rubee would also bring all of their supplies, including camping and travel gear. There really was only one comfort they both insisted on—a sturdy canvas campaign tent for their living quarters, a second large one for Niles's studio, and a much smaller third one that Rubee used for cooking.

"Are you Mr. Dewy?"

He hated answering to that name, especially when the question came from a stranger. Taking a peek over the edge of the tabloid he was reading, Niles found a tall, thin Negro, a porter according to the blue tunic that he wore. He checked to see if the man was wearing shoes, always the sign of a generously tipped baggage handler. He was—a well-polished pair of black boots that were not exactly new but were taken well care of. Niles guessed that this young fellow was making a good living working the platform. The porter showing up and knowing the right name meant that Rubee had arrived at the station. The time to leave Washington was getting close.

"What are you up to?" Niles asked the Negro.

"My name be George. And this Chinaman over by the loading dock hired George to find you."

"How did you know who to look for?"

"The fur bag."

"Buffalo," Niles added. The bag was tanned hide and still sported long strands from the bull's shoulder cape. Strapped to the side of the bag was a long leather boot holding a Winchester .44–40 rear-sighted, lever-action rifle, which Niles had already loaded.

Niles was satisfied that Rubee had sent the Negro and not someone wanting to waylay their departure. The reason for his cautiousness had arrived along with Rubee.

"Let's go find him," Niles told the porter, and then he reached down to pick up the buffalo bag and a long case leaning against it. George reached at the same time, only to have Niles wave him off. "I carry these two."

"Mr. Dewy, it would not be right for someone to see one of George's customers carrying their own bag. Just wouldn't be right."

"Trust me, it will be all right. I'm going to carry the bag and case. You take the two valises."

"I'm not sure," George said, studying the situation with the careful eye of an experienced baggage handler. "It won't look good for George. When you have a George, you just don't carry your own bags. It ain't right."

Niles rested the leather bag on his knee and unhooked the horn and strap latches. "Come here and take a look," he invited the fellow.

The porter raised back, a bit skeptical about the offer, looking as if he expected to see a bagful of snakes.

"Hurry up. This ain't for everyone to see."

George didn't move a step, but even so, he was able to lean far enough over to see inside the bag. "These are my firearms," Niles said under his breath, also pointing at the narrow, long case sitting on the platform beside him. "I carry my guns."

"That's all you had to say, Mr. Dewy. I understand. Those two be your business." The Negro picked up the two other bags, pointing his customer in the direction in which they would find Rubee, never once quieting down. "George has handled many gentlemen just like you. Their guns were theirs—never let George come near 'em. Soldiers, card men ... one fellow was just back from the wilderness. You know the folks. George never let on that he know'd anything. Besides, if I did, no one would hear."

Even walking behind him, Niles could sense the Negro's sudden shift in mood. The man's shoulders stooped, his head bent down until his chin almost touched his neck, and Niles guessed that if he could see into the man's eyes, he would see sadness.

The Negro straightened slightly, regaining some of his proud posture. "Someday, George'll have hisself a couple of fine guns. Yes, sir. Don't know what George would do with 'em, 'cept he'd have 'em."

Against Niles's better judgment, he asked a question. "What would you do with these guns if you did have them?"

George looked over his shoulder, looking at his customer as if the man were the dumbest person on the platform. "Go out west."

The Negro's answer alerted Niles to a possible danger. He'd better not encourage this fellow with more information than he needed to know—which was nothing at all.

George started parting a path through the press of people, hollering, "Let us through!" Unlike Niles, the porter acted not a bit nervous about attracting attention. "Please move! Excuse us, please." The fellow was just as polite as he could be while toughing the two of them in and out of the crowd—and around them, when possible—always pushing against the mass of travelers clogging the platform. Niles was surprised at how easily their move to the loading dock had been accomplished. George was a good man, at least able to lead him quickly to their train's baggage cars.

"Mr. Dewy!"

Niles heard Rubee right away. He looked quickly in the direction of the voice, and he found his traveling companion not far away, sitting atop the lead of two four-wheeled dollies, both loaded with their baggage. Niles took note that, for this part of the trip, the Chinaman wore a tan suit, a straw topper, and a shirt and tie already limp from Washington's swampy humidity. Another one of the man's traveling accessories also was in place—a pair of green-tinted glasses worn tightly against the bridge of Rubee's nose.

"Have you read the news, Mr. Dewy?" Rubee's first question was the one that everyone else on the platform was asking. "Very interesting, don't you think? I see you have your equipment with you; we may need it."

Niles hefted the buffalo bag over his head and then did the same with the thin wooden case held under his arm. He left the long case on the platform next to his feet. "Shame about Mr. Custer. Don't you think? Sure fortunate we got his picture when we did. Too late now."

Rubee laughed. "Yes, you will make a lot of money now from those pictures."

Niles slowly shook his head at the magic of photography—to have an image of a dead man staring into his camera lens for an eternity. If he had been a religious man, Niles might have believed that only God could make a picture. But Niles was no God, not even a lowly angel. Some people might even consider him the devil himself.

"Other news today is just as interesting, Mr. Dewy." Rubee had already folded one of the tabloid sheets into a neat little square, which he tossed down to Niles. "Read in the corner."

Niles caught the paper, turning it over until he found the article that had caught Rubee's attention. He quickly moved his eyes down the story, seeing what it was about and what made it so interesting to them. The words *gold* and *Black Hills* were enough for him to read. Niles now knew where they were heading this summer. His suspicions had been on the mark; Custer, gold, and the Blacks Hills would have been tough for them to pass up. The news from the Missouri River settlements bordering the Sioux territory reported that a shipment of gold dust had safely made it out of the Black Hills in the Dakota Territory. Apparently, the gold traveled out of the Black Hills first on mule pack and then by wagon caravan, finally going by steamboat down the Missouri. The story explained that the gold was on the last wagons out of the Black Hills before President Grant's executive order closing all freight roads across the Sioux reservation. The miners already in the Black Hills or caught trying to get to them would be considered outlaws. Grant's order might be enforced by troops blocking the main routes into the gold camps—the same route that Niles figured they would follow getting to the Black Hills' outlawed goldfields.

This time out, they might go beyond the end of the road, choosing someplace that legally did not exist. It was exactly the kind of place to which the pair was drawn for their annual business ventures.

The Negro tried to look over Niles's shoulder. "What's the paper say, Mr. Dewy? George never has time to read much."

"It's about gold out west, George."

"That's where you two are headed? Out to find some of that gold? I'll be damned." The Negro knew none of the details about a trip into the territories and was not afraid to hide it. "Them Indians'll kill you two as sure as we all standing here today. Just like they did the general."

Niles lifted the buffalo bag and rattled the contents. "That won't happen, Mr. George. Making sure that doesn't happen is my job."

George was done talking. He enlisted four additional porters and quickly had a chain of men unloading the dollies, transferring the luggage and cases to the baggage car. Some of the cases needed two men to move, while others were small enough that one man could easily carry two. The train's baggage handler tagged every item that came through the car's door. "I'm only tagging you on the first leg of your trip. You will be changing trains!" the man yelled at the Chinaman, scurrying around the dollies and shouting out orders when necessary.

"We understand!" Rubee hollered back over the noise and all of the commotion.

Niles stayed along the fringe of the confusion created by their boarding. He kept track of the loading's progress, but most of his time was spent watching the people jamming the platform around them. Niles's nerves had already taken on a sharper edge now that they were actually on the move. It was healthier for all if he imaged this might be an ideal time for somebody to try taking off with their baggage. That would be unfortunate for Niles's picture making and for Rubee's commerce. From now until they returned to Washington with the summer's profits, Niles knew that their biggest threat would come from thieves, not the law or Indians. The pair had been jumped a time or two on past journeys. Blood had been spilled, and several lives had had to account to Niles's arsenal. So far, they had lost nothing, and Niles and Rubee had always made it back to Washington.

"Mr. Dewy!" A woman hollered for his attention. "Mr. Dewy! Behind you."

Niles did not look, not wanting to encourage whoever she was from calling for him again. Only Rubee and the porter knew the name. How did someone else come to know his name? Who was she?

"Mr. Dewy, are you ignoring me? It is not nice for a gentleman to ignore a lady."

Suddenly, it came to him; Niles recognized the voice. It was Sarah Culbert. When he turned to look for her, he spotted her immediately. She waded through the crowd like a true lady, letting the gentlemen tip their hats and move out of her way, making a path. Behind her, a porter weighed down with her luggage tried to keep up in her wake.

"I am so glad that I found you. The press of all these people made it very difficult."

Niles tipped the brim of his hat. "Miss Culbert, what a surprise for me."

The woman was dressed in a wide hoop dress similar to the one she had worn to the British affair, though it was somewhat less formal. And Niles noticed that, in the light, her face was that of a lady—creamy white with lightly reddened cheekbones. Whatever she was doing here, Niles could tell that she was as cool and in control as she had been the night they'd met.

"You are looking particularly handsome today," she said, making sure that he saw the deliberate study she made of him.

Her attention sharpened his nerves even further, but he was getting used to that reaction when he was around the woman. Besides, he was quite comfortable with his appearance. His hair had been cut a few days before, he had taken a scented bath that morning, and his clothes were clean and pressed. Niles's traveling attire was stylish. His dark frock coat and trousers were made for summer wear, his neckwear was fashionable, his boots were polished, his mustache was trimmed, and his black bowler was brushed. Add a couple of pistol belts, and that would be how he would look for most of the rail trip.

Niles looked around behind the woman to see if someone was looking for her. Everyone in the crowd that he could see was ignoring them. "You're looking wonderful—cool and so fresh on such a steamy day. Are you coming or going?" Niles asked, hoping to move their encounter along.

"Nice of you to ask. I'm coming and going, so to speak. I am coming here to find you, and I am going with you."

Niles did not know what to say. He looked over at Rubee to see if they were being watched.

Miss Culbert followed his gaze and saw Rubee for the first time. "That is the same Chinese from the legation party, isn't it? Are you two traveling together? Won't this be cozy?" Sarah saw the nervousness rise in Niles and thought best to maybe divert the conversation some. "I am just returning from Philly. You know … all of the celebration stuff."

"How was that?" Niles asked, relieved that the subject had changed, giving him a chance to find a way out of the situation.

"Fine dinner parties, brunches, receptions, ceremonies, you know. And Father and I were invited to all of them. But a week of stuffiness is about my limit. You look like the kind of man who could celebrate for a long time if you had something to celebrate."

"As I told you, I don't get many invitations. That's just not my side of town. But I will take your word about the parties. Perhaps later you can tell me all about them, Miss Culbert."

"I thought we had agreed on Sarah."

"Not in public. Not exactly the gentlemanly thing to do … it might be going too far."

"Well, I'm not going to spend the next couple of months being called Miss Culbert."

Niles studied her face for a hint of what she meant. Fear suddenly took grip of his stomach and rolled up his body. He turned to find Rubee, who was now in the baggage car. The dollies were empty. They would soon have to settle into their Pullman compartments. This was no time for surprises. He wanted to be as careful as he could when it came time to ask the next question. "If I might inquire, what exactly do you mean, 'next couple of months'? What are you planning for the rest of the summer?"

"Traveling with you, Niles," she told him as if it already were a well-known fact. "You are going to hear about those parties sooner than you thought."

For the moment, Niles lost all consciousness of the crowd, the trains, and the station. All he could see was Sarah Culbert. She was surrounded by a bright nothingness. Not even sound. Somehow, her image survived being swallowed up by the void. He had never experienced anything like that before. Niles had no control over what was happening. The sensation slowly started retreating, gradually allowing him to gather his senses enough to feel Sarah holding his arm.

"Are you all right, Niles? You look dreadful," she said, her voice calm and gentle.

"It's probably just the heat and humidity. Add all of this commotion and a pretty face, and it made my head spin for a moment."

"You will feel better once we are all settled in and on our way."

"You're not coming with us."

"Oh, yes, I am! Give me one good reason why I shouldn't." She had her arms across her chest, her folded umbrella ready for battle and a cold gaze staring him right in the eyes. Niles had suspected a certain strong headedness during their first meeting. Now he was convinced that Sarah Culbert was not a woman who could be told what to do. As if everything had been settled, she moved on to the next matter. "Where are we going?"

"This is not a trip for you."

"Do you mean just me? Or do you mean that this is not a trip for a woman?"

"I don't think you should make the trip, Sarah. You don't understand. We'll be leaving the train, taking steamboats, and finally using horse and wagon. Nearly everywhere we'll go, we'll have to constantly be ready for thieves, Indians, and even crooked lawmen. There will be dozens of ways you could be hurt. Or killed."

She studied him, appearing to give some thought to what he had said. "Sounds like a challenge. Just what this lady wishes. A challenge. And you certainly are that, Mr. Niles Dewy."

"Sarah, this is not a good idea."

"I think it's a good idea. It's my idea. Not yours. All you need do is accept and enjoy. It'll be fun, Niles. A big adventure."

"Big adventure," Niles said to himself in frustration.

"I have already purchased an open ticket. We will work out the details later." She turned to her porter. "Follow me," she ordered, and Niles watched the woman wade into the crowd, which let her pass with a flourish of tipped hats and appreciative smiles from the men along her path. He knew that he would see her again—no doubt on the train. Now he had to inform Rubee about their traveling companion, but Rubee's news came first.

"Mr. Dewy, our porter, Mr. George, has made an offer which you must consider. He wants to make the journey with us, handle our luggage. Help around camp," Rubee told him. "I have not agreed yet to his offer, nor have I told him where we are going."

"He'll find out soon enough. And I have news for you, my partner. It's a long story, which I will share with you later, but a lady I met at that British affair last week spotted me on the platform and also has decided to travel with us." He hoped that he had made sense.

It was still hard for Niles to understand what had just transpired between him and Miss Culbert, let alone try to explain it.

Niles and Rubee looked at each other, shaking their heads in disbelief. Nothing had to be said between them. Each knew what adding to their entourage meant. In the end, it could at the very least cost them some of their profits and quite possibly even their lives, as well as the lives of their traveling companions. It had always been just the two of them, and they were not fond of change.

"Rubee, I know the woman is not going to take no for an answer. We are probably going to have to put up with her for a while. I'm pretty sure she will tire of our schedule and return. She need find out nothing. We aren't going to open anything up until we're in the Black Hills. And she is not going that far. So maybe no problem." He tried to keep his voice down so that everyone within earshot didn't hear. "George is an easy decision. We say no and be done with him."

Rubee and Niles were the only two left in the baggage car. The train's baggage handler, the extra porters, and George were gone—or *almost* gone. George stood on the platform a polite distance away. Their baggage filled one corner, leaving enough space for Rubee to do a little cooking for them. The rest of that side of the car was stacked high with wooden crates. The other end of the car was a mess of mailbags and passenger luggage, leaving a clearing only around the wide door.

"This is no place for a lady friend. It is not a good idea," Rubee told him.

"I've told her that, but the woman won't listen."

"You must change her mind."

"How? I don't think the lady's mind is in the practice of being changed very often. Who knows? Adding a woman might add to our cover."

Rubee left Niles in the baggage car, going over to their traveling luggage sitting on the platform under George's watchful eye. Before he reached the bags, Rubee turned back to Niles and said, "Maybe partway, but not into Dakota Territory."

"I'll try to explain that to her," Niles replied. He stood in the car's door and watched the crowd. Not one of those people would ever imagine what he and Rubee were slipping right under their noses. Out of the corner of his eye, he saw Rubee point George in his direction. The Sarah Culbert problem seemed to be out of his hands. He could only hope that their trip went reasonably smoothly. So far, the beginning had been a little rough, and now he had to deal with George.

An extra pair of hands would be nice.

Mr. George and Miss Culbert did not know it today, but they might have been inviting their own deaths by tagging along on this trip. Niles and Rubee were always very aware of the invitation they extended every summer, but these two had no idea.

It took the Negro only a few steps to travel the distance to the car where Niles waited. "Mr. Dewy, I want to—"

"Stop right there. This is not a grand tour we are embarking on, Mr. George. This is a business trip. This is work, Mr. George. Work! Do you understand?"

"I'm sure it is, Mr. Dewy. But George got it figured out you are heading west. This is a chance for me to work my way there."

"I don't care about any chances you may or may not have. I only care about the chances we take if you come along."

Niles repeated the arguments he had recently used with Miss Culbert. Separated from family. Wasn't safe. No trains. Custer's massacre. Indians. Highwaymen. Yet each new danger only seemed to excite George even more. All that Niles could do was to explain their return plans to the man.

"And in the end, we are coming right back here to Washington. We are not staying out there," Niles told him. "And I am not so sure that it would even be in our best interests to leave you there. You might want to give it some thought—real quick. You may wish you never met us on this platform, Mr. George. Joining up could be very dangerous. Life threatening. Do you understand?"

The look on George's face turned serious. His jaw tightened, and Niles could see his cheekbones twitching as the Negro ground his teeth. Niles hoped that the fellow had finally gotten the message and that he'd realized that this was not the way west for him.

George acted as stubbornly as Miss Culbert. Niles could almost see the man digging the heels of his boots into the platform timbers. The man stood there saying no with such determination that it twisted his whole body. "If you're trying to scare me off, saying you might shoot George, no, Mr. Dewy, you ain't figured it out. George ain't coming back. Wherever you leave him is his new home."

"George, I'm sorry. I don't want anything to happen to you," Niles said. The porter appeared to accept the decision. His head lowered, and his shoulders sagged. "That's the end of that; you're not coming," he told him. Now on to the Miss Culbert situation.

Just then, Niles heard the lady's familiar voice coming up behind him. "Of course he's coming. You don't expect this lady to do everything herself. Of course he is coming."

"Sarah! I don't want the porter coming. Rubee and I do just fine."

"If you don't take him, I am, Mr. Dewy."

"Sarah, please. It's going to be—"

"Choose your words well. Remember you are a gentleman."

Niles shook his head, his frustration returning all over again. Yet, if she were coming along, he did not want the two of them to start off on the wrong foot. "It's just that it is going to be a bit awkward. That's all. Just awkward."

"As well for me, Mr. Dewy. I am not accustomed to traveling with three men."

Niles was out of patience. He picked up his valise and buffalo bag and then turned to go find their Pullman accommodations. "Later, I am sure, Miss Culbert," he said, dipping the brim of his hat slightly. After a few steps, he stopped and snapped around, startling George so much that the fellow jumped. Pointing right at him, Niles issued his first order. "If you're coming on this trip, you're going to have to learn how to use a gun. Learn to shoot. Shoot to kill. Trust me, you'll need it."

Chapter 3

"Sit down, chink!"

"I can explain," Rubee said.

"You can't explain shit. Now sit down and shut up. Nigger, we don't allow train jumpers in this town. You're going straight to jail."

"He is not!" Sarah Culbert had stayed quiet long enough. She had kept her mouth shut ever since the sheriff had hoisted himself into the baggage car for an inspection.

Finished with cuffing George, the sheriff turned his attention toward Sarah. "Now you had something to say. But I'll warn you right off, unless you can tell me some reason you ain't a whore, you better keep your mouth shut." The sheriff left George standing in the middle of the car, his chained hands resting on his belly. There was a smile on the lawman's face that Sarah did not like. It was not a sweet smile greeting her. It was a lust-fired grin, the kind that contorted the man's face as he studied her.

Sarah got herself backed against the car's wooden side, with the passenger baggage on one side and the open door on the other. The sheriff pushed himself closer, blocking her vision with his broad body. She could smell the sour stench on the man's breath when he asked, "Do you have any idea what the price is for a whore to pass through my jurisdiction?"

"Sir, if you are an officer of the law, then act like a gentleman!" Sarah was ready to show her own determination, shoving him away the best she could and then pointed a steady, anger-stiffened finger at George. "And this man is in my employ."

"Classy. But that proves nothing, 'cept maybe you're a rich whore. Besides, if you're so fancy with a nigger boy and all, why you riding in the baggage car? They throw you out of fine folks' accommodations?"

Sarah made her decision. "How much money do you want?" she asked, drawing a little closer to the sheriff's face. Her eyes were unblinking as she stared into his. Her clenched teeth ground back and forth, which in turn flexed her cheek muscles. And when she spoke again, her voice did not waver. "If I can pay the fines, will you let us go? The train is leaving soon. So if I can take of this business, we will be on our way."

"That's a good idea, lady. But I'm afraid money won't pay your fine. It'll take something a little more personal."

Sarah remained close to the man's face and then did something very unladylike; she spit right in his face. And she didn't miss. She hit her target square on, leaving a dribble of saliva running down the sheriff's left cheek. "Is that personal enough for you, Sheriff?"

The lawman went into a hollering rage. He grabbed for her hair but instead got a hold of the straps on her dress, ripping them and uncovering her shoulders. "When I'm done with you, you'll wish you were a whore," he said, pushing his body against hers, this time strongly enough to pin her to the wall of the car. Sarah started kicking and screaming, kicking the man any place the toe of her shoe could reach, slugging whenever his grip loosened on her shoulders, at the same time hollering a string of curses in his face.

George used Sarah's attack to make one long-legged step, putting him right behind the sheriff. With one hand, the sheriff held Sarah by the throat, and with the other, he drew his revolver and turned enough to aim. "Move away, nigger, or something might happen to missy here!"

George stepped back helplessly.

"All aboard! All aboard!" The conductor walked along the length of the train getting his passengers back inside. He stopped to check inside the open door of the baggage car. "Train's leaving in a couple of minutes, folks," he said, unaware of what was happening. Then he saw George with his hands cuffed and the sheriff with his gun drawn.

"I'm Sheriff Bill Clay," the sheriff said to the conductor. "You're in my jurisdiction. May I ask you if these people are ticketed on this train?"

The conductor moved his head farther into the car to get a better look. "They are," he confirmed.

"Where did they get on?" Clay asked.

"That I can't say. They were on board already when I started my shift. Is there something wrong here, Sheriff?"

"All that proves is that you ain't a stowaway, nigger," Clay said, motioning George toward him. With his free hand, he unlocked the handcuffs, and then, with a wave of his pistol toward the door, he said, "Now get the hell out of here."

Sarah straightened her dress around its bodice where Sheriff Clay had torn it. "Sir, this man attacked me, and I'm going with my man, George," she announced, starting for the baggage car's doorway. "I refuse to spend one more minute with such a vulgar man. Mr. George, will you help me down, please?"

"You stay!"

"Why should I have to?"

"Because I say so, that's why. And this is official business to ensure that justice is served."

Sarah pointed an angry finger at the sheriff. "What is wrong with you? I am not staying. The only justice you are planning to serve is what is in your pants, not that badge you are wearing on your chest."

The sheriff ignored her, turning instead to the conductor. "I have reason to believe, sir, that these people are involved in some kind of illegal activity. I have been notified that they may have contraband, and that is why I checked the baggage car first before contacting you. Can you hold up the train while I do a thorough search of their luggage?" he asked.

"That is completely out of the question, Sheriff Clay. This train is already late, and I'm not going to add further delays because you have a hunch. I can tell you this—since I came aboard, all of them have been polite, showing not one sign of doing anything against the law. No. I can't allow you to hold up this train. We're leaving," the conductor explained.

"I understand," Clay agreed. "But may I stay on board at least until the next stop to have an opportunity to search their luggage?"

"Only until the next stop," the conductor answered. "After that, you need a ticket like everyone else."

"Thank you. Now like I was saying, nigger, you can leave with the conductor. The two of you stay here. I may have some questions for you."

Chapter 4

Several of the polished cases already sat open and empty. Tripod legs, developing trays, bottles and cans of chemicals, and other parts of the photography business cluttered the floor. Clay emptied each case, checking every small compartment and tray divider inside. He was too busy with the cases—tapping and knocking at the wooden sides, tops, and bottoms—to pay attention to Rubee or Sarah.

Sarah had been watching the sheriff's antics long enough. And when she nudged Rubee, she was answered with a shrug. Even if it attracted the sheriff's attention, she had to say something. Sarah had run out of silence. "What are you looking for?"

That was enough to draw the sheriff away from his search. "I don't know what you're hiding, but something hid, I'm sure, and if you're not telling, then I have to look for it myself," Clay said, and then he teased the two with a sorrowful expression. "Hope nothing gets damaged," he added. But it was clear from the way he said it and the way he conducted the search that being careful was not his way.

Despite the agreement he had made with Niles, Clay was not using Rubee to help go through the cases. He was looking through each case himself, one at a time, taking everything out of the case, no matter what was found inside, leaving Rubee sitting beside Sarah and watching as the man juggled the equipment. So far, nothing had been found or damaged.

"Let Rubee help, at least. It will speed up this pointless search."

"I got time. You should hope it takes me time," he told her. The strange smile she witnessed earlier had returned. "When I'm done here, we have something to finish," he said before going back to his search of the case.

"I'll know then what you're looking for, Mr. Clay," Sarah said, flirting with her voice and in her eyes. Clay was no dumb man; he knew when to pay attention.

"Now what do you suppose that would be, little lady?"

"Whiskey?"

The sheriff snapped his fingers and then slapped his hands together. "That, too! I knew you were all up to something. Whiskey runners. That's what I got myself here, ain't it? A gang of whiskey smugglers."

"No, Sheriff, that is not exactly what Miss Sarah meant." It was Rubee who had finally spoken.

"What, then, you damn chink? What the hell do you know?" Clay threatened, drawing his pistol to wave at the Chinaman.

"Leave Rubee alone."

"Easy to do, 'cause I'm going to be alone with you," Clay said, taking a step toward Sarah.

She ignored the man's advance, keeping her own plan on track. "My husband carries a personal case along whenever he travels. Fewer complications, he claims."

"That's it. One case of whiskey." In a near panic, Clay turned his back on the two and confronted the pile of cases and luggage still piled against the wall. "Which one is it?"

Sarah questioned Rubee before answering, getting a smile and an approving nod. Rubee had a pretty good idea of what she was up to, and it would definitely help.

"The one in the middle, near the top," Sarah told him, pointing at the case she was describing.

Clay immediately scrambled over the baggage, taking no care at all where he stepped, until he was able to grab the handle of the case Sarah had pointed out. Pulling the case with one and still holding the pistol in the other, he stumbled his way back to the open floor space. "Stay put," he threatened, waving the gun at them again. The lock was easy to open. Looking inside, the sheriff's smile turned into a grin. "Just like you said, lady."

"Tennessee whiskey."

"The best," Rubee added.

"Shut up! You're still hidin' something. What is it?" His pistol waved back and forth between Sarah and Rubee. "Don't think getting me drunk's goin' to help you jack shit." He picked one of the bottles, broke the wax seal, and then twisted the cork. He took a tentative sip at first, making sure that it was what it was supposed to be, and then he tipped the bottle back, taking a long drink.

Sarah and Rubee smiled at each other, pleased with what they had accomplished so far.

After sundown, the sheriff lit the car's kerosene lamp so that he could continue. He was half through the cases and had just finished his first bottle of Niles's liquor. Up to that point, he had yet to find anything but photographic instruments, just as everyone had told him. The whiskey began to slow him down, jumbling his search, which made Rubee more nervous that the sheriff would drop and break a case.

But when Clay began knocking his knuckle against the inside bottom of one of the larger cases he had emptied, his liquored senses noticed a difference in the sound. He carefully listened to his knocks, trying different parts of the bottom. He lifted the case, testing its weight, and then he turned the box upside down to tap the bottom. It made the same sound as the inside.

"This is hollow," he said, somewhat amazed at his own discovery. So was Rubee. Sarah had no idea what was going on. Clay studied the brass fixtures and joints holding the box together, giving each one a close look, sliding his fingers along the edges and looking for a way to get in.

"I'll betcha there's a phony bottom." He examined the case again, top to bottom. "I don't suppose you'd tell me how to get in, would you, chink?" Clay's speech had a slur that had not been there before, and Rubee noticed that Clay found it difficult to balance himself against the car's sway.

Clay put the empty case down on the floor so that he could get another bottle of whiskey, and then he walked circles around the case, time after time, looking it over while he sipped out of the new bottle. He managed to get himself dizzy, and he slumped against the stack of bags. After sitting for a while, he shook off the whiskey's effect and returned to the box again, reexamining the case's interior, turning his back to Sarah and Rubee.

Rubee used the opportunity to poke Sarah's arm to get her attention. When she looked, Rubee held a finger to his lips. "I will take care," He slipped into the car's shadowed corner across from them. It was hard for her to see what Rubee was doing, so Sarah simply kept an eye on the sheriff. When she heard the voice, she was expecting to see Rubee.

"You picked the wrong one of us as the whore."

The sheriff was as surprised as Sarah was to see who walked out of the shadows.

It was a naked Chinese woman whose color against the dark shadows was a golden tone. Straight black hair fell over her shoulders and the tops of her breasts. Her hands held a long, silver tube, offering it to the sheriff. Nothing would distract the sheriff as he watched her approach. Sarah used the chance to crawl into the corner behind her, curling up and trying to feel safe. She decided that this was not the time to know what was going on.

Sheriff Clay was not sure what to do. "I thought you were a fellow. What the hell's goin' on here?"

The woman stopped near the sheriff. "This is what's going on," she said, slowly reaching over to hold the sheriff's hand. Carefully, she moved his hand to her breast and pressed the man's palm against her. Leaving their hands where they were, she began moving the man toward a cushion of luggage. "Here," she said, guiding him to a seat. He sat, looking back and forth at where his hand was and the nude woman.

"Where'd ya come from?"

"Shh, we answer questions later," she whispered, holding a finger to her lips. "Let's do this right. The Yellow Doll's way."

"The yellow what?"

She straddled the man's lap, moving closer to his face as she sat down. Clay moved his free hand to grab the other breast being offered. The silver pipe was laid in the cradle made when she pressed against the man's hips, freeing both her hands to pull his face closer. She began nuzzling Clay's cheek and then moved her kisses down his face until she was able to rub her hair against his neck.

"Have you ever had a China lady?" she whispered in his ear.

Clay was getting too busy to answer. He grabbed her by the shoulders and lifted her body up and down against his groin a few times. The final time she was pumped down, she clamped her knees to stay in place and began rotating her hips against Clay so that he would stop the rough stuff. "I can feel you understand how to do it the Yellow Doll's way," she said as she pushed her breasts into his chest. That was an invitation for the sheriff, who began to move the woman so that he could get at his pants. Again, she clamped down, stopping his try. "No, no. Not yet. First, have a smoke. That is the way of the Yellow Doll. You'll find out what I mean," she told him, grinding her hips more slowly but a little harder against his crotch.

The sheriff showed a brief look of suspicion, but it was not enough to deny him. "Hell, give me the pipe. I'm ready to smoke up a storm." Sheriff Clay had to let go of one of her breasts to hold the end of the pipe between his lips. He watched the woman use the lantern to set fire to a twig and then hold the flame against the other end of the pipe.

"Breathe," she encouraged him. He filled his mouth with smoke only to begin choking and coughing, spewing a gray cloud everywhere. When he caught his breath, he asked, "What is this stuff?"

"Try again," she encouraged. "Not so much this time."

"This ain't tobacco, is it?"

"Try."

Clay tried again, taking little puffs that he could draw into his lungs instead of one big one.

"That's right," she told him, showing her approval by increasing the pressure of her rotations. "Once more, and I think we are ready. How about you, Sheriff? Are you ready?"

"Let me take my pants—" he said, squirming to get at them, but his arms fell to his sides like weights were attached.

"Soon," she whispered, holding the flame to the end of the pipe one more time.

He was unable to resist, inhaling the smoke once again.

Clay stopped.

The pipe was taken away, and he was gently pushed back to lie across the bags. His eyes stared at nothing in particular, and his breathing was slower and much deeper. Finally, the muscles in his face relaxed. The woman waited beside him until his eyes finally blinked closed, and then she crawled off his lap and moved to the open door.

"Niles!"

At first, all they could see was his head as he hung over from the top of the car above the door. "May I come in now?"

But nobody answered; they just weren't in the humorous mood. Niles had a grip on an iron rod decorating the top of the train car. Using that to secure himself, he slid his feet down the inside of the open freight door until they found one of the hinges. From there, it was a matter of sliding from hinge to hinge down the doorframe to the floor like using a rope ladder.

"I would tip my hat, Miss Culbert, but I left it in the room." Niles let the words *Miss Culbert* sink in. "It could get blown away, you know. Out here, the wind and desperados might blow it away. Must be careful now, right, Miss Culbert?" He hollered to be heard over the noise of the train.

Sarah was so angry seeing him show up this late that she paced around the car's open space. "Thank you for all of your protection, Mr. Gunslinger."

"Looks to me like everything was handled just fine without Mr. Dewy shooting anybody." Niles looked at the sheriff's mess and began picking up the pieces and righting cases while he talked. "What would we have done if I'd had to shoot a lawman?" he asked, stopping his work for a moment while he waited for her answer. "This works," he finally said so that he would not waste any more time.

"You two have done this before, haven't you?" she questioned both of them.

"It has worked before, Miss Culbert. Sorry you were here to see it work this time," the Chinese woman apologized. "Thank you for your help."

"What help? I kept my clothes on!"

"Setting Sheriff Clay up with the whiskey."

"Well, all right," she said, accepting both the apology and the thank you. "You're right; I was involved."

After several hours of fear, Sarah still had to burn off some anger. Niles was her target. "What's all this talk about Mrs. and Mrs. Dewy?"

"Oh, I hope you don't mind," he interrupted.

Sarah blushed, kind of swayed back and forth. "Well, I kind of liked that idea. All right," she confessed, and then she immediately stormed away from Niles like she wished she had never said it. "You're acting like some snake coiled up under a rock, and I'm not in the mood to get myself bit."

It was no time to get into a talkfest with the woman, so Niles tried to pay no attention to what she was saying. He did use the opportunity when she paused to catch her breath to tell her what her next assignment was. "Get started on his clothes."

"What?"

"Get those clothes off him. Naked," Niles explained. "I'm certain, Miss Culbert, that this isn't the first time you've undressed a man. Come on; we don't have much time." When she did not move, Niles reminded her, "Now!"

Sarah bent over to pull Clay's boots off. Niles went back to the cleanup, making a mental note that she had not responded to his remark about undressing men. When he looked around, he found her unbuttoning the shirt, ignoring him entirely. It was good enough for Niles. "Rubee, take care of yourself. I'll work on the camera."

"Rubee?" Suddenly, Sarah remembered. "Is he a he, or is he a she, or is she a he? Please help a very confused lady."

"Now you know one of our secrets. Happy?" Niles questioned.

Sarah could see that she was walking on very thin ice with Niles. "Happy … unhappy … what are all of the big secrets? I am just confused and would like to know if I am traveling with a man or a woman. Hells bells, the next thing I know, you're going to have rouge on your face."

"Only if I get too close to you."

"Don't even think it!"

"You're right; now is not the time. Get back to work," he told her.

Rubee returned from the car's shadows again looking like Niles's manservant. The camera tripod was waiting for the camera to be mounted, and Sheriff Clay was minus boots and socks, shirt, pistol belt, and the top half of his long underwear.

Niles had taken the belt and draped it over his shoulder like a bandoleer. "Don't stop there," he said, urging Sarah. "You haven't finished." When they had the camera box mounted, the hood attached, and the glass plate inserted, he finally checked to see if Sheriff Clay was ready. He was ready. Sarah had left him lying on top of the luggage in a twisted mess with his arms and legs going in four different directions. It was not a very pleasing picture in Niles's opinion.

"Rubee," Niles called, motioning to the body.

The problem was quickly fixed. Now the sheriff was flat on his back, head propped up, arms stretched wide, and his legs spread so that nothing could be hidden.

"Hold the flash tray," Niles ordered Sarah. "Hold it by the handle. Turn your face away when we're ready. Wouldn't want you to singe those lovely eyebrows or catch your hair on fire." Niles made a few more adjustments, slipped under the hood, and hollered, "Ready!"

The flash powder ignited, catching the Illinois sheriff's nude body on the plate. Niles reached from under the canvas, took the plate's sleeve from Rubee, and secured the exposed plate inside it.

"We're set." That was all that Niles had to say. Rubee knew the routine. They had packed the camera gear many times, and the two quickly had the instruments in the proper cases, stacking them back in the corner of the car as though they had never been disturbed.

"Time to go," Rubee announced.

"Go? I'm tired of not knowing what's going on," Sarah told them. She sat on one of the larger cases. "Kindly tell me what it is we are doing next."

Rubee moved to stand beside her. "We are going to crawl up to the roof and move to our compartments," Rubee told her. Where we will stay."

"Roof! Now wait just one cotton-picking minute—"

"We have very few minutes. This train's about to make its next stop," Niles said, cutting her off as he started climbing up the doorframe. "I'll go first and give you hand!" he yelled over all the train noise.

"Thank you, but no, thanks. I grew up with brothers and have been dared to do riskier."

"Have it your way, but I'll be up there if you need me."

"You're next," Rubee said, giving Sarah a gentle nudge toward the door.

She took the hint. She swung her skirt out of the way and began following Niles's route. She carefully used the hinges as steps like Niles had, and it was easy for her smaller fingers to find handholds along the door's edge. When she was close enough, Niles reached down to give her a hand, and now that she was hanging out the door of a moving train, Sarah decided that it was best to accept the help. Using Niles's grip to pull herself up, she got a hold of the car's roof railing, and with Niles's help, she pulled herself up onto the roof of the baggage car.

"What about him?" she asked, pointing down into the car.

"He'll be taken care of in the morning." Niles made a pretty good guess what her next question would be, so he quickly cut her off. "We stay in our cabins!" He yelled so that Sarah could hear. "George's there already."

Rubee's last task was to spill some of the whiskey over Clay's mouth and chest and then prop the bottle under the man's arm. The sheriff's first empty bottle got wedged against his leg. Then Rubee scurried up the doorframe, using Niles's help to crawl onto the roof.

Chapter 5

July 11, 1876

"How'd you feel back there?"

"Council Bluffs? Or do you mean in the baggage car?" Sarah asked, snapping so that even her words would have little contact with Niles.

"The train."

"I never felt like I was going to be harmed, if that's what you mean. It only turned crazy when … well, you know what went on. I did feel like I had been left in the dark. What the hell's going on around here?"

Niles chose not to answer.

"I felt you were worthless. Worthless! I felt it was up to me and Rubee to protect ourselves, not you." As far as she was concerned, their conversation was over, and she went back to watching the river's shoreline move slowly south.

Ever since the train incident, Sarah and Niles had avoided each other. On the *Prairie Rose*, that was easy; Niles stayed mostly in his cabin with the camera cases. George could usually be found fishing from the side of the boat, a skill he boasted worked "wherever ya find water."

And Sarah?

The woman wandered the boat day and night, it seemed, watching sunrises, sunsets, the clouds floating across the top of the river water, and the sandbars and riverbanks floating alongside. The shorelines were full of wildlife and wilderness that changed the farther north the *Prairie Rose* paddled. Watching the scenery was Sarah's big event on the boat, and the long days steaming up the Missouri River were an ideal time. The only problem she had with her sightseeing was that she had to wedge herself against the railing where there was usually standing room only. There was very little space on the two decks. Most of their baggage was lashed down to the aft deck, along with freight, wooden crates, and boxes stacked on every foot of available deck space. And where there weren't crates, the decks were piled with cords of firewood for the boat's steam engine.

Rubee preferred staying out of sight except when it was time to fix a meal. One of the pleasures that Niles looked forward to when traveling with Rubee was their meals. Among her many talents, Rubee was a magician with the menu of the day—morsels of meat or fish, often fresh, were spiced with the dried vegetables and seasonings tucked away in the canvas pockets of the cooking bag. With the steamboat captain's approval, Rubee set their kitchen up on the boat's top deck, where wide sheets of tin covered the wooden floor decking around the engine's smokestacks. The cooking was done in a wide, metal pan resembling a prospector's mining pan, except with a handle. It would be heated so hot that when the sprinkles of Rubee's spices hit the skillet, an explosion of aroma would suddenly fill the air near the outdoor kitchen. This was one of the private pleasures of Rubee's cooking that Niles enjoyed during their journeys. But as tasty as Rubee's cooking was, the meals had turned into pretty somber affairs, beginning with the train incident and only getting worse after the Council Bluff argument.

The Council Bluff battle started at the train depot the minute they arrived and escalated into full-blown war as Niles and Sarah had argued their way to the Missouri River, landing on the eastern edge of the Nebraska town. Sarah was not turning around and going back to Washington either because she wanted to or because she was being forced to. Niles made it very clear that he was not going one step farther with Sarah and George tailing along. And to show her that he meant it, he had hollered at her that he was "willing to stay in Council Bluff until she got bored and left on her own." This threat caught Rubee's attention, but Sarah's own vocal assurance made it clear that she would never go back until the trip was completed, and returning to the capital city with Niles was the only way that she would do it. As soon as it was clear that Sarah was bound to win the argument eventually, a barrier of silence had immediately gone up between them and separated the two as they steamed up the Missouri.

Niles was still mad at her. He knew that it had been the wrong decision to let her come along, and now he was probably madder at himself than he really was at Sarah. Besides, Niles figured that, now that they were halfway to Fort Pierre, it was time to at least act civilized with each other. After all, there was still a long way to go before they were all safely back east. Niles knew that the feud between the two had to end, or, as Rubee had pointed out, it could endanger their own trip.

"You seemed to handle the sheriff's advances rather well. I might guess even practiced," Niles said when he had found her on the lower deck standing at the railing and watching the river scenery flow by.

"You're getting personal, Mr. Dewy."

"No more personal than you asking me questions. I'm a photographer. What don't you believe? I live in Washington, as you know. Need I remind, you have been in my house?"

Sarah's look drilled through Niles. There was a look of horror on her face, as if she were shocked by the thought that she had ever let this man touch her. That is what Niles felt, and he was not far from figuring the woman out.

"I want the man to tell me the truth. That's all. It can't be that hard to do."

"Is that why you were so eager to jump aboard back in Washington? Because you spent the night at my house?"

"Maybe. I don't know," she stammered, facing away. "I didn't know then that you might be up to something dangerous. I felt you were a trusting and honest man. A gentleman!"

"Well," Niles mumbled, congratulating himself on his acting job. "I told you. I told you exactly that. The trip is going to be dangerous. No place for a lady. Don't you remember?"

"Let's not start the argument all over. I cared that night in your brownstone; it was the wishes of the lady to be there. Is that so hard for you to understand?"

Niles turned away, embarrassed by this kind of talk coming from the lady.

"Is it because we spent the night together that you won't tell me the truth?"

"That's exactly why I have told you the truth."

"Have you now? Why is it, then, that nobody in Washington has ever heard of a photographer named Niles Dewy? You don't sell them, do you? That's why your house is full of your pictures you never let anyone see. Please know I feel like one of the honored few. And I thank you for that."

"You're welcome. I am happy you enjoyed some of the work."

"Enjoyed! What is wrong with you? I admire your work, and I enjoyed being with you! Is that so hard for you to figure out? That is why I don't understand. What is it about you that makes you hide your work? It's very powerful stuff, Niles. Railroad work crews, isolated soldiers, battlefield hospitals, Confederate veterans' hospitals, mining camps, trading posts … yet, as far as I can tell, you never let out them out of your house. How do you make a living if you don't sell your pictures?"

"You are stringing together a very exciting spider's web of intrigue, Miss Culbert. How can you even believe yourself? Where are you coming up with all this make-believe?"

"Make-believe! I'll have you know a congressman's daughter has many ways of getting information. In Washington, never underestimate what can be found out about a person."

"In such a short time?"

"If need be." She stopped sparring and stared at Niles as if something had fallen into place—maybe another piece of her puzzle. "All those pictures are a road map of where you have traveled, aren't they?" she asked as her face brightened with a new theory. "And if you're not going there to make photographs you can sell, then why are you going there?"

"Sarah, you're going a little far. I'm a photographer. I happen to like making pictures of distant, raw places. What is so hard to understand? You're beginning to sound like that sheriff, and that scares me."

"Niles, I don't care what's going on. I just don't like not knowing what's going on. I think you know that part of my makeup."

Niles remained silent.

"Well?"

"I would say you don't like being lied to, strung along, tricked, or kept in the dark. Am I close?"

"That's right."

"Then don't keep me in the dark. Why weren't you afraid?"

"When? The baggage car thing?"

"Ya."

"Most women have seen the smile on a man's face when he has certain ... shall I say ... expectations. Even I have seen such men's smiles—the one like the sheriff was wearing and you have worn, Niles Dewy," she added.

"So that's all?"

"No. I suspected I would either be killed or raped and had decided to kill the son of a bitch first."

"Kill him? You have never killed," Niles speculated. If she had, he would have to rethink their whole relationship. Protecting Rubee and their cargo was his job, and if this woman became a threat to either, Niles would have to act.

"Not yet. But that was not the first time I have come close to murder. When it got to the point when it didn't look like you were coming back, I would have shot him with this," Sarah said, pulling a small pistol out of a pocket of her dress. Niles recognized the gun, a four-shot Colt Pocket .41 with the two-inch barrel. It could be very effective in close quarters, and he had no doubt that Miss Culbert knew how to use it.

"I seem to remember you telling me the first night we met that you didn't like guns."

"I said they were awful, not that I would never use one. Believe me, if the pistol didn't work, I would have strangled him, smashed in his head with a box, set him on fire, whatever I could do to kill that man and save myself." Sarah's anger had returned, and it was again focused on Niles.

"Don't be mad at me. I was on the roof of that car from the minute the train moved. What was I supposed to do? Yell to you that I was there? Not a good plan, Miss Sarah."

"Admit it, Mr. Dewy, the only reason you were there was to protect your damn camera cases and Rubee. You could have cared less about either George or myself."

"Not so," Niles said, trying to defend himself.

"Stop lying to me, Niles. Just stop it! Whether you like it or not, I really do like you. So please tell me what Rubee is all about. All right? Do you have any kind of answer for that?"

Niles kept his mouth shut.

"Or will you tell me what was in that pipe? Don't say it was just some strong tobacco."

"Tobacco," he told her right away. "Special Virginia tobacco we use for trade. It's a very strong smoke. Some can handle it, and other people are overwhelmed."

"Overwhelmed is not the word for it. It laid the sheriff out."

Niles shrugged. "What can I say?"

"You can start by saying the truth. Do you know anything about what's going on, or are you really stupid and haven't a clue?"

Removing his hat, Niles made a deep bow. "You have caught me, Sarah. I'm really stupid. You uncovered me. That's my true identity. Mr. Stupid. A know-nothing."

Sarah ignored his attempt at humor. She still was not satisfied. "Answer me this—are you a gunman for hire, Mr. Dewy?"

"What happened to being stupid? And you asked me that before."

"You didn't answer me before, either."

Niles was tired of all of their round and round. "Yes, I'm a hired gun. And I'm hired to save pretty ladies ... usually from themselves."

"Don't joke with me anymore, Mr. Dewy."

"My guns are protection. Many of the places I go to make pictures are not the most law-abiding places, and keeping harm away from my camera equipment sometimes takes a certain amount of—what shall I call it?—bluster."

"Protect pictures you never sell."

"That's your opinion, Miss Culbert. Besides, I like guns. Guns are as close as I come to a hobby. Something I can relax with. Like making pictures."

"You're strange, Niles."

"I like collecting guns, target practice, hunting, cleaning—"

"All right. I believe you."

"Thank you, Miss Sarah."

"I accept that part of you, Niles. But it doesn't explain Rubee or that smoke."

"Sarah!" Niles spun completely around, slapping his hands against the side of his head as if he were in pain. "Why won't you accept? Give up."

"It's not a question of giving up, Niles. It's a question about knowing the man I care about."

"What? How can you care about a man you claim not to know?"

She didn't answer and instead let her eyes find his.

"Sarah, it's now time you leveled with me. What are you up to?"

"Niles," she said, pausing as if she were forming the words in her head. "Niles, I haven't been completely honest with you." Sarah fell silent again. Niles thought that she looked like she was about to cry or lose her nerve, but he had no idea what to say or how exactly to act. So he waited to see what came next. She looked away, and then, as she began to speak, she returned her gaze to his face. "Niles, I'm living in Washington with my father." Sarah turned away again and folded her arms across her chest for safety. The woman's stare fixed on the Missouri River's southward-drifting shoreline. For a moment, she looked like she was about to jump the railing and swim to that shore, escaping Niles and what she was going to say.

No matter the answer, Niles didn't want to ask the next question. But he and Rubee had to know. "Why, Sarah?" Niles asked as she still stood with her back to him. "What are you running from? Is it the law? Your father? A dressmaker you stole thread from? Tell me."

Sarah turned around. "This isn't funny!"

"Sorry." Niles saw the seriousness of the matter as soon as she had turned so that he could see her face. Her arms were still crossed, and her throat muscles stiffened along the side of her neck. Her eyes invited no intruders.

"I live in Washington with my father because of you, Niles Dewy. I was a nurse in the Confederate hospital you came and took pictures in. I've been trying to find you ever since. I'm not running from anything. I am running after something."

Chapter 6

When the town council heard that their sheriff had been arrested naked and drunk, he was doomed. Within hours, Clay was fired. The former sheriff decided right then that he was not going to let that gang get away with what they had done to him. He was free to go after them, fueled with a certainty that he was right about the four. Why else would they have humiliated him so? The next morning, Bill Clay boarded a westbound train, this time as a ticketed passenger. It had been easy to follow the group's route. All Clay had to do was ask around at each station stop until he found someone who had seen them.

He arrived at Council Bluffs on July 12 and found the place clogged with people in a state of suspended confusion. A hired hand who hung around the depot told Clay that he had helped move the group's luggage from the train down to the river landing only two days before. The landing along the Missouri River at Council Bluffs was busy with all sizes and types of river traffic. From shallow-keeled steamboats to hide canoes, William Clay would have no trouble finding the transportation he could afford. The Council Bluffs railroad bridge was the northern-most crossing of the Missouri River, turning the river settlement into a hub for all of the travel coming from and going to the high plains territories. Starting at Council Bluffs, a boat could go upstream all the way to Fort Benton at the Great Falls of the Missouri River far north in Montana Territory. Miners and prospectors and every size, shape, and description of fortune seeker crowded the docks, all trying to get to the same place—the new goldfields discovered in the Black Hills up in Dakota Territory. And they were all stranded. The backup had started with the news of Custer's battle, keeping many of the boats docked until the Indian trouble was taken care of. Very few boats of any type were willing to travel as far upstream as Fort Pierre, which was a couple of hundred miles north. And the main Black Hills road started at Fort Pierre on the west bank of the Missouri River, where the old fur-trading post was now being used by the gold seekers to stock up with the last supplies and necessities they would need to cross the prairie.

It took the better part of Clay's first day on the docks to find somebody who had seen the strange group and knew something about their plans. There were many who had seen the four—it was hard not to notice them—but no one could tell him where they went. Retracing his path back along the landing, he asked once more.

"You bet I did. I'm a dockhand, and I see most everything. If something happens behind curtains or doors or behind my back, I hear about it."

"I'm sure you do, but what about this group? Where did they go?"

"They were quite a sight, that nigger and Chinaman and the fancy lady and gentleman. Can't tell ya what they was up to, but I can tell you they was up to something. Sure, I know where they went."

"Where?"

"The Black Hills, mister. Where you been? Damn pilgrims! Wherever you've been, ya ain't been payin' attention. All roads be leading to them Black Hills ... some godforsaken place called Deadwood. I loaded them on the *Prairie Rose* myself, the last side-wheeler to get out of here. Ever since, I been sitting here the last two days with no work."

Clay reached in his pocket, fumbling among his coins. "Will this help out?" he asked, offering the coin to his informant. "Where's the boat taking 'em?"

"Fort Pierre."

"The Black Hills?" he asked.

"I can tell ya they ain't goin' to San Francisco! Say, can I give you a hand with your things once the boats is runnin' again?"

"Not necessary; this is everything," he said, patting the saddlebags draped over his shoulder. He raised the rifle in the air again and patted the pistol on his hip. "This is all my baggage, mister. It's all I need to get to them Black Hills."

"Ya better have a bagful of crazy with ya; you'll be needin' it," the dockhand added.

Getting to Fort Pierre was now Clay's problem, along with the hundreds of others trying to do the same thing. He looked like many of the others who were stuck. He was unshaven, wearing the same outfit of clothes that he had been wearing for days, and he was low on money. All that he had in his pocket was his last pay and a few gold coins he always had stashed away for emergencies. His railroad tickets to cross Iowa had used some of his cash. But his success in tracking the group this far and now knowing where they were going made the cost unimportant to Clay. His looks might fit in with the prospectors, but unlike them, he was not in search of his fortune. Clay was in search of revenge, a far deadlier fortune to seek.

He searched the saloons lining the streets near the river, asking around if anybody knew about any boats leaving for Fort Pierre. That seemed to be the question of the day, and the closest answer was rumors of boats avoiding arrest by the army by sneaking out in the middle of the night. Clay gave up when there were as many men sleeping it off in the saloons as there were standing along the bar, and he decided to find a spot on the docks to spend the night so that he would be there when the river came to life again.

"Mister, mister. Wake up!"

Clay heard the words before he became aware of what was being said, but he remembered his whereabouts before he opened his eyes. He had fallen asleep with his hand resting on his pistol holster, and with a sudden jerk, he pulled the sidearm free and grabbed for the man who had woken him up.

It was the dockhand—the fellow who had helped him the day before. But knowing the man was not enough for Clay. Neither his aim nor his grasp of the man's shirt wavered.

"It's all right," the fellow said. "I ain't shanghaiing ya."

"What're you doing, then?"

The dockhand studied Clay and his pistol for a moment, looking as if he were trying to decide whether what he was doing was right or not. "This be no way to treat a body who might have what you're looking for."

Clay let go of the man's shirt, but he held his aim until the guy had stepped back.

"I don't know who you are, mister. And I don't want to know. All right? I just thought you might …" The dockhand hesitated. "All I thought was that you might be in the market for some departure news."

"I'll pay you what I can." Clay reached into his money pocket. "Two dollars—that all I can spare. Either take it or I'll wait for cheaper news."

The dockhand took the coins and checked up and down the dock, making sure that no one was close. It was about a half hour before sunrise, and only a handful of people could be seen anywhere on the docks. It was obvious that the river life had not yet come alive. "If you want to go to Fort Pierre, I know a boat leaving this morning."

"What boat?"

"The *Janet*. She's a keel loaded with supplies, but she's willing to take on twelve passengers. And if word gets out about it, there'll be a riot down here. Come on, I already made a deal with the capt'n to hold a space for you. So if you want to go, follow me."

Clay hesitated, wondering if this was a setup to rob him. If that were the case, why didn't he jump him while he was asleep? Just to be safe, Clay kept his pistol in his hand and then followed after the man.

"Hurry! They're shoving off." He heard the dockworker ahead of him, but Clay was already running about as fast as his body would go.

"Here. It's still here. Hurry up."

Clay saw the man standing on the landing where a keelboat was beginning to drift away. Its mooring ropes were already free, and the boarding ramp was just being pulled up.

"Hold it!" the dockhand hollered. That was enough to stop the ramp midair.

"Let him on!" a man from the boat yelled, but Clay did not see who it was on the crowded deck. The ramp lowered until it was as close as it was going to get to the deck, which was drifting farther out into the river. Already, there was a two- or three-foot gap between the end of the ramp and the deck, but Clay was not worried about falling into the Missouri River. Getting wet was not a problem. He was more concerned that he would miss the chance to keep pushing ever closer to his targets. And now he had a pretty fair idea of where they were heading—the Black Hills of Dakota and a mining camp they were calling Deadwood.

Chapter 7

July 18, 1876

"If you had to, would you kill her, Mr. Dewy?"

Niles had already asked himself that question many times, beginning at the train station in Washington, and with the last 170 miles waiting ahead of them, he still answered the same way. "There's no reason," he replied to Rubee's question.

"There may come a time when you have a reason. And that time is fast approaching for you and Miss Culbert. She is going to find out. You know that."

"I understand," Niles agreed.

"Mr. Dewy, I feel this is a very different journey. Very different." The two were riding far ahead of Sarah and George, a formation they had fallen into soon after leaving Fort Pierre. "Our cargo travels on its own clock."

"I know."

"I can feel the time for this shipment is now very close. I also feel Miss Culbert does not want to be smudged by the truth of our secret."

"This Deadwood camp we're heading to ... I'm afraid it may smudge us and our secret," Niles admitted.

"I, too, have a fear about this Deadwood. And fear, Mr. Dewy, is not worthy of smugglers such as us. But this time, it may be wise to respect our fears."

"If you're worried about time, I can speed us up—push on a little faster. Sooner there, sooner gone."

"No," Rubee said, studying the western horizon that seemed to wrap around them. "It is not a matter of speed, getting there and back. It is the time we must be in Deadwood that makes my skin crawl."

Niles thought about Rubee's words. Over their years together, he had come to respect not only her wishes, but also her insights. She had always proven to be a wise partner. But she seemed to be a little skittish about the gold camp they were heading toward—this Deadwood place. All that he knew about it was that, at this time last year, it did not exist, and now it was the richest gold strike ever to hit the United States. It was bigger even than the California rush back in '49 or the more recent strikes up in Montana. All that he and Rubee knew about the place was that it was this summer's golden opportunity. Niles and Rubee's unease tickled his instincts to recheck his weapons, assuring himself that each was loaded and ready for any target.

The river breaks were beginning to flatten out some, but the craggy slopes were still ideal for anyone planning to ambush them. The Winchester lay across his lap. He was confident that rifle fire in this type of terrain was his best defense. Later, when they were on the prairie, he would carry the Buffalo gun, the single-shot Sharps .50 caliber, the famed firearm that "shoots today and kills tomorrow."

Their two days loading up on supplies at Fort Pierre had them well provisioned for the prairie crossing. They had four horses, along with saddles, blankets, and other riding gear. There were a few bottle of Tennessee whiskey, four pack mules and pack frames, and Sarah had traded some of her jewelry for a Navy Colt, a gun belt, and a carbine for George, who had kind of become her de facto protector. They had pemmican, smoked fish, dried buffalo berries, chokecherries, and some honey.

There were some proper traveling clothes for Miss Sarah, who had insisted that she would pay Niles back as soon as they got back to Washington. "Or you can collect sooner if Mr. Niles wishes," she had told him. The woman was still trying to get Niles to bed down with her again, but from now until they were out of Deadwood, Niles did not want to confuse matters with whoring.

Niles's generosity also bothered George. "Can't pay ya now, Mr. Dewy, but George'll work off all what's owed for the horse and such. Promise. And I'll even buy one of them mules from you. Just you wait. When we reach them Black Hills, I'll pay ya. Why, them ol' miners never seen the likes of George pick 'em up and lay 'em down better'n this nigger boy."

"What are you going to do to make all this money?" Niles asked. He added, "Sticking with us may just get you killed, you know that?"

"Wish you wouldn't talk like that, Mr. Niles."

"Just being honest, George. Just being honest. So what are you going to do?" Niles asked again.

"Get rich."

"Mind on letting me in on your little secret to riches?"

"Yes, sir. They call's 'em the Black Hills, don't they? Well, George is as black as a fry pan … we's made for each other, Mr. Dewy. Black Hills, black George. Yes, sir. Every time I hear them say the Black Hills, I hear 'em callin' my name. Yes, sir, they callin' this momma's boy."

"You might end up only with a mule and horse as the sum total of your riches. You know that, don't you?"

"They'll work harder than me; they's younger than George."

"How old are you? Tell me the truth."

"Nineteen. Swear," he told him, raising his right hand high. "How old are you, Mr. Dewy?"

"What's gotten into you asking a mighty personal question like that? Make sure you never go asking a lady that question. I'm thirty-six."

"How long you been doin' what's you doin'?"

"I've been traveling, making pictures for nine years."

"Are you rich?"

"Wow, now! George, why you being so nosy?"

"Don't mean to be nosy. Nothin' like that. I just tryin' to figure how long it's goin' to take me to get rich. That's all George meant, Mr. Dewy."

The teamster Niles had hired on with had been in no mood to wait around with the rest of the freighters stuck at Fort Pierre. Bosh was his name. "A proud son of Mother Russia," he had explained to Niles when they'd first met.

"No government son of a bitch going to tell this old Russian when and where he can go. I'd sooner drink ox piss before this boss'll let some slithering government snake tell me what I can do. I don't care if it be the tsar himself. I'll cut off the balls of any white or red that gets in our way and stuff'm limp pizzlesticks right down their squawking throats. If'n I was a swearing man, I'd tell you Bosh don't do no damn rules. There ain't no goddamn rules out on them prairies or in no gold camp, 'cept to keep your scalp and get rich quick and get out. That be it."

At least Niles and the freighter agreed on one thing, even if their way of expressing it differed. "First night you're out, meet up with me at Willow Creek. You should be able to do them eleven miles in a day. If you ain't there by sunup next morning, I leaving, and you can catch up with me whenever you feel like it." Those were the only directions that the teamster had seen fit to share with Niles.

The July heat had baked the freight trail, crumbling the gray gumbo and edging the axle-deep ruts into a fine clay powder that covered everything—horses, mules, riders, packs—with a ghostly makeup. It was an uncooperative route for mounted riders. Either the dust was too deep for a horse to get a good footing, or it was strewn with jagged chunks of clay sharp enough to slice an ankle. It was not an easy ride for the four of them. The horses would veer one way, stepping for sure footing, and the mule would go the opposite direction, tugging the rider back and forth in the saddle in an effort to stay aboard. It certainly was not ideal for the four of them to gain their horse sense and riding legs after weeks of train and riverboat travel.

A dust devil of twirling gray headed down on them, following the sides of the draw they were riding up. The riders tucked their heads down to keep the dust out of their eyes and mouths as the wind swept by them. "Can only get better!" Niles hollered back to the others.

Sarah and George rode together, as they had been since leaving the fort, usually keeping enough distance between themselves and Niles and Rubee so that they weren't constantly eating their dust. But every time Niles twisted around to check on them, it appeared that the two had found plenty to talk about, and it was not odd for him to catch them even laughing—not an easy reaction to the heat and treacherous trail. They were an odd sight, the two of them—the Negro kid on a big black-and-gray draft horse and the white lady on a small bay mare, riding side by side and having a grand old time as if they were sharing a Sunday ride.

"If I heard right, you told that sheriff back in Illinois that George isn't your real name."

"Yes, that's right." The Negro looked away, studying the side of the draw and looking as though they might give him a way to explain. "George ain't my real name ... just sort of a nickname, Miss Culbert," he finally told her.

Sarah rode on for a while and then turned to him. "So, come on, let's hear it."

"Hear what, Miss Sarah?"

"How you get this nickname?"

"That's easy. Every Negro working the rails takes on the name George, honorin' Mr. Pullman."

"George Pullman, the railroad man?"

"That be him. He built the cars we does most of our work in, so they calls us all George."

"What'd you momma name you?"

"Joshua Monroe."

Sarah rode on for a while. Finally, she turned to him again. "Well, Mom and Dad Monroe have a very fine son. You can tell them I said so when you next see them."

"Just a momma."

"No pa?"

"No, Miss Sarah."

"Well, she did a very fine job raising a young man like you. You can tell her I said that."

"I certainly will, Miss Sarah. I certainly will, and I tell her what a fine lady you is who said it."

"So where did the Joshua Monroe handle come from?"

"James Monroe."

"Your daddy?"

"No, President James Monroe, our country's fifth president. He's born in Westmoreland County, Virginia, on the twenty-eight day of April. See, I was born on the twenty-eight of April, too, in the same Virginia county, so my momma named me after a president of the United States."

"What else you know about James Monroe?"

"He was our president from 1817 up to 1825. And Mr. Monroe, may he rest in peace, died in New York City on the Fourth of July 1831. Ain't that something? A president dying like that on the Fourth of July?"

"Well, that's Monroe. How about Joshua? Now where did that come from?"

"Oh, that be easy, Miss Sarah," he told her, breaking into a wide grin. He cleared his throat, sat up straight in his saddle, raised his arms to heaven, and began singing, "'Joshua fit the battle of Jericho … Jericho … Jericho. Joshua fit the battle of Jericho, and the walls came tumblin' down.'" He then hummed a verse and was just about ready to start in again. "'Joshua—'"

"I got it," Sarah quickly interrupted. "You weren't the only one who went to Sunday school." After Sarah stopped chuckling over George's musical outburst, she had something else that she wanted to ask. "Do you think Mr. Dewy and Rubee are made-up names?"

"How'm I s'pose to know something like that? All I know to call 'em is their name, and that be Mr. Dewy and Miss Rubee."

Sarah watched the two riding far ahead of them. Finally, she turned to George. "Oh, forget it. I'm just trying to pass the time. There's just so much nothingness I can look at. That's all."

They rode on in silence for a while until George moved his horse a little closer to Sarah. "May I ask a favor?"

"Sure. You won't get me in trouble now, will you? What is it? Speak up."

"Miss Sarah, I'd appreciate it if you just keep callin' me George. Don't be letting on about Joshua Monroe. Would you do that for ol' George?"

Sarah laughed at his request. "Sure, George, you got my word, even though I think Joshua Monroe a good fit for you. Maybe start using it when we get to Deadwood. Think about it. No matter what you call yourself, it is a pleasure knowing you," she said, extending her hand to shake his.

They had yet to release their grip when out of the corner of her eye, she saw Niles fall off his horse, soon followed by Rubee doing the same. Then she heard the gunfire!

"Indians, Miss Sarah! Get down!" George hollered, getting himself out of the saddle as quickly as he could, still holding Sarah's hand, which he used to drag her down with him.

Niles hugged the edge of one of the clay ruts, the Winchester already smoking from the couple of answering shots he had fired off. A quick glance between shots told him that Rubee was unhurt, trying her best to hang onto the reins of her horse so that it would not run off and join Niles's, which had been spooked off by the sudden outburst of gunfire. Niles focused his aim again and saw that the attackers weren't Sioux. They were dressed in white man clothes; they wore floppy hats, not feathers, and each wore a bandanna covering his face. Niles counted three so far. Two were riding at them from the left side of the trail, firing revolvers, and the other was coming at them from the right, using a rifle. The solo rider was maneuvering his horse down a game trail cut into the eroded side of the draw, giving him scattered safety from a crevice or shallow wall of clay, where he would use the cover to fire a number of shots before moving his horse along the narrow trail to the next bit of shelter. His companions on the other side of the draw had no cover as they charged down the gentle slope, zigzagging their mounts as their only defense against Niles's return fire. Niles picked those two as his first order of business, counting on George and Sarah to pin down the third one on their right. The river breaks had suddenly gone from a hot afternoon to a heated battlefield, and the acrid smell of gun smoke began to fill the air as the ground around the four travelers exploded from missed shots, sending dust and dirt into the air around them.

George had managed to hang on to the big draft horse, although the animal was not cooperating, tossing the Negro back and forth as it tried to break free, keeping George from the task at hand, which was supposed to be returning fire.

Pressed against the ground and flat on her belly, Sarah wiggled closer to George. "Give me that gun! Toss it!" she hollered, trying not to lift her head too much. The next time George's horse spun him around closer to Sarah, he tossed the gun to the ground where she could reach it. She scooted toward it and picked it up. In the same motion, she was on one knee, pistol held with both hands. She cocked it and fired. Her first shot went wide of the rifleman, exploding a chunk of clay more than ten feet to the side of the gunman. But it was close enough to get the fellow's attention before setting his rifle sights on the Negro and now the woman.

Niles's first few shots were wide of their marks. He forced his breathing to calm, squirmed into a more comfortable position, and relaxed his arms and hands before resting his elbows on the ground. He braced the Winchester's stock against his shoulder, focusing his eye on the rifle's rear sight and then the front bead. Then he saw his target. The spot on the man's chest looked to be only a few feet away. Niles did not hear his shot or feel the rifle recoil, but he clearly saw the bullet tear away shirt and flesh, pushing the man out of his sights as he fell from his horse.

George had been pulled to his knees when the big draft animal had reared back on its hind legs. But the animal's antics trying to free itself were George's only protection as he was yanked around, bobbing up and down. The rifleman took a little longer to steady a shot at George, and Sarah used the man's hesitation to carefully aim her next shot. She did not see where it hit, but it did not hit the attacker, who skillfully swung his horse around to get a better angle and fired again into the melee where George and Sarah were making their stand. Sarah was unable to get another shot off right away, because the mule bucked right in front, knocking her to the ground again as she ducked under the tangle of reins.

"They're not doing so well!" Rubee yelled over to Niles, but he did not care to look, for he had the second rider in the rifle sight appearing as close as if Niles were peering at him through a spyglass. He watched the man trade his empty revolver for a loaded one that he had stuck in the front of his belt, but before he could fire off a fresh round, he disappeared from Niles's sight, and the rifle stock jerked against his shoulder. The powder-blue sky was all that Niles saw where the attacker had once been. The riderless horse veered away, making a wide turn back up the slope. He quickly crawled 180 degrees around so that he could join the battle going on behind him.

Sarah was finally out of the way of the bucking mule. She searched for the rifleman who was taking aim at them again, but his aim was momentarily averted by the sight of the riderless horse running up the opposite hillside. When he twisted in his saddle to take up the aim again, he presented Sarah with her best clear opportunity. She steadied the Navy Colt's aim and fired. She followed immediately with a second round, but the sound of the shot was cut short by a piercing scream that echoed off the sides of the ravine and across the draw.

Niles was ready to fire at the rifleman when he saw the squirt of blood from the center of the man's chest shoot at least a foot into the air. The rider fell into one of the crevices clawed by wind and rain. His horse continued down the steep trail as if nothing had happened. George's horse and mule sensed that the shooting was over, and they gingerly circled each other as the meadowlarks' musical accompaniment once again carried on the wind.

"Them birds singing your praises," George said to Sarah. "Lord Jesus, Miss Sarah, you just saved this nigger's life."

She handed the Colt back. "Return the favor someday," she told him before turning to see if Niles and Rubee were all right.

Niles waved and then motioned them on. She heard his voice carry on the wind as he said, "Get moving!" Sarah watched as Niles helped Rubee gather up their horses, mount up, and then head up the draw, continuing their westward trek in search of the Russian's freight wagons.

"Didn't figure you'd show up!" the freighter hollered even before the four had all dismounted. It was sunset, and the prairie was wearing a golden robe when they were led into the bull train's Willow Creek camp. The white canvas covering the wagons' cargo hinted a yellow shade, and the narrow ribbon of the creek drew a honey-colored line across the grass-covered plains.

"Didn't give me the full lowdown on your traveling companions," Bosh said to Niles as he was working on removing his horse's saddle.

"Four. That's what I paid. Four people."

"A yellow-skinned chink and a nigger boy?"

Niles carried the saddle over to the wagons, dropped it on the ground next to one of the wheels, and turned to the freighter. "Good-paying passengers, Mr. Bosh. Fine folks, don't you agree?"

The freighter studied the group, setting his gaze on Sarah, who was undoing her saddle. "She'll get ya a pot of gold!" he told Niles, accompanied by a low whistle.

Niles fixed his own gaze on the freighter. "You goddamned foreigner, you've got a squaw's crotch for brains."

"Think what you like, but ol' Bosh seen all kinds comin' and goin' from them Black Hills, and Deadwood'll change a person. Place'll make a preacher man screw a whore, and the whore'll be singin' in the choir. All I's telling you is you got yourself a mighty fine gold mine right there. Yes, sir, she be a strike-it-rich madam there in Deadwood," Bosh said, pointing at Sarah.

Before Bosh could lower his arm, Niles had a pistol jammed against the man's throat. "I'll take your advice under consideration. In the meantime, you better clean up your act around the lady."

Bosh lowered his arm slowly, his eyes locked on Niles's. "Whatever you say, mister. You be the paying customer."

The revolver pushed a little more firmly into the folds of the man's neck, pressing against his windpipe. "I'm glad to see you respect the lady," Niles said, lowering the pistol.

"Oh, you can bet ol' Bosh'll respect the lady," Bosh said, rubbing his neck. "Hope you ain't as touchy about the chink and that there colored boy."

"What's wrong with you, mister? Russians hate everybody?"

"We love Mother Russia but hate the tsar. Bosh is the top bullwhacker, and folks do what I say out here, just like them oxen," he added, waving his arm at the herd of oxen grazing on the other side of the wagons. "Keep the chink out of my way, and if that ant's ass gets in my way, I'll tie that pigtail of his around the horns of my team's wheeler." The freighter went on listing his rules and pointing at George. "And you, nigger. No pissin'!"

"Ever?" George questioned.

"Can't you hear, darky? I don't want you leavin' a mark for other coloreds to follow. No pissin'!"

"You ain't right, bull man. You ain't right," George said, throwing up his arms in frustration.

"Them Sioux caught the Metz in Red Canyon, just east of the Black Hills, right where we're headed ... murdered three and got off with a nigger woman. Boy, you better believe them Sioux made damn sure she'd never piss again."

"Sorry to hear about the fine woman," George said, moving across the camp to get right up in Bosh's face. "But this here's a mighty big, empty country, and I'll pee wherever I want. And every time I do, I'm goin' to spell you name, whatever it is."

"If'n you do that, you'll be pissin' your life away. Boshcovich Stovkonikog Petronid—and if you got any water left, don't forget to dot the i's." Turning back to Niles, Bosh asked, "Didn't run into any trouble coming up the trail, did ya?"

"Naw. No trouble," Niles answered. "Why'd you think we'd have any trouble?" he asked, figuring that Bosh was the one who had put the highwaymen up to their little ambush.

"No, I knew you can handle any trouble might be throw's your way. But something might happen; you just never know. Hard telling. But these ol' prairies will make a man careful, and just wait—Deadwood'll make you downright worrisome."

The freighter was not Niles's only worry. The Russian had failed to mention that there would be other folks traveling with the ox train beside themselves. There would only be two others, but Niles knew enough about playing poker that he sensed that they were a pair to draw too.

First was the kid—not a paying passenger. He would have to walk the whole way, prodding the oxen along. "Meet John Sutherland. Least I think that's what he callin' hisself today," the Russian introduced. "He's a walkin', talkin' lie. Can't believe a word that half-wit runt tells ya."

"What makes you say that?" Niles asked.

"First off, he tells me his name's McCall—Jack or such handle. Then he starts in callin' hisself Sutherland. Tomorrow, he'll call himself Jesus Christ," Bosh explained, obviously disgusted that he was even wasting his time talking about the runt. "Bet my lead ox the kid's as empty-headed as they come."

Judging from a distance, it was hard for Niles to figure out what size load the runt's head carried around. The kid was shorter that most—probably not more than five feet tall if even that—and skinny as a split rail, but his face was kind of pudgy looking, with a nose bent to one side as if it had been broken at some point and never set properly. His mouth was nothing more than a pencil-thin line—no lips to speak of. At best, he was a repulsive-looking fellow.

"Ain't got a penny to his name, either. He ain't got enough meat on those bones of his to even make it worth my time whippin' off. I'll work the dumb son of a bitch to death. Swear I'll kill him. Scrawny chickenshit!"

"You leave my chickens out of this," said Bosh's other passenger—a paying customer, but there was no telling what price she had paid or how she had paid him. She would be considered quite a looker in the gold camp, but her focus seemed to be always directed to the willow cages of chickens tied to the sides of the freight wagon. "My lack of money is going to be short lived," she declared to anyone interested in hearing. "I'll start off serving eggs ... then my own hurdy-gurdy joint ... and then I'll get me a real-life saloon—a sure road to riches in Deadwood, even if I do say so myself. I'm fixing to come away from those Black Hills the richest lady in Dakota Territory. Just you mark my words."

"I believe you," Niles agreed with her.

"Kitty LeRoy," she said, extending her hand. "Most folks just call me Kit. Been whoring since I was ten. Highest paid first-time girl to ever hit Texas. But this around, I going to be the highest-priced egg lady in Deadwood Gulch. Yes, sir, mister. Kit's going to be a full-fledged lady this time around. Yes, sir, an egg lady. Kitty's Egg Emporium. Come one, come all, gents, get them scrambled, fried, or hard-boiled, and I ain't talking about your brains," she sang out. "No, sir, I ain't going to spread my legs ... not right off, anyhow."

"Please, Miss LeRoy," Sarah implored. "Can't anyone speak with a civil tongue out here?"

"My tongue does a lot of things, sweetheart, but civil ain't one of them." Niles watched the two hardheaded women face off. This could prove to be a very entertaining prairie crossing.

"You married?" Kit asked her. "Sold it for good, I'll bet, and you're kicking yourself mighty hard right now, figuring you could have made a sackful of gold there in Deadwood. Well, marrying never been known to stop a whore before."

"I am married," Sarah announced, hoping to put an end to the conversation.

"I know'd it. Which one of these fine fellers you hitched to? The darky? You and the Chinaman make a fine pretty pair. Whoa! No, it's you and fancy guns over there," Kit said, giving Niles a rather seductive once-over.

"Sarah and I are husband and wife," Niles confirmed, no more comfortable saying it now than he had been saying it to that Illinois sheriff.

"I just knew it. What's a pair like you up to? Honeymooning in the Black Hills of Dakota? What do you do for trouble, Mr. Fancy Guns?"

"I'm a shooter—"

"I got that!" Kit interrupted.

"No, I'm a photographer. Rubee is my assistant, and Mr. George there is our porter," he explained, introducing the rest of the traveling party to her.

Letting out a low whistle, she said, "What a handsome little family."

"We get along," Niles said.

Bosh had heard enough and headed out to check on the ox herd. "A stinkin' pit-tail, a nigger boy, two whores, a hired gun, and a half-wit. Blessed Russia!" he said, offering a mocking prayer toward heaven. "The devil's going to dance when this gang hits Deadwood."

Chapter 8

If William Clay had known that morning when he was running along the Council Bluffs river wharf what it would be like to spend more than two weeks on a keelboat with little deck space, boat hands, a half dozen passengers, and freight tucked all around them, he would have thought twice about jumping aboard. Now that part of the trip was behind him. He had finally made it to Fort Pierre, where he would either find the four or it would be the starting point for the next leg of his manhunt.

The fort was located practically in the middle of Dakota Territory, on the west bank of the Missouri River. It was on a grassy plain about a half mile wide and maybe a mile long, trapped between the river bluffs seventy to eighty feet high on the west and a broad expanse of the Missouri River on the east. It was nearly two hundred miles straight east of the Black Hills, and every mile was on the Sioux reservation.

Even though Clay had never ventured far outside of Illinois, it was easy for him to have conjured up in his head what a frontier outpost should be like, and Fort Pierre was his first-ever look at such a place. It met most of his expectations and then some. Ten-to twelve-foot-tall whipsawed log walls made up four sides with a guard tower perched on top of the palisade's northwest and southeast corners. Dozens of Indian tepees occupied the river plain to the north of the fort, and the camps of hundreds of stranded prospectors surrounded the fort like a small town. Makeshift businesses of every shape and description dotted the plain, selling everything from New Orleans' girlie postcards to hand-drawn maps of the Black Hills gold strikes. Games of chance of every variety were available to any and all comers, and more than one saloon offered expensive, watered-down shots of whiskey, usually served across a couple of pine planks balanced between barrels. Walking up to the fort from the river landing, Clay saw two tepees with a line of miners waiting outside for what he suspected were the favors of some soiled dove—probably a dirty Indian dove at that.

Once inside the walls of the fort, Clay noted the layout. A barracks ran along nearly the length of the south wall, a storehouse along the west, and a stand-alone building was occupied by Sutter's store. There looked to be a cookhouse and a smokehouse, and just off the central yard was a regular-looking, two-story house sporting a porch and real glass windows. On either side of the main gate were corrals for horses and mules.

"Goddamn Sioux keep trying to run 'em off if I don't run them injuns off first," a man guarding the stock with a lone Civil War vintage musket had told Clay as he stood there checking out the available horseflesh.

Everywhere he looked, he saw idle men filling their time with boredom. The place seemed to be overrun by hundreds of fortune seekers waiting to move on to the gold camps in the Black Hills; they sat, stood, lay on the ground, and engaged in all manner of devices, keeping themselves occupied and killing time. Card playing, checkers, and napping appeared to be a handy pastime for some, but most simply sat around watching the carnival play around them. Like the men stranded in Council Bluffs, they were stuck at Fort Pierre for the same reason—the government had declared the Sioux reservation off limits to whites and was stopping all travel into the Black Hills. Those who tried were considered outlaws and were subject to arrest. If they resisted, the army had orders to shoot to kill.

Clay saw no soldiers or marshals or fences preventing them from taking off. But the reason soon became obvious to him, and it was a reason looming a lot larger than the threat of being arrested.

Custer!

It had not been a month since the Sioux and Cheyenne had massacred Custer's Seventh Cavalry on the banks of the Little Bighorn River up in Montana, only a few days' ride northwest of the Black Hills.

Coming up from the river, Clay had overheard dozen of questions.

"How did the Indians ambush the troops?"

"Where did the murdering savages disappear to?"

"Did they move up to the Canadian territory?"

"Are the Indians heading to the Black Hills to attack the gold camps?"

"Where is the cavalry? Chasing them?"

"Where is the trail from Fort Pierre to the Black Hills blocked by roving war parties?"

And along with all of the questions that Clay had already heard, there were many stories making the rounds at the fort about those who had already lost their scalps.

"Ed Sadler, Johnnie Harrison, Gardner, and feller went by the name Jack were found naked and scalped near Peno Springs."

"Jim Hogan got hisself killed near Fort Pierre Road."

"They buried Old Man Herman where they found him."

"That old river man, Captain Dodge, was caught by savages who tortured the poor bastard so bad it was an act of kindness when the Sioux finally killed him and put him out of his misery."

"Three men with their faces shot off were found just eleven miles west of Fort Pierre near Willow Creek."

It was talk that the sheriff from a quiet little county in Illinois was unaccustomed to hearing. Well, so be it. Clay tried shrugging it off. After all, he had made it this far, all the way to the edge of Indian Territory. And so far, all of the rumors of the Sioux threat were not

David A. Soma

enough to keep him cooling his heels on the banks of the Missouri River for very long. No, the lust and vengeance eating at his insides gave no second thought to the Sioux threat. He was going to finish what the China girl had started. No doubt about that. Clay had had plenty of time already to play over and over in his mind what he was going to do with the two women. The only thought he had ever given to the gunman and nigger traveling with them was to kill both of them the minute he laid eyes on them.

It had not taken Clay long to realize that he had really gotten himself to a frontier wilderness in the middle of nowhere. Except for the riffraff population stuck at Fort Pierre, the country around him for hundreds of miles in every direction was empty of people. That was except for the Indians, who apparently had an argument with anyone trying to enter their sacred Black Hills, which meant that the Sioux had an argument with William Clay.

Clay had never been the hunted one. As a lawman, he had always been the hunter. And in those few times when he had actually had to go after someone, it was never a life-or-death deal—mostly vandals, drunks, and brawlers. The biggest danger he usually faced was some name-calling, cussing, and maybe a wild, inebriated punch. Soon after his arrival at Fort Pierre, Clay came to the sobering realization that, out here in the territories, he could be attacked at any time and face death, and the only one he could count on for protection was himself. A gnawing fear settled in the pit of his gut, causing him to glance over his shoulder more than once, and he knew that it was not going to go away until he was back in the States and surrounded by civilization. It was a fear that at any moment could take control of his head.

And it was probably that same kind of fear that was covering his prey's tracks. Clay was pretty sure that those four renegades he was chasing must be pretty confidant that the fear of being scalped by the Sioux would prevent anyone from following them.

"Cocky little shits!" he grumbled as he worked around the inside of the fort. "You're sexin' and shootin' ain't going to protect you out squat shit. I ain't fallin' for it, and the devil's fear is going to have to come along for the ride."

His first order of business was to find any news that he could about the four. Did they make it to Fort Pierre? Did anyone see them or talk to them? When did they leave—and how? And along the way, he would have to outfit himself.

His first stop was back at the corrals. There was no news about the four, but a mare—way past her good days—was all the horse that Clay could afford, costing most of his silver dollars, the leather vest he had been wearing, and a pair of socks. Considering his current circumstances, the horse had been costly, but Clay was glad to have it.

Next was Sutter's store, where, for the last of his silver, Clay got himself two boxes of cartridges, jerked antelope, crackers, beans, coffee, and a bit of a lead. A buckskin-clad trader told him, "Colored boy did come in. He looked around, didn't buy nothing, and walked out. Haven't seen him since."

"Did you see his shoes?"

"Mister, I don't go around looking at folks' feet. What are you, some kind of lawman? Bounty hunter? Why you askin'?" The trader eyed him. "This feller do something?"

"That's nobody's business but mine. Did you see the nigger's shoes?" Clay asked again. "I'm trying to figure out if he's ..." Clay hesitated, trying to decide what the trader wanted to hear. "If he's the feller I'm supposed to meet up with here. All I knows is he said I'd know him by his shoes."

The trader stared at him, his facial muscles twitching some. "Laced up, high-topped boots. Polished up real fancy like," the trader told him. "Hope that's your friend. Now get the hell out of here. I got other customers."

A horse, some food, extra bullets ... not a bad start, Clay thought to himself as he surveyed the fort. Now all he needed was more information. He was sure that the four had been here. Maybe they were still here, or, if not, maybe someone had seen them leave. He decided to move his inquiries out to the grassy river plain surrounding the fort. South of the fort where the freight wagons were parked, he came upon two men who told him that they might know something.

"What's information like that worth to you?" one of them asked him right back.

"Half box of cartridges. I'll trade you bullets for news," Clay told them.

"Well, in that case," the fellow who had struck up the bargain began. "Since the news of Custer hit the fort, no freighter in his right mind going to take off across those prairies … might just lose everything—team, wagons, freight, scalp. But I'm pretty sure two bull trains were crazy enough to try it and took off for the Black Hills. An army of gold-hungry prospectors went with the first one, just daring the Sioux to attack, but the second one was this here Russian freighter—think he go'ed by the name Bosh—took off the other day way before sunup. Talk around the freighters is he only had some half-wit hired hand with him—"

"And that whore who'd been doing business under one of his wagons," the other man interrupted. "The son of a bitch is flat-out crazy if'n he thinks he can hold off the whole Sioux nation with a whore on one side and a half-wit on the other!"

Clay's frustration let go. "What this got to do with the chink and nigger?"

"Them four you be asking after … well, they took off the next morning. I'll bet my claim, that ol' Russian freighter got hisself a mighty handsome fee for given them four a private ride."

"But they didn't leave together. That makes no sense."

"Sure enough does, mister. Takes a bull train more'n a day to make it up those bluffs and out of the river breaks. Eleven miles and you got to do it in one day; there's no place to camp in those breaks."

"You'll roll right back down them hills if you stop," the other man added.

"What's that got to do with those other four?" Clay asked, a bit confused by this frontier topography.

"Riding through those river breaks is a heck of a lot faster. Leave a day after and you don't waste time. Meet up at Willow Creek and then you're off and runnin'. Bulls can start makin' go time out on the flats. Got it? No time wasted."

Clay was still confused, but it was beginning to make sense—especially if the four didn't want anyone to know when or with whom they had left Fort Pierre.

"Where's that Russian freighter headed?"

"Bosh? Straight west to the Black Hills."

The other fellow quickly added, "All roads leadin' to Deadwood from here."

That was it; Clay had finally pinned down their final destination and how they were getting there. "Sticking close to an ox train ain't fast, you dumb shits!" Clay exclaimed. All of a sudden, Clay could feel his luck changing. After less than half a day at Fort Pierre, he had what he needed, and as long as he had sunlight left in the day, he was going to stay after them.

He followed the Black Hills road up through the Missouri River breaks with only a vague map in his head of the route that lay before him. Landmarks he had heard of were sketchy at best, and he was not even sure if they were along this same trail. The only compass he had was to follow the wagon ruts worn into the prairie sod by the countless freight trains that had already made the trek between Fort Pierre and Deadwood.

He reached forward in the saddle and patted the old mare on the neck. "I'll have me some fun screwing them ladies. Maybe the chink first, making that white watch, seein' what coming her way ... and then I'll kill the bitches!" The mare's ears twitched, finally twisting around toward her rider, throwing her neck around so that her eye could see him as if she had understood what he had said. Clay slapped the ends of the reins at the horse's head. "Damn nag!" he swore. He had taken a liking to talking to himself; it kind of broke up the monotony of the seemingly endless ride. For the Illinois fellow, hearing his voice roll over the prairie as if it were his own bird song was something he never could do in the tree-clogged east. And besides, Clay had grown to like the sound of his own voice and what it had to say, so he kept right on talking to the wind. Maybe, just maybe, he calculated in his mind, if anyone did catch sight of him—like some savages, for instance—they might leave him alone if they saw him riding all alone across the prairie talking up a storm, thinking that he was a crazed lunatic. That would be just fine with him. "I know where you secret's hid … I know, I know. May not know right now what it is, but I know where you got it hid." He sang as loudly as he could, and then he fell silent, listening to the fading sound of his voice taking flight over the prairie until it was muffled by the emptiness. "I'll take apart those stupid-ass picture cases one side at a time, and wham, bam, thank-you, ma'am, I'll be rich—ass-kicking, son-of-a-bitch rich! What's in there? Gold? Paper money? Counterfeit money? Fool's gold? Marked cards? Whatever it is stashed inside those cases, I know'd it's worth a fortune, 'cause you're going to die for it."

Pushing himself up in the stirrups and waving a fist at the sky, he hollered, "I smell it! I can smell me a rich man!" As the wind swirled around him, he caught a whiff of his own odor. Weeks of no bath or change of clothes, exhaustion, fear, hatred, and revenge had tainted his sweat, and he wrinkled his nose at his own smell—a stench far from the perfumed aroma of pampered wealth.

By Clay's figuring, he was maybe another day closer to his prey. He had been plodding along the wagon ruts for nearly thirty-six hours, never stopping, always keeping the western horizon as his goal. But as his second night descended over the dusty, powdered, pale sky, and a bank of thunderheads snuffed out even the starlight, the mare stumbled over the side of one of the wheel ruts that neither she nor he saw. "Goddamn piss-ant luck," Clay grumbled. It became obvious to him that they should probably go no farther. He had not rested since the boredom of the keelboat, except for a nap or two in the saddle. He needed sleep, and so did the mare. They were crossing what appeared in the dark shadows to be another one of the dry streambeds that webbed the prairie, its deep-cut channel offering the only shelter around for their night's accommodations.

Clay dismounted and undid the saddle, using the reins to hobble the mare for the night, and then he made himself as comfortable as possible against the eroded side of the stream. He had not spied a tree, let alone a stick, since leaving the Missouri. Unless he could figure out some way to burn dirt, a fire was a distant luxury, so he settled in for a cold supper of jerked antelope and crackers.

No fire for cooking coffee and beans.

No firelight to keep him company.

No snapping and crackling of burning wood to lull him to sleep.

Never before had Clay been unable to build a fire. Back east, now becoming a distant dream, he always had plenty of wood for cooking, heat, light, and comfort. "You bastards," he grumbled, ripping another piece of the dried meat off with his teeth. It was dark and uncomfortable, and the jerky tasted like dirt. "I was just doing my job, and look what you shitheads did to me!" he said, justifying his revenge as he slipped deeper against his saddle.

Bright light popped through Clay's head as the sharp rays of sunrise pried his eyes open. He jumped to his feet, dropping the rifle that had been resting across his lap. The sun was already a ball of yellow light sitting on the edge of the eastern horizon, but the morning breeze was still cool with a hint of early morning freshness as it fanned the tall grass, which reflected silver and gold depending on how the wind caught them. "Damn!" He swore his first prayer of the day as he reached down to retrieve his rifle. Next to it, he discovered the remains of his supper, picked up the piece of dried meat, and shoved it in his mouth for his breakfast.

"Horseshit! Horseshit! Horse-goddamn-shit!" he hollered over and over as he gathered up his gear and half dragged it toward the hobbled mare. "I should leave ya here for some damn Sioux to gut out. He'll eat ya. Be like eatin' poison. Serve them savages right! Nope. I might get damn hungry out here, but I'll eat grass or dirt if I have to before I'll chew on some damn ol' horse meat," he told the mare as he slung the saddle over her back.

He untied the reins from around her ankles and shoved the bit between her teeth. Just as he was about to swing up into the saddle, he spotted his fear.

Sioux!

He stepped out of the stirrup, making a quick scan of the surrounding horizon. He saw no more of them. "Maybe they ain't seen us," he whispered in the mare's ear. "Not likely," he added, knowing that they must stand out like a sore thumb.

Clay tugged the mare across the gravel bed as the Indians began slowly riding toward him, weaving around each other as if they were braiding a rope, spreading farther and farther apart with each loop. He crawled up against the side of the stream's eroded trench. "Come on, come on," he said, urging them closer as he sighted down the rifle barrel. "Just a little closer."

His first shot went somewhere, but nowhere near the riders. The Sioux were smart enough to stay out of rifle range. They returned fire. The two shots echoed over the empty prairie, but they hit the sod well in front of his protective trench. Crouching behind the earth breastworks, he waited for more shots. "Single-shot rifles," he whispered as he carefully peeked over the edge of the trench. They had ridden closer, and now that the battle was on, Clay felt much calmer. For the next quarter of an hour, they exchanged gunfire, peppering the prairie and filling the air with bluish clouds of spent gunpowder.

Suddenly, an arrow whistled over his head. At first, he didn't know what the sound was, having never before heard an arrow cut through the air. He fell to the ground, hugging the empty streambed for dear life. "Where'd that come from?" he asked the mare, but the horse's only answer was a look of fright in her big brown eyes.

Carefully, he peered over the edge of dirt again and saw a lone rider much closer than the others. His speed and accuracy with a bow and arrow was far more evident than his comrades' rifle shots. Already, a halo of arrows stuck along the edge of the trench, competing with the tall grass.

Clay knew that he had to fight back—or else they would just overrun him and then have their fun with him. He raised himself over the edge of the prairie and aimed, following the rider until he had the rhythm of the horse, and fired. He watched the Sioux crumble and then slide off the side of his horse, landing facedown in the grass. Arrows and bullets hitting the edge of his trench sprayed him with clods of dirt, forcing him once again to hug the streambed. He heard a sickening thud and saw a dark squirt of blood splash across his pant leg. He looked up just as the mare looked down at him before her legs gave out, and she crumpled to the ground. At the first break in gunfire, Clay raised up, rested his elbows on the edge of the prairie, steadied the rifle on target, and fired. Then he quickly ducked down again. Only when the gunfire and whistling arrows let up did he chance another look. The rider at whom he had last fired was sitting on the ground, looking stunned from the jolt of the bullet that had pushed him off his horse. He first heard the horse galloping toward him, and then he felt the ground around him shudder. In the flash of an eye, the horse and rider sailed right over the top of Clay, landing in the dry creek bed behind him and throwing up dust and gravel as the Sioux lunged at him, a pistol aimed. The Indian's first shot hit the mare. Clay's eyes watched the Indian slump forward with the clarity of fear, and only then did Clay realize that he had fired the rifle and killed the man. Oddly, though, his attention was riveted to the Indian's horse that slowly walked over to the edge of the wash and began nibbling on a clump of grass.

Clay scrambled back to the protection of the ledge. Taking a chance, he looked over and watched his visitors riding away, probably to lick their wounds and regroup. Just as quickly as they had appeared, they rode over the horizon, and Clay was all alone, left only with a stillness like he had never heard before. Even the ever-present wind and whisper of the blowing grass sounded eerily quiet, and that scared him half to death.

Chapter 9

"I'm a mighty famous man."

"Good for you," Niles congratulated. "Now what makes you so famous?" Niles continued, asking Bosh's hired man.

"Wild Bill Hickok hisself killed my brother down in Kansas. Abilene, Kansas. Shot him in the back over a couple chickens. Wild Bill Hickok hisself. You know who Wild Bill is, don't ya, easterner?"

"You're famous because Bill Hickok shot your brother in the back?"

"Over some damn chickens," the teamster added.

The wind had to be just right, but from his seat atop the lead wagon, Bosh could hear some of their talk. "Last week, he said his brother was killed with Custer. Take your pick!" he yelled.

"I'll kill you!" screamed the little fellow. He had exploded, losing control. He spun around, hollering, "I'll kill ya! I'll kill ya!" He threw the ox rope to the ground and then began pointing the stick he used to prod the beasts at Bosh, punctuating each "I'll kill ya!" with a jab. Then, as suddenly as the outburst began, it ended. The man turned, picked up the ox rope, and began walking, slamming the wooden prod against the lead bull's hindquarters. The whack did not please the bull; he swung his head around trying to gore anything within range, bellowing until it echoed off the rolling grass itself. His cries set the other bulls off, which apparently had been waiting for just an occasion to issue their own challenges.

The runt's temper was now packed into his five-foot hickory pole, madly goading the ox along with sharp jabs in the ribs or lashing out with the leather whip, showing no mercy for any animal within reach. The runt was mean enough, as well as an expert manipulator of his instrument of torture, swinging it in circles a few times over his head before directing the lash to a spot on the animal singled out for punishment. The beasts' bloody cuts were immediately tortured by a swarm of flies, which made them even more vicious and ornery, and, to Niles's way of thinking, downright dangerous. The half-wit was seldom, if ever, in an agreeable state of mind, and now he freely applied his viciousness to the suffering animals under his charge.

One by one, the bulls started losing their own tempers, bellowing, twisting, and squirming against their yokes, jabbing horns at the empty air, threatening person, whip, fly, or sky. The train came to a dead stop, which set off the whippings again. The bulls' orneriness took on a stench of its own. While tearing at their leather harnesses, shaking the very wagons, the animals were shitting and peeing all over the ground, each other, the front of Bosh's lead wagon, Niles, and anyone else dumb enough to be close.

Bosh's whip snapped only inches from the runt's head, striking with such force that it made a sound like the crack of a rifle—enough so to fool Niles into reaching for one of his pistols, but it stopped the hired hand swinging the whip in midair. "Knock it off, shithead!" Bosh hollered. "I'll cut you open and leave ya for the flies. Move 'em like ya had a head, or we'll have nothing but you to pull us to Deadwood!" Bosh yelled, aiming the whip's staff at the fellow. The two teamsters soon had the team moving again, away from the stink hole they had created, maybe even at a faster pace than before the tantrums and all of the bellyaching.

The pastimes to choose from for those riding along with the bull train were either staring at the empty plains or talking to the empty-headed. But after the severity of the high plain's loneliness took hold, the choice became staring at the empty-headed or talking to the empty prairie. They all were suffering the effects of high plains isolation. Sarah complained that they were lost, making circles instead of moving forward, and Bosh was the most lost of any of them. Suffocating was George's description of the wide openness, as if it were closing in on him under a sky so heavy with heat that it surely was collapsing. The constant wind whistling in their ears was enough to drive some insane if they listened for long. But even the wind could be hushed by the silence that left your heartbeat ringing in your ears. It was the quietness of the place that numbed the mind the most.

Niles had enough of the looking after the first day, so he made a habit of riding along with one of the other travelers, talking if the person were so inclined. Kit was always ready to swap stories, George always had questions that needed answers, Rubee's philosophical discussions could be almost as boring as watching the grass blow, and Bosh was a born talker, but his stink and even dirtier mouth would leave Niles feeling like he was covered in slime. Sarah and Niles were now far friendlier than on their ride up the Missouri River, and ever since leaving Fort Pierre, they had been spending their nights together under a wagon, so during the day, they often stayed a more comfortable distance from each other. Even from the most talkative, he would sometimes be met with a wall of silence, which he shrugged off, knowing that there was plenty of time to try again before they reached the Black Hills.

Bosh's hired hand never had much time for talk. The poor fellow's routine plodded along day after day—hitching the oxen up in the morning, walking step for step alongside the bulls all day, and finally unhitching the oxen at night. Whatever the fellow's reasons, as soon as Niles approached, his face contorted into an expression that really did unmask him as a madman. He would pull his tattered sombrero over his face, ending their talk before it began. At least Niles could get a grunt or two out of an ox. The runt's one distraction was Sarah and Kit. Whenever there was a break, the women would find him hanging around, watching their every move. It was the only time that he had a smile on his face. "That ain't no 'let's be friends' smile," Kit warned Sarah. "It's a 'look in my pants' smile. If he ever shows up at my place," she said, using her hands to cover her crotch, "I'll cut it off."

Niles had figured that striking up a conversation with the kid might be a good way to spend some miles. When Niles felt that the dust had settled from the outburst and that all of the bellowing had quieted down, he forged on. "This is another one of your make-ups, ain't it?" he asked, trying to sound as sympathetic as he could. Niles did not want to stir up the man's temper again and have to dodge the stick's wild swings. "Please don't get me wrong here. Bill Hickok's probably shot a man or two, but never in the back, so I would guess that your brother wasn't one of them."

"You know who Wild Bill is? Huh! You some friend of his?" The man pushed the brim of his hat up, and Niles saw the runt's face suddenly take on an even darker look.

Rubee and Niles never considered Bill Hickok a friend, but they had crossed paths with the man on numerous occasions, first near the end of the Civil War. They had known the man as a renegade Union scout, hired security for the railroad work gangs or gold shipments from the Colorado mining camps, and a lawman in the railhead towns who easily and often stepped over the line separating law from outlaw. No matter where he was or what his job was at the time, Bill was always happy to see Mr. Dewy and Rubee make their unexpected appearances. They had spent time with the man, swapping lies and conducting business. He loved having his picture made and enjoyed the pleasures of the Yellow Doll's many offerings.

"Which brother was that now? Brother Sutherland or Brother McCall?"

The runt didn't answer. Instead, he stood there trembling and glaring down at the ground. Niles noticed that the man's neck muscles were straining again. Even through the fellow's scanty beard, he could see his gaunt cheekbones twitching. His grip on the hickory prod tightened, turning his knuckles white.

"Jack or Jim or whoever you are, you're crazy out of your head, little man," Niles told him before walking away.

"I'll kill you for that! Jim Sutherland'll blow your head off, mister!"

That got Niles's full attention. He had killed over less threatening words. But as soon as his hand moved toward one of his pistols, the fellow went for the pistol tucked into the waist of his trousers. By the time he even touched the pistol, Niles had drawn, aiming the barrel only inches away from the man's forehead.

Having a gun aimed at his head didn't seem to scare him off. He went ahead and pulled the rusty gun out, anyway. Niles pulled the hammer back slowly so that the fellow could hear loudly and clearly the cartridge that might just kill him falling into the chamber. That still did not stop him from waving his gun at Niles, pointing it every time he hollered, "I'll kill you! I'll kill you!" until the gun fell apart, its barrel landing beside his moccasin, leaving only the grip to wave harmlessly in the air as Niles walked away. It was hard to tell whether the poor man kept quiet out of anger or disgrace. Never before had Niles had the bad fortune of having to face off against such a pathetic soul.

Afterward, Rubee cautioned, "He is the type of man who will creep up behind you, Mr. Dewy, and shoot you in the back of the head."

Niles agreed. "I am guessing that's the only way the little runt can defend himself."

"All men are mad," Rubee said. "Some less than others."

Their only landmarks along the way were the creeks and washes that the bull train crossed. On the second day, they did not make it the fifteen miles to Lance Creek, but they did make good time following Willow Creek for nine miles.

On the third day, they navigated over a divide of Lance Creek's tributaries, crossing them just below the fork.

Day four was ten miles long, and they set up camp on the dry, treeless banks of Frozen Man Creek. "Change that to Thirsty Man Creek in a big hurry in this July heat," Sarah joked. The congressman's daughter looked far from the Washington receptions and dinner parties. Her hair was tucked up in a tight bun on the back of her head, and she wore a blue bandanna to keep the sweat out of her eyes and wind out of her hair. After the first day on the trail at the Willow Creek campsite, her wardrobe changed from the riding skirt and high-necked blouse to linen pants and a loose-fitting shirt.

Their fifth day ate up the miles, according to Bosh—and who else would know? From sunup to sundown, they traveled twelve miles to the shores of Cottonwood Creek, another one of the prairie's lies. There was no water and certainly no cottonwood trees. They carried plenty of water for themselves and the animals, but it was difficult to find enough wood for a fire to bring coffee to a boil or to allow Rubee to cook a campfire delicacy.

The prairie does make people crazy, Niles and Rubee knew. So that was the only explanation Niles had for George's preference for spending time with Bosh. "Might just be a freighter someday, Mr. Dewy. Maybe that's how George gets hisself rich," the Negro explained to Niles and Rubee one night.

"Come on, George. This prairie's touched your mind. Start thinking straight. Deadwood's got to be better than this," Niles told him.

"This peace and quiet feels good. You understand, don't ya?"

Rubee nodded. "Yes, I understand."

"Besides, out here, you can't tell George where to go or what to do. I'm my own boss."

The next morning, the train porter was back with Bosh, riding his draft horse beside the lead wagon and listening to the bullwhacker spout off about the Deadwood-to-Fort Pierre trains.

"My wagon's loaded high with mining equipment, building materials, wood stoves, ammunition ... a few cases of guns ... tools, and barrels of dried apples, flour, rice, and sugar. There are crates loaded with coffee, tea, jerky, and even canned fruit. There are fifty-pound bags of dried beans and potatoes and even a bundle of *Bismarck Tribune* telling all about the Custer battle at the Little Bighorn for them who's smart enough to read."

George watched every move Bosh made with the ox team. Bosh drove ten yoke of oxen—twenty animals—plus two extra hitched to the rear of the train in case of a need to trade with the Indians or if an accident downed one of the yoked critters. The bulls were the Texas breed, sporting horns four to five feet across, which they could swing around with such force that they could go right through a man. It was an attack the oxen mounted any time people came near them. Sarah and Kit noted that there was little difference between the temperament of the bulls and the hired hand. The yoke of oxen pulled a string of five wagons lashed together with iron chains like railroad cars steaming down the tracks.

Every morning, the hired hand first harnessed up the wheelers, which were the animals nearest to the lead wagon. Then he moved to the leaders at the head of the team, adding the pointers and wings to the yokes in between. The routine was repeated in reverse every night before picketing the bulls in some belly-tickling grass close enough to their camp to keep any Sioux from walking off with one.

Bosh's whip was similar to that of the hired hand—a hickory staff that was four or five feet long with a long length of braided leather fastened to the end. But Bosh's was different from there on. Attached to the whip's end was another leather string that was a couple of inches long and wider than the end of the braided whip. "The popper don't make so many cuts on the animals," Bosh explained. To show George, he snapped the whip over the horns of a bull, making a pistol-like noise, which encouraged the ox even more than an actual blow.

"He'll kill 'em," Bosh said, pointing the staff at the hired hand leading the front team.
"Son of a bitch beats the piss out of 'em. Ain't going to make it to Deadwood that way." Then he snapped the whip out again, this time aiming over the runt's head. When the whip popped, the poor fellow almost lost his pants because he jumped so fast. George and Bosh burst out laughing as the teamster turned and pointed his staff at the two. "I'll kill both ya assholes! Kill ya!" he yelled, and then he turned his back on them again and gave the lead bulls a hard yank, which they responded to with wild swings of their horns, trying to hook their tormentor. All the challenge did was get the bulls whacked over their heads.

"If the runt owned his own steers, he might treat them better," Bosh told George. "Take me, and I'll get them fleshed up on that sweet grass along Spearfish Creek. When they're meaty enough, I'll butcher 'em out and sell the steaks in Deadwood for a chunk of gold each. Yup! You want to eat? Line Bosh's pockets with gold, you hungry bastards."

"How do you get back to Fort Pierre?" George asked.

"Dumb-ass nigger. Buy a cheap, worn-out team there in Deadwood, drive 'em back, rest 'em up, and take off for Black Hills again."

"Got it all figured out, don't ya?" Niles said, riding up to the wagon.

"I got you figured out, picture man. I'll bet you're a faro dealer. Damn parasite, showing up at every mining camp to suck the gold out of the prospectors' aching muscles."

"I do like showing up at fresh places like mining camps. But making pictures is why," Niles explained. "My gambling is getting there and getting out."

"Ain't getting me, Dewy. Nope! This son of Mother Russia spends his gold buying whiskey and women."

"And bulls," George reminded him.

The trail kept stretching on west over the horizon. Finally, on the sixth day out, they made it to Grindstone Butte after a grueling twelve miles of steep, rolling hill country. The bulls struggled to pull the train up the hillsides, taking a lot of punishment from the teamsters. Coming down the other side, Bosh rode the brake and reined in the team so that the wagons would not take off. All day was hill after hill with hardly a level stretch of trail anywhere.

Bosh declared that they were halfway to Deadwood Gulch the next day, one week after leaving Fort Pierre and only four miles west of Grindstone Butte. "Welcome to paradise, ladies and bastards. Deadman Creek the nicest cemetery on the Dakota plains."

"Trees, shade, water ... it a waste on the dead, Mr. Bosh," George told him.

"You got that right, nigger. Hell, you've got more thinking in the colored head of yours than the dumb-ass half-wit. Called it

Peno Springs up until some freighters got themselves scalped right here, right where we's sittin'. Every one of them poor bastards was pinned to the ground with Sioux arrows. Right over there," he said, pointing where the oxen were grazing. "Say Crazy Horse hisself did the scalping, cut off their balls, then rubbed the dead men's blood all over his own body—"

"I think that is quite enough, Mr. Bosh. I don't need to know the grisly details. Please," Sarah interrupted.

"You'll get used to it, missy, after you've cut off a few balls," Kit told her.

"That's only half the story. Since they was murdered, a lady ghost has been seen floating over the place where they died," Bosh added, pointing again at the same place.

Other than its gory past, Deadman Creek was an oasis in the sea of grass. Elms, cottonwoods, and a few box elders offered a shady refuge from the beating sun. There was a spring, its water cold and crystal clear. The rest of the day was spent watering the stock, collecting a huge pile of firewood, napping in the shade, and the women hung some canvas for a makeshift bathhouse for themselves. Niles's instruction was to keep the runt away while the two women were bathing.

"It's about time you start cooking," Niles suggested to Rubee as they built a fire.

Pointing an accusing finger at Niles, Kit said, "I saw the look on your face, mister. Don't even think of my chickens. You'd be eatin' my livelihood."

Dancing a jig to a Russian tune only Bosh could hear, he said, "'I'll eat your livelihood." He grinned a bit more than he should. "Lay back and spread your legs."

Kit glared at the freighter. "You fat bastard! Screw your asshole then eat shit."

"Shut up! Both of you, please!" Sarah hollered. "Please just shut up, won't you? No one here's a prostitute. For God's sake, no one's buying or selling sex, never—"

"Thanks for the prayer, lady, but don't you even think never out here," Kit interrupted.

Rubee sat quietly, watching for Niles to suggest what they should do. A shrug of his shoulders was it; it was not the answer that Rubee wanted.

Rubee stood and stepped closer the fire. "Ladies and gentlemen, we are all prostitutes in one manner of speaking or another." Sarah hung her head in defeat, and George laughed under his breath, wondering what Rubee was up to this time. Bosh didn't take being called a prostitute standing still. He took a step or two toward Rubee until Niles moved between them.

"We all sell something," Rubee continued. "But we are not talking about prostitution. I believe Mr. Dewy was suggesting now would be a fine time for me to show off my cooking skills."

"Got my vote," George spoke up.

Sarah and Niles clapped, cheering Rubee's decision.

"Your chickens are safe, Miss LeRoy. Bosh, use your bullwhip to snare a couple of prairie dogs or jackrabbits," Rubee ordered.

"No gunfire," Niles added. "Let's not announce we're here. Hell, the smell of Rubee's cooking will do that."

When Bosh returned an hour later, he added four prairie dogs and three gray jackrabbits to the dinner's menu.

"Good hunting," Niles congratulated. "Told you it was a damn smart way to make sure the Sioux don't hear you shooting your supper."

"Did ya know rabbits and antelope screw each other?" Bosh asked while he and Kit dressed out the animals.

"If I was a gambling woman, I'd bet you watched. And I'd bet it made that Russian pride between your legs as hard as one of those hickory sticks."

"Jack-a-lopes. Sioux call 'em that. Jack-a-lopes. Only place in the world you find 'em is on these Dakota prairies," Bosh went on, ignoring Kit's taunting.

Bits of prairie dog and rabbit, dried mushrooms out of Rubee's cook bag, freshly picked prairie onions, fresh sage, and a sprinkling of Rubee's spices simmered in water until a rich sauce coated them. The runt wanted to add to their supper, so when Bosh was not looking, he cut open a gunnysack of potatoes, counted out seven, and tucked them in the fire's embers. When one of the baked potatoes was laid on Bosh's plate, he said nothing, obviously happier with the meal than hollering about the theft. Sarah and Kit wandered off into the bushes around the edge of the trees surrounding the springs and discovered a bramble patch thick with berries. Sarah tasted one, reporting to Kit that it was "as sweet as sugar." The two quickly had a hatful of the berries picked for dessert.

The sun was beginning to ride the western horizon when the meal was ready. The aroma of Rubee's prairie dog and rabbit stew hung over the campsite, and the smell of brewing coffee was so heavy that they could almost drink the air itself. Niles needed to make a contribution, but all he had was some after-dinner refreshments. He uncorked one of his bottles of Tennessee whiskey and passed it around the campfire after the meal when everyone was full and lying back to gaze at the canopy of stars overhead.

"Back home, never seen a sky full of stars like this, Mr. Dewy," George said before taking his turn with the whiskey. "It's like the sun exploded and made thousands of little fires. What do you think of that?"

"Nigger head's smart," Bosh said, giving the hired hand sitting next to him a poke in the ribs.

"I'll kill ya!"

"How many times you gonna kill me, runt?"

"Every time."

That night, under the low-reaching branches of a cottonwood, Sarah and Niles slept together.

"How much you charge him last night?" Kit asked Sarah the next morning.

"Nothing!" Sarah snapped back as Kit's insinuation. "I gave him everything he wanted for free!"

"Just remember what I said; don't give it away. If you can't sell it, sit on it."

That day, they continued past sundown, making up for the lost time. The festivities of the day before were quickly forgotten, and most of the day, everyone stayed to themselves, trying their best just to ride out the day. Fourteen miles from the springs, they finally stopped, setting up a dark, cold, dry camp at the Mitchell Creek crossing.

The next morning, while the teamsters prepared the wagons and stock for their ninth day on the trail, George, Sarah, Kit, Rubee, and Niles were sharing a breakfast of dried venison, canned peaches, crackers, and water when a distant popping sound interrupted the dawn's quiet. It was very far off, but even to hear the faint popping gave Niles a jolt of excitement. Another bandit holdup or Indian raid would be welcomed entertainment for Niles. The others in the party might not have agreed, but Niles liked to continue sharpening his edge the closer they came to the end of the road, always checking his guns, ammunition, eyesight, and reflexes.

"We have company, ladies and gentlemen," he said. He walked around to the other side of the wagons where Bosh was tightening ropes. "Hear that?"

"What? All I hear is you pumping in and out of that wife of yours all night."

Niles barely let Bosh finish his words before there was a pistol jammed into the man's fat belly. "Told you once never to talk about the lady that way. If I have to warn you a third time, I'll stick this barrel up your ass and shoot you inside out. Got it?"

Bosh stared into Niles's eyes briefly and saw that he might just do it. "Ya. I hear gunshots. Behind us to the east. A long way east."

"Gunshots? What are you up to this time, you ugly Russian?"

"Bosh is up to nothing, as you say."

"Just like you were up to nothing when we were ambushed by those bandits east of Willow Creek?"

"Ya, that right. Bosh is up to nothing."

"You're up to your head in nothing. Who's back there?" Niles demanded. By now, he detested the freighter and would find great pleasure in blowing him away.

"Sioux, pilgrims, freighters, army, outlaws—"

"Oh shut your damn mouth. We're all outlaws out here."

Bosh ignored Niles's order. "Probably all of them's breathing down our necks. You scout if you want to know. Bosh thinks the army's protecting the generals. Ain't no army of prospectors, 'cause the Sioux'd leave 'em alone. Could be another freight outfit, but when we left the fort, there wasn't a freighter anywhere ready to leave." Then, studying the eastern horizon, he added, "Could be hunters."

"Hunters. You're so goddamn smart you probably shit through your mouth so you can save up words. There ain't enough buffalo out there to waste that many shells."

Bosh stuck a filthy finger in his mouth and then pointed it in the air. "Sioux," he said, grinning.

"Does your wind tell you who they were fighting? Sounded to me like it was a small group, not that many shots. It was a short battle—"

"Someone got run off, or someone lost their scalp," Rubee interrupted. "Mr. Dewy," Rubee said, bowing toward him. "Mr. Bosh." There was another bow. "Perhaps we should go."

"I told you, ya filthy little yellow-eyed chink, to keep out of my business." Bosh was about to pull Rubee off the horse, when suddenly, from thin air, Rubee had a two-foot-long silver stiletto stabbing into the freighter's throat. At the same time, Bosh again felt the barrel of Niles's pistol, this time jammed into his back. He slowly let go of Rubee, lowered his arms, and stepped to the side. "Like I was just saying, let's go," he said. "The little slant-eye's right."

Chapter 10

Flies.

Hundreds of flies.

Yet it was hard to count even one fly. The buzz of each fly, though, could be heard. It was an agitating sound that grew louder as more flies joined the feast.

Dark clouds of flies swarmed over the dead.

Coal-black flies gorged their craven appetites on the dying flesh.

Black, shimmering dots scurried from the carcass of Clay's dead horse to the dead Sioux. They crawled across the eyeballs, up nostrils, in and out of ears, and so many got inside the gaping mouths that it looked like the dead were chewing on black, fuzzy balls, torturing the two grateful dead who felt or knew nothing. Clay used the feeding frenzy to pass the time trying to follow one fly in and out of a body crevice.

Sometimes, Clay thought that he could see the dark clouds capturing the ghosts of the dead, only to shatter the spirits into hundreds of pieces when the bugs flew their separate ways. "You're going to hell. A never-ending, buzzing purgatory's waiting for you." Clay had to deal with his own hell; constant buzzing was a hell for the living, as well, tormenting Clay more than the plain's isolation. The sound felt like it was drilling through his ears, into his head, first setting his nerves on edge, but as the morning grew older, Clay's temper grew until it took control. He made himself ignore his companions in the wash, dead and alive, trying to aim the rage at the Indians hiding somewhere around him. With every noise, every flicker caught in the corner of his eye, he just knew that it was the Sioux returning to finish with him and pick up their dead.

"Come on!" Clay yelled, no longer crouching behind the wall. He stood in the wash, screaming at the prairie and waving his rifle in the air over his head. "I'm right here! Or can't you stinking redskins see me, you blind bastards?"

He then turned his temper loose on his dead horse, giving it a kick and sending a black cloud of flies into the air. "You think this is pretty damn funny, don't you?" he asked, giving the horse another kick. Pointing at the sky, he said, "All you're good for now is food for them damn buzzards. Me? I killed for a horse they'd sell to rich men back at Fort Pierre. Rich men!" he screamed as he landed another blow. "More horse than you ever was!" His kicks grew to one punch after another until he exhausted himself. "Rich man, you son of a bitch."

Since the raiding party disappeared, Clay had been twisting and turning, ready to confront any sound—the sound of blowing grass, meadowlarks landing and taking off, even the dead Indian's horse still grazing on the scattered weeds along the edges of the dry wash. That horse was Clay's escape. Just catch it, mount, and ride off. Somehow, Clay felt it that might not be so easy. Before that could happen, his concern was still the return of the Indians, expecting them to ride over the grassy slopes at any moment.

A few hours after seeing the last Indian, Clay chanced crawling over the gravel bed toward the dead Sioux. He retrieved the Navy Colt pistol flung aside by the dying man. "Your stinking chief's going to miss you, gunfighter," he grumbled while examining the revolver. Moving to the body, he found tied to the Indian's buckskin belt a leather pouch of bullets. He loaded the gun's empty chamber and then stuck it inside his own waistband, jamming the pouch of cartridges into his shirt pocket. On the other side of the belt, a red, yellow, and blue-beaded sheath held a horn-handled knife. At first, Clay shied away from taking the knife. He was set on leaving it behind, sure that its sharp edge had been used to scalp white men. "That's stupid!" he yelled at himself, tugging the sheath free from the belt. "I got a few haircuts of my own in mind," he told the dead Indian, slashing at the air with the blade.

"Might just be fun teasing the girls. Slice off a clump of hair or two when that Chinese woman or blonde whore don't do what I tell 'em." Then he started acting out the knife's future, imagining how he would use it on the girls, shredding dress sleeves, popping off the buttons, cutting the bodice laces underneath, letting them feel the pleasure of the blade scratching down their skin as he shaved off the rest of their clothing.

Clay smiled for the first time all morning. "Maybe tattoos on their cheeks," he said, adding, "Top and bottom cheeks, of course!" He giggled.

His arsenal had grown, but it was of little help waiting for the Sioux to return, and it did not arm him against his own fears. He had convinced himself that he was immune from fear. Now he cowered in fear in a trench dug by Mother Nature's armies in this vast, empty battlefield.

Rolling the deadweight of his horse back and forth, Clay finally got the saddle off. He propped it up against the side of the wash and went after the brown-and-white mare wandering the creek bed maybe a hundred yards away to the south. "Here I go, Chief Dead Ass," he said, stepping over the Indian. "Could've brought a lariat with ya," he told the corpse. Clay knew himself well enough to know that having a rope would be useless. Roping animals in an Illinois county was very seldom called for; it was usually reserved for a rabid dog or runaway milk cow. Nope, his first encounter with a near-wild Indian pony was going to be empty-handed. Clay's other choice was leave the horse behind and walk to Deadwood.

"Easy, girl," he said over and over as he drew closer. "It'll be fine. I'll treat you like a fine Chicago whore. Yup, that I will. Easy, girl. Easy." Clay was only a couple of yards away from the braided rope reins dragging across the ground, studying on the best way to snatch the rope. "I'd take a bath, shave," he whispered, careful not to do anything that might spook the animal. "Comb my hair back, rose water. I'd treat them ladies right fine," Clay said, slowly reaching for the rope. He moved his hand before the horse could react. "And they'd treat me just fine," he said, grabbing the rein. "Huh! Gotcha, bitch!" He gave a tug, tugged again, and with the third try, the horse's stubbornness let go, and she began following his lead. Getting the saddle on her back did not go as smoothly as Clay had suspected. The pony stood quietly while her blanket and the cinch ropes were taken off, but when Clay picked up his own saddle blanket, the horse's eyes went wide and wild, and she shied away, pulling Clay along with her. Clay shortened the lead, working his way close enough again, and then he tried to throw the blanket on her back. This time, she wiggled and bucked a little, sending Clay's saddle blanket flying.

He pulled her near the Indian blanket. "You can't get around me, bitch," he told the horse. "Try this on for size," he said in a smooth voice as the horse let him return the old blanket to her back. "Now let's see what happens next."

The horse looked away from Clay and snorted a time or two but did not move away. Her twitching flanks were the only sign that she was not yet won over. On top of the Indian blanket, Clay gently placed his own. The pony was still suspicious. Like a wagging finger, she threw her head up and down, yanking Clay's arm along. The saddle blankets held on, but as soon as Clay started lifting his saddle, the horse began twisting, throwing her head, pulling back on the rope, and trying every contortion she could to keep the saddle off. Clay tired of fighting the animal, gathered his rifle and canteen, and led the horse out of the wash. "Waste my time, damn squaw. I'll tell you this—you got the manners of a Chicago whore."

He felt ten feet tall now that he was out of the wash like a lone tree surveying the prairie. The hot air no longer had the burned-dust smell rising off the sand and gravel. Standing above the wash, the air carried the scent of grass, and there was a breeze cooling the heat, giving Clay a shiver the first time he felt it through his sweat-soaked shirt.

He turned, looking back at the wash and seeing the ditch really for the first time. Camping in the dark and hiding in it never gave him a chance to study his fortress. Above ground, it did not look as deep as Clay had imagined from the bottom, and it was actually narrow enough that maybe he could jump across. The longer he looked at the wash, the dead Sioux, and the horse, the more it churned his belly, feeling more and more like his stomach was being forced up his throat. Without any further warning, green-colored bile exploded from his mouth. There was nothing else, just the bitter acid. He put his hands on his knees so as not to fall over, letting the rest of the convulsion work itself out of his system. They were dry heaves, heavy blows to his stomach, sending sharp pain through his body, prying apart his throat and mouth, waiting for vomit that would never come, gagging Clay with every spasm. And then it would start all over again. The choking brought him to his knees gasping for breath, and there was a sour taste in his mouth. Once he was able to breathe again and his stomach had quieted, Clay felt like he had just taken the beating of his life, and he was sure that his insides were black and blue.

Suddenly, he realized that if anyone were watching, kneeling as he was, it must look like he was offering a prayer over the dead. He jumped to his feet. "Damn grave," he said, spitting some of the foul scum in his mouth into the wash. "Assholes!" he hollered. "You taste like shit. Amen!" Saying no more, he turned west, following the ruts of the Deadwood road, leading the Indian's horse behind him.

He asked himself, *Will this prairie ever end?* He had been watching the endless reach of the plains since the keelboat had sailed past the mouth of the Platte River a couple of days south of Fort Pierre. He did not want his mind to empty like the land, spending much of his traveling time planning his revenge. And the two women had become an obsession, possessing his thoughts so completely that they stirred excitement in his belly and often stiffened his cock. Sometimes, the empty landscape became a backdrop for his visions of the women's faces and bodies as they squirmed beneath his weight as he was poking them. And in the end, his mind was set on killing them both. Clay's mind wandered in between the land of poking and the land of killing as he crossed the endless prairie.

What more could he do with them?

What could they do for him? Two naked, bald women lying at his feet. What possibilities. Not like the whores who let him get in and out of them and then showed him the door ... he would keep these two around for a while to play with. In this wilderness, nobody would give a damn what he was doing to the women, except maybe the nigger and that slick gunslinger who claimed to be the blonde's husband.

"Husband, huh!" Clay hollered at the prairie. "Before I kill him, I'll make the son of a bitch watch me poke his wife." The idea sent a rash of goose bumps up his arms and a lusty tickle deep in his groin. He reached for the bone-handle knife and began slicing the air. "Then I'll cut off his balls and jam his limp penis inside his wife," he said, sneering. "She'll be married to ya then!" The image of jamming the man's part into her mouth while he was screwing her stiffened his penis again.

"Time to look for the Sioux," he said, trying to shake off the hardness. "Like screwing. Like killing," he added.

He searched the prairie and found no sign of danger. He did discover since leaving the wash that they had been moving right along. Clay's make-believe world had masked the hours of walking, step after step lost to his fantasies.

By Clay's way of counting, his catch was on their ninth day and should be pretty worn out by now, lulled into the monotony of their slow progress. With the Indian pony, daylight, and some luck, he could still get a few miles closer to the freight train and maybe even catch them. "The Sioux ain't helping you get away. No, sir! I'm still coming," Clay yelled at the invisible prey.

To keep his mind off the women, he set his sights on the western horizon. The wind was calm, allowing the heat to grab onto everything, reminding Clay of a magnet he had seen one time that attracted metal shavings. The monotony of watching the July heat along the horizon, watching it boil like a kettle of water and sending shimmering waves of steam into the air, had the same effect on him as his daydreams. Again, he was thrown into a trance, a mindless walking routine.

Mindless walking ...

Walking ...

The heat ...

Boiling horizon …

The sound of the horses …

The sun had made little progress sinking from its midday high. Clay was moving along, mesmerized by the dancing heat, when the faint sound of a distant explosion coming beyond the west's horizon shook the plains into the here and now. The noise snapped Clay out of his daze, but all that remained of the sound was its echo fading away as the prairie soaked it up. It sounded like a small bomb going off. Clay desperately tried to remember what he had heard. *It was not the crack of a carbine,* he thought. It was more like a small bomb. It had to have been a high-caliber rifle, or he would not have heard it unless they were right over the next hill. It was clear that the sound came from ahead of them and not behind. Far ahead of them. *Who'd be shooting gophers with a buffalo gun?* Buffalo hunters? Clay had seen nothing but bleached bones cluttering the prairie, not one sign of a live beast.

The fancy gunfighter, he thought. "Showin' off, ain't ya?" he yelled, knowing that the words would fall to the ground unheard. Clay tried to remember if he had seen a high-caliber rifle when searching the baggage car. "Could have it hidden," he said, giving himself a good excuse. "You hide a lot of shit, don't ya, you screw asses?"

Indians?

"That's it!" The raiders who attacked him this morning had caught up with the bull train. "Close," he whispered, listening for a second shot. Why were the Indians not firing back? Scared off by one shot? If they were the same band that had hit him, they had several firearms. One less thanks to Clay, he congratulated himself, patting the bulge made by the Colt tucked in the waist of his pants.

He leaned closer to the horse's ear. "If I can hear their gunfire, we can have our fun tonight," he said.

Chapter 11

July 30, 1876

Madam Mustache stood smack-dab in the middle of the trail where there were no longer ruts carved in the prairie sod. It now wound along a boulder-strewn trail with a rapid, foaming creek on one side and pine-covered rocky side hills on the other. The woman's shape was nearly as round as some of the boulders rolled aside to clear a way for the bull trains. Her legs seemed to start at her knees, or at least that was where her dress was hemmed. *Dress* was a loose description of the getup. Starting from ground up, she wore a pair of beaded Indian moccasins and canvas miner's trousers, and the dress over that unbuttoned halfway up the front to her neck, under which she showed off layers of scarves—red, blue, pink, green, and gold, each draping her chest like a wave from a falling rainbow.

Eleanor "Madam Mustache" Dumont is a looker, Niles thought to himself, and then he could not help laughing out loud. "Depends on who's doing the looking, I guess," he said, shaking his head.

"Champagne's on me!" she shouted as soon as her newest mark was close enough to hear. She waved a goblet in one hand and a green glass bottle in the other. "Welcome to Deadwood Gulch, mister, the shiniest spot in these black mountains!" she hollered out, waving the green bottle over her head. "Champagne, French champagne straight from New Orleans. Nothing finer. Seein' how the prairie didn't bake ya and the injun's didn't scalp ya, your first libation's on me. After that, you're on your own."

While she talked, she moved toward them, skipping from rock to rock, jogging around others, and even jumping a few that she could manage. She looked like a child's ball rolling down the hill.

What a welcome to the Black Hills, Niles thought, and he laughed. "Eleanor Dumont. Still peddling that soda water?" he asked, hollering so that she could hear.

The woman stopped, straining her neck as she squinted for a better look through the ever-changing pattern of flickering light and shadows cast by the trees and sun as they danced the day away. That is how Niles and the rest of them had felt since leaving the prairie. Everything about the Black Hills seemed to be a dream; the air was of sweet-smelling pine, and it was so cool in some of the deepest shadows near the creek that it gave them shivers. They were tired and beaten by the prairie. But somehow, these shadowed hills they had entered had given them a brand-new strength, and they had pulled out of their sunburned selves as if the trees had grabbed a hold and given each a good shaking out.

"Well, I'll be a goatherd's bitch. If it ain't the picture man. It sure's heck must be the truth … all roads leadin' to Deadwood this summer!" the woman yelled as she ran toward Niles. "I'm fixin' on dying a happy, rich woman," she said, adding loud yelps along the way for punctuation every time she maneuvered to avoid another sharp, stony edge for fear that it would puncture her. "I have a hunch you might as well take my gold right now and save me the trouble," she complained to Niles, carrying on in the middle of the trail and presenting a leather sack from a pocket in her outfit, waving it in the air. "Might as well take all my worldly goods. Tell me to my face—nobody in the gulch will have any money left to buy a bath by the time you leave," she challenged him. Waving the sack again, she said, "What money I have will go right into that pipe," she said, showing her mock frustration by kicking at loose stones until one of them turned on her, not being as loose as she had imagined. It hurt the toe enough; her face grimaced from the sudden pain. "They're going to smoke up their gold now that you showed up. All that gold going right up in smoke. Melt it down and smoke it away. I know all about that black tar," she said, registering a knowing nod.

Niles had settled in to take a long listen. He had not forgotten how the woman could carry on.

"She's with ya, right?"

"Who?" Niles asked, trying to sound as innocent as he could.

"Don't try to give this barber a close shave, sonny."

To a few like Miss Dumont, Bill Hickok, and short list of others, Rubee and Niles were familiar travelers. What they all had in common was making the edge of the frontier their business at one time or another in the last ten years. Niles felt that they were being lined up like billiard balls waiting to bump into each other as the frontier grew smaller and smaller.

Madam Mustache Dumont was one of those frontier folks who knew that, when the picture man made an appearance, the Yellow Doll and opium had arrived. "Damn it!" Dumont cussed finally, slapping her middle. "If I didn't like the shit so much," she admitted, shaking her head in resignation.

"And the money," Niles reminded her. In their past encounters with the woman, Eleanor had never been slow in arranging a place to open an opium den along with her other enterprises. "Are you open for business in Deadwood?"

"Everyone needs a shave and a grave. Backdoor bathhouse, barberin,' and buryin', it's the first place you come to entering Deadwood."

"How many burying holes you digging, Mustache?" Niles asked.

The woman feigned a bad back. "I've dug my fingers to the bone. Deadwood's a dying place."

"The only damage to your fingers was the pain you felt paying some poor grave digger." Niles laughed.

Mustache looked a bit disgusted. "Only two this week," she said, straightening up. Niles suspected that she was working herself into some kind of serious. Without thinking, he reached for the pistol on his left hip and quietly cocked it. It was a business decision that he was sure to make more often. "It's enough business to keep my mustache trimmed," she told him, ruffling her namesake, a thin mustache across her upper lip. "Besides, buryin' business up here gives me the shakes," she said to Niles like she was confiding in a close friend. *That's what she is,* Niles thought while listening to her. An addict is always the dealer's friend. "These hills' dark canyons and shadows can give ya the dying willies if ya let 'em."

Atop the spheres that made up Eleanor's body sat a head ball crowned by a haircut advertising her skill. She knew one way to cut hair and one way only—put a bowl over the top of the customer's head and chop away with whatever you have handy. "Dull knife, scissors if you're lucky. Hell, I chew the damn stuff off if I have to."

"You're not traveling alone, are you? Where is she?" she asked.

Rubee, Kit, and Sarah were fifty yards or more behind Niles, still hidden from Dumont by the pine and underbrush where the trail bent along the creek. George was even farther back. He had told Niles when they had first entered the Black Hills that he wanted to enjoy the cool pine-scented breeze all by himself. "Smells so fresh and clean, Mr. Niles, that it's like George is smellin' new." And Niles understood, himself feeling the shivers that the place sent through his chest.

For some reason, the Black Hills planted a very strange feeling in Niles. Maybe it was the shock of leaving the prairie so abruptly. But so far, he had been unable to put his finger on the nervous tingle itching inside his chest until Mustache's diagnosis. "Dying willies," he whispered to himself as he studied the shadows. That's it—an eerie sort of feeling like he was walking down a dark alley. Looking up the canyon walls just on the other side of the creek, they could easily be walls of buildings restricting him, blocking his escapes, and blinding his aim. Out on the prairie, Niles could see forever. They could set the Sharps aside now; they were in the Black Hills.

At times, the prairie had left Niles feeling naked, unable in any way to fight off the sun and the wind. The prairie had its way with you, and little could be done to hold it at bay. The Black Hills wrapped themselves around the riders, clearing the dust from their nostrils with the clean, almost peppermint odor of pine. Out on the prairie, where they had traveled days between watering holes, these Black Hills seemed to be crisscrossed by a maze of creeks and streams that at times made the air itself smell like water. It was not the stale, fishy, slow-water smell like the Potomac River back in the federal city. Here, the air felt like it was part of the water, suspending spray as it dashed against and around canyon walls and rocks. Niles had read about oases of water and shade discovered in the great sand deserts of Africa, much as the Black Hills was an oasis caught in another kind of desert—a never-ending prairie.

"How did an outlaw like you get past the Sioux?"

"Could ask you the same question," Eleanor shot right back. "Hell, picture man, I know how you got through," she answered herself, using the hand holding the goblet like she was drawing a pistol out of a hip holster. "As for me, them mighty Sioux take one look at my face and they're so confused whether to scalp my lip or my top knot that I'd walk right by 'em like I wasn't even there," she said, ruffling first the mustache and then her bowl-cut hair.

Hearing the ring of more horseshoes echoing over the sound of the creek, she twisted herself to see around Niles just as the riders made the turn in the trail. Dumont studied the sunburned and dusty pilgrims as each made the turn. "One, two, three. Bringin' your own pictures with you this trip," she said, sounding very sober, not at all like the cheerful barber. "Never figured you to be one runnin' girls."

"Nothing to worry about, Mustache," Niles quickly corrected, introducing each rider as they came out of the bend. "Sarah Culbert," he said, pointing at the lead rider. "And Kit LeRoy—she's the chicken lady there. She's going to set up a cafe."

Eleanor squinted to get a better look at the third rider coming around the corner. Rubee's hat was pulled down, the long braid pinned underneath and a bandanna covering her face from nose to chin. Dumont waddled closer, looking at Rubee and studying what she could see. "Slant-eye, that you?" But the ring of more horseshoes falling against stone and announcing the arrival of still another customer for her enterprise cut Dumont's scrutiny short. She could make out another rider through the trees, but the thick underbrush of berry bushes kept Eleanor bobbing back and forth, trying to catch a glimpse between the ponderosa pine and the shadows. Then she set her eyes on the bend in the trail. She first saw the nose and then the long face of the horse, its ears twitching from the sound of rushing water.

Dumont let out with a loud rebel yell, "Looky here! Y'all got the first nigger I'd seen up in the gulch. Downright traveling with a crowd, ain't ya?" she hollered back at Niles. "A chicken woman, a fancy lady, a nigger." She turned her scrutiny back toward Rubee. "It's you, ain't it?" she asked.

Rubee pulled down the bandanna and then removed the hat.

"I knew it! I knew it!" Eleanor shouted. "Come on, gold's a-waitin'. Champagne's on me!" she yelled, offering the goblet to Sarah. "If you get tired of one fella," Dumont said, laughing and waving the green bottle in the air, "come on over to my place, the Backdoor Bathhouse and Barbershop—Badlands' end of the gulch. You'll be as pretty as gold to all them lonely fellas. And they'll pay a pretty sack of gold dust to let you wash their backside. No offense, picture man!" Dumont hollered.

"None taken," Niles said.

"I take offense!" Sarah's temper snapped, her glare darting back and forth from the plump woman to Niles and then finally resting on Kit. "Is that all you women do out here? Sell yourselves?"

"Can't carry around nothing more valuable than all them girl parts," Dumont told her, getting as close as she could to performing a sexy sashay, but then she hesitated, obviously rethinking offering the goblet to Sarah. "What you saying, missy?" she asked, slanting her eyes suspiciously at Kit. "This chicken woman set on selling more'n eggs?"

"Eggs—that's it," Kit assured, reaching behind to rattle one of the chicken cages tied to the saddle. "Maybe a beefsteak on the side, but a basket of eggs'll be my sack of gold."

That bit of news put Dumont back in her jovial mood. "Skinny girls always get more men than us big ones," she said, turning away from the riders to retrieve a mule hobbled near the creek. "But trust me, us big girls know how to make everyone happy. Come on, follow me, and I'll lead y'all into Deadwood. We got ourselves a right pretty parade here," she called out, spurring the mule. "Y'all can fix me supper tonight, lady. I'll be your first customer. Fry me up a batch of eggs. Them yolks as hard as a gold miner's heart."

"You should be a poet, Miss Dumont," Rubee said.

"No money in that," Dumont told her. "Any more of you?" she asked, looking down the trail. "This is quite a bunch to take off across that prairie all alone."

"We were with a bull train until a day and a half ago," Sarah offered. "But the vulgarity of the teamsters sent us ahead."

"Dirty-minded, stinkin'-body teamsters … that's money in Madam's pocket," Dumont sang out, hearing the news.

"Sorry, only two of them," Niles told her.

"And one of them's a runt who'd get lost in you and never be seen again." Kit laughed.

"Oh, well, there'll be more after them. Fort Pierre must be like a dam ready to burst." She slapped the mule's hindquarters with the end of the leather reins, which only made the animal twist around and try to bite her instead of speeding it up. This prompted a brief battle between the two. Dumont swatted the animal with the reins, and the mule tried to bite back. All the while, Mustache kept up her end of the conversation. "You and that Yellow Doll can disappear quicker'n mercury runnin' off a mirror, I swear. Then, poof—like smoke—you show up here." Dumont managed to bring the mule to a standstill, leaving her looking at Niles instead of up the trail where she intended to go. "What is it with you two?"

"What happened to your Nevada City dreams? That's where you were heading the last time we saw you," Niles said, hoping to deflect any more questions. He hated questions. Questions in general had never been a conversation starter for Niles. A question required an answer, and when they were traveling, answers were never were easy to come by.

"Lord of leapin' lizards! Where are you?" she asked, waving her stubby arms wildly. "Deadwood," she said, answering her own question. The woman produced a pistol from the folds of her costume and took two quick shots at a dead ponderosa wedged between the rocks along the bank of the creek. "That's what happened to them Nevada City dreams. Deadwood!"

All of the horses shied away from the ricocheting noise. The mules kicked up their hind heels, Eleanor yelled, and George joined the commotion, kicking his mount into a gallop and passing the rest of them, rounding the next twist in the trail and disappearing. The sound of his shouts and the ring of metal horseshoes against stone echoed long after he was out of their sight.

"Let me give ya the lay of the land, picture man," she began, sidling her mule up to Niles. "Plenty of beans and boomtown whiskey. More get-rich schemes than smart brains to make them work. Got a dance hall, fancy-dressed lawyers from back east, but we ain't got no law. No law, did you hear me?" she said again, and then she turned on Niles. "And a Chinaman called Long Ears running a butcher shop and opium joint. Don't buy the meat 'less you like dog or horse," she warned him. Then she hesitated before continuing, "Long Ears makes sure he makes the money and not you. Don't tell me I didn't warn you."

Niles and Rubee had planned on it being the case that someone would already be peddling opium in Deadwood. That way, they would be able to arrange a sale of their entire load to one person instead of staying longer and selling the opium a pinch at a time, one addict at a time. The longer they stayed in Deadwood only increased the chances of trouble. Niles considered Dumont's news promising for an early return to the States.

Eleanor slowed her mule so that it would make a nice, gentle turn, pointing her in Niles's direction. "I ain't the only friend the Yellow Doll's got in the gulch," she said. "I seen Bill Hickok hangin' around Long Ears's joint." But before Niles could react, she kicked the mule around again, and off they trotted.

Bill Hickok. This was the second time his name had come up since they'd left Fort Pierre, and Niles knew that it would not take Hickok long to discover that they were in the gulch. He loved to pose in front of Niles's camera, even going so far as to wear a fancy getup, get his hair and handlebar mustache trimmed, and get his boots polished. Underneath the dandy front was another opium addict. A dangerous one. One side of the man was the congenial gentleman gambler and upholder of the law. The other side of the man was the opium addict, disposed to bullying and threatening to get his supply of the drug rather than paying, and this Bill Hickok was the killer. When opium was around, Bill could be dangerous, not caring what he had to do or whom he had to do it to in order to get his fill of the narcotic.

"Come on, still have a ways to go and money to make 'fore tomorrow's sunup!" Eleanor yelled out.

"I am not waiting for morning. I'll pay for a bath tonight!" Sarah hollered back, hoping that the woman had heard.

Niles laughed watching Eleanor nearly roll off the back of her mule, trying to twist around to seal the deal with Sarah. "Nickel for the bath. Nickel for the soap. Nickel for the towel. Don't s'pose I could interest you in a shave?" She laughed.

"Don't tell me!" Sarah hollered back. "If I did, it would cost me a nickel."

"Bang! The lady got it right. Everything costs a nickel … 'cept buryin'. That's fifty cents. Just the hole, mind you. I'm not in the coffin-building business. I'll plant ya in a hole and cover ya up. Fifty cents is as fancy as Madam Mustache goes."

Riding behind Sarah, Kit moved a little closer. "These layers of travel we're wearing's as good as wearing a mask. Hell, lady, as you are now, no one in Deadwood Gulch'ld have any idea you were such a pretty-looking thing. I'd think twice about that bath," she told her.

Rubee overheard Kit's advice. "She's right, Miss Culbert. In some places, it is good not to let people know who you are. Deadwood may be such a place."

Sarah rode ahead. "I am sure you are both right, but this lady needs a bath, and she's getting one. I will handle the consequences of a clean life, thank you."

After more than two hours of winding alongside the creek, the trail gradually climbed into the forest overlooking the sheer stone cliffs that pinched the water into a narrowing gorge. From there, the riders could see maybe three quarters of a mile up the canyon. The same creek they were following split the gulch in two, each side beached by a sand-and-gravel plain several hundred yards wide in some places before a thin pine forest reclaimed the lower reaches of the hillsides. Above that and up the barren slopes to the mountains and the cliffs that crowned them, it was easy to see how the canyon had earned its name. The sides of the gulch, whether they be rock or gravel, were cluttered with dead trees—seventy- and eighty-foot-long logs bare of limbs and branches. The trees were straight as a rifle shot, countless numbers thrown against the sides of the canyon like sticks. And it was like that as far as they could see—an entire forest long ago felled by a force as powerful at that time as the gold rush now consuming the gulch.

Mustache kept them to the high south side of the stream, sending tiny avalanches of stone rippling in their wake as the horses and mules picked their way around the deadfall and boulders. Below, along the creek, they spotted their first prospectors working the gravel beds, most using pans to wash through the gravel, though a few already had elaborate sluice systems constructed. The gulch widened, making a broad, fairly flat plain already host to a handful of log shanties, campaign tents, small corrals, and a few wagons.

"Bet you ain't seen civilization like this 'tween here and the Missouri!" Eleanor hollered to her entourage.

The trail continued westward up a gradually widening canyon, where plenty of ponderosa pines crowded the creek and the neighboring hillsides. They crested the saddleback of a low hill and maneuvered the horses and mules around a tree-studded rock outcropping. Before them was Deadwood.

Mustache had warned Niles not to let the first impression sour him on Deadwood. "Low end we call the Badlands, here under the brown rock cliffs," she said, pointing to the layer of rock towering over a bend in Whitewood Creek. "Up canyon's Main Street."

The slopes had been cleared of most trees. A few log buildings appeared open for business, and according to Eleanor, no matter what they advertised, they were in the business of selling whiskey.

Just below the hill sat Madam Mustache's Backdoor Bath, Barber & Burying. A canvas draped over a couple of poles hung in place by ropes tied to a ten-foot-tall pine stump made up the roof and a side of her place, and true to her advertising, there really was a back door. The woman had constructed a pine plank wall that was maybe eight feet high and eight feet long, and she'd somehow tricked it into standing upright. In the middle of it was a door. The wall was not attached to anything; it stood on its own, a one-wall building ready with a door—a door that went nowhere. Farther up the road from Eleanor's back door, the bare skeleton of a frame building sat waiting to be closed in, and from there on up, Deadwood's main street appeared to be a collection of tents and log affairs of varying degrees of engineering know-how and boomtown ingenuity.

Niles chose a level area on the hill overlooking the Backdoor for his campsite. He could see all of the comings and goings around the bathhouse. It was an easy rifle shot. Moving downhill a short distance, his pistols would be in good range. Just after they had put up their tent and started a fire, Kit and Sarah were off to the bathhouse.

While the women took their baths and did what they needed to do to feel ladylike again after their prairie crossing, Rubee prepared a meal that sent a cloud of aroma drifting on the wind and blowing through the gulch. If they had been opening an eating establishment, the smell alone would have lined up customers. A stew of wild onions, dried garlic, and mushrooms served over boiled rice, along with beans prepared with honey, black pepper, and onions, was the feast welcoming them to Deadwood.

"An ancient Chinese tale tells how, long ago, the gods sent the ox to man's world to help the farmer plow more land for rice. When the ox returned to tell the gods of his time with man, the beast proudly proclaimed that now man could eat three meals every day. The gods were horrified, telling the ox that it was supposed to only help enough to feed man one meal every three days. To correct this mistake, the gods sent the ox back to man's world to bear the weight of its error for the rest of time."

After the meal, George, Eleanor, and Rubee went down the hill to the Backdoor with the larger of their two tents. Niles sat watching the shadows of the three appear and disappear in the Bathhouse's flickering campfires while he drank Kit's strong coffee leftover from supper, using the time to clean and reload his guns. The camera gear would wait until morning to be unpacked—not his guns. And he could do this familiar routine—removing the cylinders, dismantling the barrel assembly, swabbing the metal clean, and dabbing oil in the firing mechanism—with his eyes closed. It was exactly how he felt when he used a black box to develop photographs inside the tiny tent. Sometime around midnight, George and Rubee returned to the camp, walking out of the night and into Niles's firelight. "I'm takin' a nap 'fore sunrise," George announced as he wandered off into the dark to bed down. Sarah and Kit were sharing the tent, along with Kit's chickens, which she swore up and down would lay eggs by morning now that they had a roof over their heads.

Niles was not planning on eggs for breakfast. The kettle of water boiling for Rubee's tea and a freshly brewed pot of coffee was far more reliable than Kit's eggs.

Rubee walked among the photography cases, selecting the ones with the false sides and moving them near the fire. In the light, the polished finishes were hidden under a cake of trail dirt, which Niles began cleaning away.

The clasps holding the top hinges together were undone, and then, using a small implement, Rubee removed the brass screws, loosening a tin cap fastened to the top of each of the four sides. Beginning with the front of the case, Rubee slid out of place a thin wooden panel, one precisely fitted to the front. There was another for the back and one on each side. Behind the wood veneer, sandwiched against the case's outer wall, a piece of parchment paper covered a thin sheet of opium, which Rubee carefully peeled free of the case. The drug had been pressed to a thickness of the brim of a hat. It was pliable like hat felt, and it was sticky and as black as charcoal.

When the last case was back to its original configuration, the unloading of the opium was complete. Five camera cases, four sheets of opium per case, and twenty sheets of the drug were 133 pounds of opium.

Dawn was still maybe an hour away.

Now came the wait for tomorrow. Niles sat back, a new cup of coffee to warm the mountain's night chill. The opium always intrigued him. It could be molded into whatever shape was required for its transport and sale. The drug created its own secret life, much as Niles Dewy was created. Opium made everyone who came in contact with it an outlaw. And, in the towns from Deadwood to Hong Kong, the secret opium trade flourished because of the invisible people who moved it around the world. Opium was a black, shadowy presence much like the images captured in a Niles Dewy photograph.

"Welcome to Deadwood, Rubee," Niles offered, holding one of the sheets aloft like a victorious garland. With the coffee cup in his other hand, he raised a toast in Rubee's direction.

"We are here now," Rubee said, returning a slight bow. "This is the time the opium chose."

"Good! Here's to being on time," Niles said, raising the cup again. "I'm not sure what day it is. I lost track of that little detail somewhere back on the Missouri. I think it's still July. It was July when we left Washington," he said. But Rubee was not forthcoming in adding details to the opium's calendar.

The two sat, each respecting the stillness and listening to the dawn. The pine needles playing on the breeze laid a soft whisper over the gulch, and the random snapping of the campfire when flames ignited pockets of pine pitch left a sizzling tail in its wake.

Finally, Rubee moved, reaching for a new log to add to the fire. "Much like a clock, don't you think, Mr. Dewy?"

Niles shrugged his shoulders in response to Rubee's question.

"The snapping of the fire," Rubee explained, using a stick to stir the coals and sending a spray of sparks into the air. "Fire is like the ticking of a confused clock, void of a clock's trust, the very sincerity common to all timepieces. You do trust your watch, don't you, Mr. Dewy?"

"When I remember to wind it."

"So it is not time you mistrust ... it is yourself you mistrust."

"Just wind me up, Rubee, and I'll tell you the time and anything else you want to know. May not be right. But I'll be telling you just the same."

Niles's jaunty philosophy brought a wide smile to Rubee's face. The beauty possible in that face caught Niles. Black eyebrows arching over black eyes invited gazing at her face. A long, slender neck held her head like a fragile piece of porcelain. Her posture, even in stillness—the lines of her shoulders, the bend in her arms, and tilt of her head—displayed a gentle grace ... poise in action rather than words. Niles could see how men fell under her spell and ultimately the spell of the Yellow Doll's opium dream. Niles often fantasized about making a picture of the face, a glass plate as delicate and as fragile as the Yellow Doll. But Rubee would never allow such an exposé. Niles had never probed the subject, but he suspected that Rubee was superstitious about photographs like some who refused to have a picture made because they believed that it would steal their souls. No, Niles suspected that Rubee's superstition was not of the spiritual nature; Rubee avoided such matters. Instead, a photograph somehow was seen as a cast of Rubee's own death mask.

"As long as there are opium addicts, there will be opium smugglers, Mr. Dewy, for many ancestors before us and many generations after. This is our time to follow the secret road."

The dawn quiet, when the few night birds were courting slumber and it was still too early for the morning songs, whispered that daylight was a hint above Deadwood Gulch. They knew that they were sharing a time—a place—that no one else could ever be a part of. Niles thought of it as a picture, a glimpse into a tiny crack in time that silently captured them at this moment ... beyond the edge of Niles's photograph, forever lost.

Chapter 12

July 31, 1876

Morning in Deadwood Gulch was a shock of black-and-white light. Once the sun was clear of the eastern rim of the canyon, trees, rocks, water, people, faces, and buildings were all either painted in a bright white or cast into dark shadows. Niles Dewy's creative trick was to play in the sliver of shadow between the two. In that narrow band of time and space is where he found his photographs.

The sound of a man's voice humming a gospel tune about as loud as one could hum a tune without bursting into song could be heard coming from the underbrush in the direction George had set himself up a small camp. "'Joshua fought the battle of Jericho ... Jericho ... Jericho. Joshua fought the battle of Jericho ... and the walls came tumbling down!'" George ended his hymn, almost dancing to his own rhythm as he walked up to Niles's campfire. "The ladies knows this already about George. I's told 'em out on the prairie. I want you'll to be the first to make it official," he said, straightening back on his heels so that he could stand a bit more erect and proud. "Here in Deadwood, you can call George the name his momma gives him—Joshua Monroe. I knows how to mark it down with a pencil on paper even, so it's all legal and Christian."

"Christian's important if something is going to be legal," Niles said. "I guess this means you've been traveling under a false name. Well, doesn't that beat all. A phony name. You, George! I never would have guessed," Niles continued, sounding a bit put out, but suddenly, he burst out with a big grin and thrust out his hand. "Pleased to make your acquaintance, Mr. Joshua Monroe. And a very handsome name it is," he said, pumping the Negro's hand.

George turned his attention to his horse and began saddling up. "Time for this old boy to get him some food and start to work." Peering under the animal as he tightened the cinch, he told Niles, "Miss Mustache's set me up with both. Yup, that be right. She told George she'd fix me a big old plate of breakfast and give me a shave if'n I'd just build her some bunk beds. Now figure this one out, Mr. Dewy; George comes all this way with you folks to these here Black Hills, and this ol' blacky's first dollar's coming from something my momma taught me young on—how to make beds. She'd be a shakin' 'bout now, singing away if she only knew what her boy was fixin' to be up to this morning."

The Negro swung himself up into the saddle and spurred the animal around. "These Black Hills fit Joshua Monroe like a good pair of britches … pockets janglin' with gold," he told Niles, almost singing out the words as he slowly trotted off down the hill. "'Lay my head on Jesus's pillow,'" he started singing. "'Lay my head on Jesus's pillow, and I'll dream of heaven's golden gates.'" After a few refrains, he stopped, turning back toward Niles and hollering, "I asked her, Mr. Dewy, what she was fixin' on doin', start up a boardinghouse of some such. You know what she says to this old boy? She says they're for something called the Yellow Doll. S'pose she's startin' up a hurdy-gurdy house, do ya? Naw!" the Negro answered himself. Turning away from Niles again, he added as he rode on down the hill, "Don't think they'd want bunk beds in a place like that, but who knows whatever here in Deadwood Gulch."

Sarah ducked out from the tent, rubbing her eyes against the bright sunrise. "Anyone seen Kit?" she asked, shuffling in her stocking feet closer to the campfire.

Niles poured a cup of coffee for her. "She left about an hour ago," he said, and then he stood up. "She's setting up down there." He pointed down the hill to a spot on the other side of the road from the Backdoor Bath, Shave & Barber.

Sarah tested the coffee, slurping a sip quite noisy for a lady, Nile thought. Then again, it may have just been that his ears had not yet adjusted to the rude sounds of the day. "She says I can give her a hand this morning. Setting up, you know. Whatever the hell she does to sell eggs." She stammered around while drinking her coffee. "Maybe in a while … if them chickens ever start laying again," Sarah added. Suddenly, she jabbed a finger into the sky. "Just helping out with the eggs. None of that bedding down stuff," she quickly added, making sure that he did not take her the wrong way.

"Just me." Niles laughed. "Our tight little bundle, snoring away," he joked, referring to how they had been sleeping together since leaving Fort Pierre—boots and hats off, everything else securely buttoned up, lying side by side like they were bound together with a rope.

Sarah reared back and slung her cup across the campfire, hitting Niles in the chest and splattering coffee over his face and linen shirt. He was still smiling, shaking as much of the coffee off as he could. He undid his kerchief from around his neck and dried his face with it. "Would you care for another coffee?" he asked, dabbing at the front of his shirt.

"Please."

He retrieved the cup from the edge of the fire pit, used the kerchief to wipe it off, and dusted off the pine duff. He refilled it and then offered it back to Sarah.

She smiled almost apologetically as she took it from his hand, and Niles had a hunch that he was in big trouble. Just as the first cup had, the second one flew at him, but this time, he had half expected it and was able to dodge out of the way—only enough, though, so that it hit his arm, soaking the sleeve with coffee stains.

"You're tough in the morning before you get your first cup of coffee in you. My only question is if you ever get around to drinking it."

"You wore out your welcome with me some time ago, Mr. Dewy. Back around the time you left me with that drunken sheriff. If it hadn't been for Rubee and your precious opium, who knows? You certainly didn't have any clues!"

"I knew you'd take a liking to the opium. Am I right?"

"That's not what I meant, and you know it. I want no part of this dirty little drug business of yours. And you know it."

"Opium has a way of making it the business of anyone who crosses its path. Besides, Miss Sarah, I haven't seen you saying any good-byes, either. I bet there were a dozen times between Washington and Fort Pierre when you could have changed course—"

"Ninety-seven," Sarah interrupted.

Niles stopped poking at the fire and looked over at her. "Ninety-seven what?"

"Number of chances I had to turn around and go back."

"Well, make it ninety-eight. Head out this morning. None of us will be around, so you can just make off with about whatever you can lug off." He turned then, leaving her standing next to the fire pit. "I am going to go make some pretty pictures. I'll be back around noon," he told her. "No more what-ifs. Get on with Deadwood, lady. Who knows? Might be a struck-it-rich miner here in the gulch itching to marry up with a congressman's daughter. That's really why you stuck it out, ain't it? You're in it for the gold like every other outlaw up here. And you figure some of the dust might just blow your way. So be it. Just make sure it doesn't blow off of my pile."

"Boy, you don't have a clue, do you?" Sarah crossed her arms, planting her feet a little more firmly on the slick pine needles covering the ground. "Can I ask you a question?"

"Shoot," Niles complied, shrugging his shoulders like it meant nothing to him. "Ask away. Makes no never mind to me."

"If we are all in it for the gold, then why doesn't Niles Dewy ever sell any of his prized photographs?"

Niles turned to face her so that she could see the dead seriousness in his answer. "Because he doesn't have to."

"Oh, I get it. Niles Dewy's handsome fee is for being a hired gun—a killer—nothing but a two-bit smuggler. No, he's not in it to feed his nasty little drug habit. Nope, not him. He feeds his habit by photographing the dead or soon to be. That's your pay, isn't it, Mr. Dewy?"

Sarah spun around, making it clear that she had heard enough, and she went about her morning chores. When next she looked, Niles was riding down the hillside, leading the top-heavy mule loaded with his photography equipment. When she could see that he was far enough out of sight, she ducked into the tent and dragged out her traveling valise, spilling the clothes out of it. Then, in each of the four corners along the bottom, she carefully peeled back a small triangle of fabric, lifting the false bottom out and revealing a fitted compartment underneath. The compartment held two .45 double-action Colts. They were sheriff's models with short barrels—steel gray with polished grips. In their own cutouts next to the pistols were four extra cartridge cylinders, each loaded, a spare box of cartridges, and a belt for the single, small, soft leather holster fastened to the underside of the false bottom's lid. She selected one of the pistols, checked the cylinder's load, and then balanced the gun in the palm of her right hand, acquainting herself with its weight and balance. She put the belt and holster together, tightening it around her waist so that the holster fit into the small of her back. Finally, she practiced reaching around and pulling the pistol out, making sure that her finger was on the trigger by the time she had swung it around in front of her. Speed of draw was not Sarah's goal; concealment, surprise, and accuracy would make up for her lack of speed.

The .45 was not the only weapon Sarah Culbert would be carrying while she was in Deadwood. A lady's innocence could be as murderous as a well-aimed shot and sometimes far more accurate.

The placer camp was long past its morning coffee. The dozen men working the claim were the ones that Niles had noted the day before when the light was all wrong. But this morning, the light was absolutely perfect for picture taking. The placer camp—with its shaft dug into the back of Whitewood Creek, the winless hoist with array of ropes, the piles of stones terracing the side hill around the shaft, the freshly split pine plank trough sluicing the creek water over their screens, the prospectors sifting the sand to capture any sign of glitter—made for a very interesting photograph. Niles's mind framed the photo with the early morning angles of sunshine painting the far side of the stream in a mix of shadows and light.

Niles reined his mare off the trail, tugged the mule to follow, and let the horse pick her way over the rocks and through the underbrush. As soon as it was obvious that he was approaching the camp, one of the prospectors picked up a rifle and began making his way toward him. Niles counted at least four other rifles lying around the placer shaft, so he raised his arms, entering the campsite on friendly terms, showing that his hands were empty of any weapons.

"Far enough, mister."

Niles heeded the warning, squeezing his mount's sides with his knees. She toyed with the idea of stopping, first slowing and then dancing from side to side until she finally found a secure place for her hooves among the rocks. "Dewy's the name—Niles Dewy. I'm a photographer!" he shouted over the rushing sound of the creek.

"Say again? You're a what?" the man asked, putting the rifle over his shoulder, but Niles noticed that the fellow had his finger on the trigger.

Taking a chance by spurring the mare a few feet forward, he shouted out again, "Name's Dewy—Niles Dewy! I'm a photographer, and I'd like to make your picture!"

The miner stopped, cocking his head to study Dewy and the mule. "You be a picture man?"

"Yes, sir, that be me. I have all my equipment right here," Niles explained, jabbing a thumb toward the mule. "Won't take but more than a minute once I'm all set up. Just have to stand still when I tell you, and magic—you're captured in a photograph."

That got the man's attention. Niles lowered his hand and smiled, knowing that it always got their attention. Army man or Indian, lawman or outlaw, Irish, German, or Chinese gandy dancers, bawdy house girls, or nurses in a war veterans' hospital—their vanity always allowed him to capture a moment in their lives in one of his photographs.

"No fellow's ever wanted to make my picture, mister. I'll be darned!" the man exclaimed. Then, as if it were all settled, the man turned and started back toward the camp. "I fought at Gettysburg, and nobody ever wanted to make my picture there. It would have been a mighty little picture, too, seeing that there were only two of us left out of our whole outfit. Now here, in the middle of nowhere, in these Dakota hills, some fella wants to make my picture. You know what, mister?" the fellow asked, turning his head to get a good look at Niles. "I figure I'm just downright lucky. Yup, lucky!"

"Never know. I might just be your lucky gold piece."

"Might bit late for that. Name's Wydell. That's my partner, Andrews, over there." He vaguely gestured over his shoulder. "We been finding color for near on two weeks now, so what's you see here is some darned near rich men."

"How rich?" Niles hollered back. Couldn't hurt to find out for Rubee how much gold a working man made here in the gulch.

"Kinda nosey, ain't ya?"

"Nope. Haven't been here long, and I'm just curious how rich the strike in the gulch really is. That's all," Niles assured him, moving the mare a few feet closer.

The man stopped and turned around to size up Niles. "Well, let me put it to you this way—you ever looked into a pouch full of gold dust? Let me tell ya, it's like looking into a bagful of sunshine, each little flake sparklin' and shinin' like you's looking right into the sun itself." That said, the fellow turned to his coworkers and prodded them back to work.

As he watched the men return to their chores, it didn't surprise Niles to notice how they positioned themselves, preening a bit and attempting to look important. He had witnessed this little dance many times, whenever a photograph was in the making and the people in the picture realized that they would be trapped forever in time.

Niles's practiced eye scanned the setting. A low, rocky knob covered with pine saplings and a tangle of berry bushes separated the placer claim from the creek bank near a point where the stream widened into a still, moss-green-tinted pool before plunging once again over rock and dead timber on its rush to get out of the canyon, free of the Black Hills and on its way to a certain death on the parched prairie.

Niles dismounted and began his preparations. He soon caught himself out of breath from rushing from the mule to the tripod and then to the developing tent and then back to the mule. His excitement and rush to make his first photo in Deadwood Gulch nearly caused him to drop one of the boxes holding the glass plates, forcing him to catch his breath and slow down. Photography had an order to it, and if he deviated from this order, the process was doomed to be a failure. Smuggling was the same way. Rubee had often told him that opium insisted on order.

Inside the developing tent, nothing more than a lightless, tiny, pyramid-shaped wigwam, Niles squatted over his work. He unwrapped a glass plate, brushed it clean, and then dipped it into the tray of viscous collodion. He was calm and relaxed now, finding pleasure in preparing to make his first picture. He flipped the tent's flap aside, ducked out, and walked over to the camera, careful not to stumble, drop the glass, or expose the treated plate to light. He gently pushed the plate into the back of the camera box, using the grooves to secure it in place.

"Ready? Everyone be still," he ordered. The prospectors all stopped what they were doing and worked at positioning themselves just so. He pulled the lens cap off and began counting, "One … two … three …" He knew that the men would all be holding their breath by now. "Seventeen … eighteen …"

Niles checked the frame, trying to imagine what the finished photo would look like. Wydell had positioned himself next to the hoist; the ropes on the spindle looked silvery. Behind him, three men stood around the mine shaft; their shovels and picks also wore a silver tint. To Wydell's right stood a tall, lanky man sporting a jaunty beaver top hat. Niles guessed him to be Wydell's partner. A pile of rocks and logs composed the right side of the frame, and on the other, the sluice trough drew a line from the lower-left corner of the frame to the picture's focal center where three prospectors stood over the saw pit where they were ripping logs into planks.

"Twenty-eight … twenty-nine … thirty," he finished under his breath. Then he replaced the lens cap. "Done!" he shouted. "You boys can breathe again."

He then released the plate from its carriage, slipped it out from under the camera hood, and ducked back into the developing wigwam.

Inside, Niles let out his breath. The flap was closed, and no light seeped in around the edges.

He uncovered the plate in the tent's reddish-tinted glow and waited for the negative exposure to bloom. Would the picture he envisioned be there? Had he done everything right? What had he forgotten? This was always a time of doubt for Niles. After all, it had been more than two months since he'd made his last photograph, and that had been back in his brownstone studio. The photograph had been of a young Negro mother and child, both shiny clean for Sunday services. When he returned to the federal city, he was going to make a print and give it to the mother. Niles knew that his photo would travel through generations far into the future, decades from the time when mother and child posed for him one bright Sunday afternoon in May.

Why was the image taking so long to reveal itself? He really disliked this part of making photographs—the wait. Had the chemicals somehow been compromised during their trip? This was the black period in the process when it was all he could do to control the gnawing anticipation growing inside his chest until it almost gagged him. The verdict would come in either a rush of exhilaration racing through his nerves or a crash so deep that he would only be able to climb out of it in the next blank glass plate.

Not yet! The plate was still black. *Not long enough,* he scolded himself. *Wait!*

The photographer's patience—like a smuggler's patience—rested on the edge of finely honed instincts … the instinct for waiting patiently.

"Patience," Niles whispered over and over. It felt like he had been waiting dozens of minutes when he knew that it had been less than a couple. He felt helpless, knowing that there was nothing he could do but wait. He never got over the sense of time involved in photography—the time waiting for the light to be just right and waiting for the image to develop. Time was frozen by the picture. Looking at a photograph, Niles was sometimes overwhelmed by a sense that he was peering into the past, into history itself, a pinpoint of time from the past. A picture of time born of a magic elixir of light and chemicals.

Finally, Niles watched the image come to life across the plate like a flower opening its petals to a soft morning light.

He did it!

He had captured time once again.

The photograph was of placer claim number twenty-one below discovery, and it turned out to be a good use for a precious glass plate and Niles Dewy's first morning in Deadwood Gulch. Now on to the next photograph, Rubee, and the opium.

Eleanor Dumont was also making good use of Niles's and Rubee's first morning in the gulch. She had George busy building the bunk beds. A fresh stack of firewood sat ready to heat the bathwater. Her flour-sack towels were washed and drying on a line stretched between two trees. The big oak bathtub she had freighted with her all the way from Denver had been drained, and she was now ready for her last chore before refilling the tub, which was cleaning out the silt and sand washed off the prospectors that had settled in a thin layer on the inside bottom of the tub. Eleanor had the tub on its side, propped against the legs of the stilts that held it above the fire. In this way, she was able to reach the bottom without tumbling head over heels into it. Aided by a pair of surgeon's tweezers, she gleefully plucked flecks of gold dust out of the mud. Her "mud money" was like the "side money" the bartenders down on the main street swept up under their scales, and every couple of days when she changed the bathwater, Eleanor routinely added another ten dollars to her profits.

"Richest strike I ever did see!" she hollered out, examining another flake of gold held in the tweezer's grip. "Heck, they be washing off more gold dust here in Deadwood than they claw out of the ground with picks and shovels in most other gold camps.

Almost makes you want to go into the laundry business, but washin' out dirty socks ain't for this lady. No, siree! The chinks can have it," Eleanor said as she dropped the flake into her pouch. "No disrespect intended, Miss Rubee," she quickly added.

Rubee was inside Eleanor's bath tent, watching the lady mine her "pay dirt" through the pulled-back flap while she unpacked the Yellow Doll's costumes. "None taken, Miss Dumont," Rubee assured her. She added, "Now where do you suppose you came up with such a trick? Maybe from the Chinese?"

A long silence settled between the two women, suggesting that Eleanor was in the midst of working out in her mind where exactly she had picked up such a profitable habit. "I suppose I could have come across it in any one of the six or seven gold camps I've tromped through over the years. But suppose I might have picked it up from some Chinaman," she offered. But she quickly added, "Might not have, either. Ya know I don't mix much with Chinamen ... or women, for that matter. 'Ceptin' you, Miss Rubee. But you know you really ain't a chink ... not like most, anyways. You're more like one of us, you know. Your getups are a sight better looking than most, and you sure can talk on mighty pretty like. No, you be a cut above most of us camp rats. I mean that. Heck, if you don't believe me, just ask anyone of the dirt-eatin' prospectors. They'll tell you right off. Even that picture man of yours knows what ol' Mustache's talking about. Hell, he knows, or he won't be following you around all the time."

"That is just the poppy talking, Miss Dumont."

"That ain't no poppy talkin', that's plain and simple whole truth and nothing but the truth, and the good Lord hisself strike me down with a mighty thunderbolt if'n I ain't telling the truth," Eleanor told her, lifting her arms wide and tilting her head back, inviting the heavens to strike her down.

An hour later, the tub of fresh creek water was warming above the fire, and Eleanor had stacked neatly folded towels on top of an empty whiskey keg next to the tub. The raja's chest of opium sat on the floor of pine needles on the other side of the tub, covered by a big buffalo robe serving as the step in and out of the tub. Rubee had supplied Eleanor with some soap and bath oils. A green silk blouse sporting red-and-gold stitching down the front and a pair of white silk pants sat on a stool at the foot of the buffalo robe step. A long red silk tunic embroidered with a green dragon that wound around the garment from the neckline down to the hem hung from a low tree branch nearby. Under the tunic sat a pair of blue slippers decorated with golden tassels, and on another branch next to it hung a cone-shaped straw hat woven with green, red, blue, and gold silk ribbons.

Rubee was neck deep in the steaming bathwater. "Miss Eleanor, are you out there?"

"Here I be, honey. What ya need?" Rubee smiled when she heard the wooden back door open and close, and then she heard Eleanor just on the other side of the canvas. "We'll parade you up and down that ol' Main Street, and come nightfall, we'll have customers lined up waitin' to get a good ol' up-close and personal look-see at the one and only Yellow Doll herself right here in Deadwood Gulch."

"You are correct, Miss Dumont. There will be many customers, but the Yellow Doll is interested in only one."

"One! Who in tarnations you talkin' about?"

"The Chinaman you call Long Ears."

"Long Ears! Why do ya want him?"

"What exactly do you know about his business?"

"Well, let's see. I guess he showed up here in the gulch ... oh, I would guess around the first part of June, give or take some. No, I'm pretty sure that's when he showed up ... didn't have my door up yet ... that's why I remember. He started up with a butcher counter; he just set up under a hunk of canvas ... stringy, tough as shoe leather, salted slabs of meat, near all of it mangy old horseflesh. He'd sell ya a hunk of it—a pound, he said, weighed out on his own scales—for a quarter. Funny thing, though, about him—he ain't like no Chinaman I'd ever laid eyes on 'fore ... you know, tiny like you is. Well, Long Ears is a giant—six feet tall at least ... tall like a tree, he is. And them ears of his, biggest damn ears I ever did seen. Listen to this, Miss Rubee, if'n you pay him for your meat with a coin, he takes and stick that ol' coin of yours right up in his ear ...

right inside them ears of his ... them's big enough to hold a double eagle, if'n you get the picture. And get a load of this—if he has to make you change, he pulls the coins right out of those ears of his. Yes, sir, he plucks you out a coin right out of his ears. Now you ever heard of anything like that b'fore? Bet you haven't, Miss Rubee. In all your travels, I'd bet my bathhouse you ain't never seen anything like that. No, sir!"

"You get to keep your bathhouse, Miss Dumont."

Then, as if she'd clear everything up, Eleanor went on, "Anyways, like I was sayin', pretty soon after'n he gets here, word starts floating up and down the gulch that he's got hisself a tent set up behind that meat counter of his, and lo and behold, for a pinch of dust, you could have yourself a puff or two of that China smoke. Well, you know this ol' gal hightailed it right up there to his tent to be the first in line to get a taste of what he's peddlin'. Makin' sure he weren't passin' off no turpentine-soaked tobacco as the real stuff—you know, Miss Rubee, just like you showed me. I know what good opium is, thanks to you and that picture man, and I sure as heck knows when it ain't—"

"And your learned opinion, Miss Dumont?" Rubee interrupted.

Dumont puffed herself way up to deliver her verdict with all of the authority her size and heft could muster. "Long Ears's got the real thing. Even went back to check it out a time or two just to make sure he wasn't saltin' the bowl up front, then slackin' off. Well, I can tell ya he's right above board, at least every time I happened to wander by. Darn it to heck, Miss Rubee, but I do like that smoking! Never took kindly to puffin' on some ol' cigar, but that tiny pipe is my cup of China tea. Know what I'm sayin'?"

Rubee understood. "Does he have a lot of customers?"

"Ya mean are folks takin' kindly to have a puff every now and then? I can tell you this—that China smoke is fetchin' a better price than gold. Oh, he's still sellin' a goodly share of meat, I s'pose. And he's had enough customers out back to build hisself a lumber-sided butcher shop. Son-of-a damn Chinaman took all the lumber I was going to use for my place. As you can see, all I got was one wall and door out of that whole load of lumber brought here by a bunch of Nebraska farmers. I didn't have the money to buy all I needed. Long Ears did! Wasn't more'n four days later that sky-scrapin' chink got hisself a four sider complete with roof, door, two windows … the whole darn shootin' match. Sittin' right there on Main Street is Madam Mustache's Bathhouse and Barber. Yup! That Chinaman built my place. And out back, well, let me tell ya, out back now, he's got two tents, and I hear tell he's diggin' a tunnel under his shop. No one s'pose to know it's there, right? But just go and ask anyone up and down the gulch, and they'll tell ya he's diggin' hisself an opium den. But not a soul hereabouts will let on they know anything 'bout it. Just you wait—them same souls who know nothing today, they'll be the same fellers standin' in line waitin' their turn on the pipe. Yes, sir!"

"Mr. Long Ears has prospered?" Rubee asked.

"Prospered? I'll tell ya so. Not only is he doin' all this building and diggin', but he gone and upped the price from a quarter to a fifty-cents-pinch of dust for a puff. Still, didn't hurt his business from what Madam Mustache can see. They still be linin' up every night."

"Why do you suppose he raised his prices?"

"Higher prices … you know what this ol' gal thinks?"

"No, but I'm quite certain you have an opinion, and I would like to hear it."

"It's my figurin' that Long Ears's supply of that ol' black tar is peterin' out. No more. All gone. Good-bye. So he's fixin' to get as much gold out of his customers' pockets as he can before he runs out. Now just think on it—how long do you s'pose the gulch's miners' justice is going to let an empty-handed opium peddler keep sittin' smack-dab in the middle of Main Street? I'll tell ya. About two seconds. No puff, no glory. Bye-bye, Long Ears, and they ain't going to let him get out of the gulch with all the smoking gold stuck in his ears. Nope! Gives more of a reason why ol' Hickok and company is makin' themselves right comfortable in front of the butcher shop. *Haw*! There ain't but one reason why those fellers hangin' around there. You know Hickok—he never stood in the same place for longer than a minute unless he was bein' paid to. Feller in my tub not a week ago said he'd come up from Colorado, and he's telling me they run Bill out of Cheyenne for sleepin' on the street. See, what's I tell ya? If'n you want my honest business savvy ..."

Rubee remained silent, sitting in the tub listening and thinking.

"Well? Do ya or don't ya?"

"Please, I want to hear."

"Well it be pretty simple-minded. This here ol' gal thinks you're the best thing to show up in this ol' gold camp as far as Long Ears's smoking business goes, ever since Hickok showed up with them Utter brothers. As long as Hickok's hangin' around Long Ears's joint, no one's sayin' so much as a peep about his prices. You hear what I'm sayin'?"

"I hear you," Rubee answered, stepping out of the tub, using a couple of the towels that Eleanor had so carefully laid out for her and then starting to get into her costume.

From the other side of the tent's canvas wall, she heard Eleanor holler out, "Got it!" She yelled as if she had just hooked the biggest catch in Whitewood Creek.

All during her bath and their little talk, Rubee had been puzzled by all of the racket Eleanor had been kicking up. "What have you been doing out here?" she asked as she pulled the tent's flap open and stepped outside. The Yellow Doll had arrived in Deadwood.

Eleanor Dumont gave her a long top-to-bottom look, letting out a low whistle. "Got to tell you, Miss Rubee, you look more beautiful than even I can remember. Oh, I've seen it happen b'fore—you goin' in there looking all dirty and muddy, ya know, looking like a feller. And then like magic, out you come lookin' like this. I don't care how many times I seen it happen, it about knocks these ol' eyes out every time. Look at ya." She waved her arms widely toward Rubee. "You got all them fancy girl parts just like this ol' girl," she told her, moving arms over her own chest and waist. "I know'd why them fellers like looking at the Yellow Doll as they drift off ... they be dreamin' 'bout you. Gosh darn it, if'n I were some feller, I'd spend my money to get a real up-close and personal look-see at you and a puff of China smoke. I'd be a payin' customer, that's a sure bet.

Darn right. Look at you. You're so dang pretty. And you know what makes you even prettier? You be my friend. Now that beats a full house every time at my poker table."

All the while she had been bathing, Rubee had wondered what Eleanor had been up to, and now she saw. "Your personal rickshaw awaits the Yellow Doll," Eleanor told her, pointing with a great flourish at her barber chair that she had somehow managed to get into the back of a buckboard wagon. "And you'll be sittin' pretty as we parade up and down Main Street," she explained, obviously quite pleased with the new use of her old chair.

Rubee and Niles had first crossed Madam Mustache's path back in the summer of 1870 when they were plying their trades in the Northern Pacific Railway's work camps. The barber chair had long ago started showing its many miles. Aside from a few rust spots, the leather seat had suffered a long cut which Eleanor was constantly poking some kind of stuffing into. One arm was missing, but the other looked as good as new. The iron-scrolled footrest was in pretty good condition; she still had the headrest, though the chair would only tilt back a few inches. With her bathtub and barber chair in tow, Eleanor Dumont had been moving from camp to camp over the years—army camps, mining camps, railroad camps—bathing and shaving hundreds of men who came on her trail. She had once told them, "Barberin' and shavin' just came natural to me during the war. I'd start around sunup shaving them boys' faces. Some of 'em I just flat-out pretended 'cause they weren't even old enough yet to've growed whiskers, but I gave them a full shave, anyway, just so they'd feel like a man. Then come sundown, I tell 'em I need to rest or I might slice their throats open. Them boys, they understood."

Rubee circled the buckboard, inspecting the moorings holding the barber chair in place. "Do us a favor," she said as she climbed into the back of the buckboard with Eleanor's help and up into the chair. "Make sure this little parade of ours goes past Mr. Long Ears's establishment."

"Deal!" Eleanor nodded. "I know'd you been listenin' to this ol' gal. I also knowed you take kindly to my paradin' idea. This ol' camp rat sure enough knows how important paradin' can be. Why,

I always figure if'n you got nothing better to do, might as well be puttin' on a good show. And a parade makes it all look important … official like. You know?"

The Yellow Doll understood. Parades and opium had been marching side by side most of her life, starting as a child growing up in Hong Kong, where her father was a licensed opium trader, watching the British army parade around. Later, when she began her service to the empire as a trusted domestic first posted in Calcutta, where her father's relatives continued her education in the poppy business, the spectacles had often included tigers and elephants. Rubee's postings in London and finally America's federal city were also places where parades were an important symbol of power.

"One more favor I must ask of you, Miss Dumont … and if you care not to be involved, I will understand. I, of course, will compensate you," Rubee added, knowing what mattered most to the woman.

"Shoot away," Eleanor said right off, and then suddenly, she thought better of it. "Ya ain't asking me to kill someone, are you? I thought that was the picture man's job. I ain't dumb, ya know. He's told me hisself what he does. I just never seen him do it. That's all."

"No, that is not what I am asking, and it is very unlikely Mr. Dewy told you any such thing. Besides, I have not been here long enough to know anyone well enough to have them assassinated." Rubee watched her physically back down.

"Well, you probably be right. It might've been just an ol' hint or just me seeing all those guns of his. That's all I meant by it. But just you wait—you haven't met up with Long Ears yet. Then, no matter what you say, ol' picture man's got his work cut out, Hickok and all," Eleanor grumbled under her breath.

"Talk of Mr. Dewy and what he does or does not do is far from what I am asking." Rubee never allowed any conversation to wander into the territory occupied by Niles Dewy. Like Eleanor Dumont and her false walls, Rubee respected Niles Dewy's false walls, partly because she had helped to construct them, but mostly because, from the very beginning, he had taken to the smuggler's secret life. Rubee was aware that picture taking was his narcotic, and he would support his habit however he was able to like any addict. In the case of Niles Dewy, his skill with a firearm supported his growing talent with the camera box. His collection of photographs was not only a record of their own travels, but the pictures also revealed the maturing of his alchemist's skills. Rubee already could see the day when he would choose to share his photographs, and that would be the day that Niles Dewy ceased to be. No, she knew that Niles Dewy had been created for the purpose of smuggling opium, a special tool used only for smuggling, and one as important to its success as false-bottomed chests, double-hulled boats, moonless nights, or bribery. Starting with the poppy farmers in India, Niles Dewy was the last link in the chain of people moving the drug onto its final destination, and this time, it was to bring it to the gold camp in Deadwood Gulch.

"I'm telling ya, this here place gives me shivers," Eleanor told her. "Ya know, some ol' camps, they just be too tough to die, but this here place, Deadwood Gulch, it be a place where hell itself will freeze over. Yes, sir, I can feel it in this here ol' gal's bones."

Rubee didn't say anything, but a shiver ran up her spine, a chill not from the cool mountain air, but a chill coming from deep inside. She climbed down from the buckboard, went back into the bath tent, yanked the buffalo robe off the opium chest, and opened its lid. She selected ten fist-sized balls, put them in her empty costume valise, closed the lid of the chest, and covered it again with the buffalo robe. She picked up the valise and went back outside. "Will you hide this for me?" Rubee asked Eleanor, offering her the valise.

"What is it?" she asked, twisting her head from side to side and looking over the bag. Rubee opened it and then tilted it forward so that Eleanor could see inside.

Madam Mustache let out another low whistle as she looked at the balls of opium. "Wow, now! I ain't never seen that much, ever. You got to be showing me all the opium in China. Right?"

"Hardly."

Eleanor kept looking first into Rubee's eyes and then into the bag. "Can't be no harm in hidin' this," she said slowly.

"If you do this for me, Miss Dumont, there is only one instruction that goes with it—no matter whatever happens, do not tell anyone you have this. No one, do you understand? And never, never give it to anybody except me. No one, do I make myself clear? Will you do this for the Yellow Doll?"

With no hesitation, she said, "Of course I do this for you. But why you trusting me? We'd know'd each other a couple of times over the years, but askin' this, you must trust, or—"

"Or I would not ask you," Rubee interrupted. "You have never given me a reason not to trust you, Miss Dumont."

"Let me stash this. No one will ever know," Eleanor told her, and for a moment, Rubee thought that the woman was going to salute, but instead, she simply shrugged, rolling her shoulders from side to side.

"Thank you. And remember now—no one but me."

"I got it hammered in stone up here," she said, tapping her head with a finger. "Hear me out, Miss Rubee. I swear to you if this ain't waitin' for you whenever you want it, I'll cut out the devil's Adam's apple right there in hell. It'll be waitin' for you whenever that 'for you' happens to meet up with us." Eleanor then turned and disappeared through the door in the lone wall.

"The wall is really there for you, isn't it, my friend?" Rubee whispered.

Eleanor returned, minus the valise, bubbling with enthusiasm. "Come on," she said, inviting the Yellow Doll to take her place. "No finer throne to be found in Deadwood Gulch, I tell ya. Now sit yourself real pretty like, and off we go."

And go they did, from one end of Main Street to the other. The Yellow Doll perched in the barber chair, bouncing along and holding onto the chair's lone arm with one hand, the other waving at the men gawking at yet another Main Street attraction rolling by, listening to Eleanor's steady song drumming up business. "Bath and shave! The Yellow Doll and a grave! Come on, boys! Wash your toes, bury your nose. Follow the Yellow Doll, men! She's the prettiest you'll ever see in Deadwood Gulch. Get a real close-up look!" she sang out. Aiming a finger at a fellow standing on the side of the road, she hollered, "What are you afraid of, mister? Taking a bath or getting up close to the Yellow Doll?"

Kit had made up her mind after a quick jaunt up and down Main Street. The camp reminded her of one of those carnivals at a county fair back in the States … folks milling around, most of them bored with no place they wanted to go. It seemed like there were more people than places for them to go, anyway. No, it did not take her long to get her fill of Deadwood's newborn Main Street. So she quickened her pace, heading back to her own little campsite. She'd had plenty of offers from the countless men she'd passed along the way, telling each of them and anyone else within earshot that she would take them all on at her Egg Emporium "right under the brown rock cliffs." That was where she had decided to set up shop; it might be a little safer there, not that far from Madam Moustache's Bathhouse and her friends. And, if all went according to everyone's plans, there would be a steady stream of customers over at Dumont's place lining up for a taste of opium and a look at the Yellow Doll. And fresh eggs for breakfast the next morning. It added up to a sound business plan in Kit's mind.

"Yup. This is my place," she said to herself as she spread out a rag quilt on the patch of pine needles she had kicked into a pile, giving her café's seating area a bit more cushion for the future diners. Using a piece of split pine and a piece of charcoal, she printed her sign advertising her eggs and leaned it against a stump beside her. Her hens clucked and strutted around, appearing as if they were quite pleased with themselves for not being lost somewhere along the way, and Kit had already been rewarded with some freshly laid eggs this morning—not dozens, but enough to open for business. She already had a pot of creek water hanging over the fire starting to boil, and now all she needed were customers.

"How much for an egg, missy?" her first customer asked.

"Most I want right now is trade," Kit told him. He offered her a sheet of canvas for a couple of eggs, and Kit graciously concluded the deal. By noon, her hens had added a second sheet of canvas, and by supper time, she was able to add biscuits to her menu, complements of two men who had traded a Dutch oven and a pound of flour if she'd throw in the shiny Mexican pistol. Kit felt that she had made a pretty good bargain.

"By sundown tomorrow and a 'pinch and a poke' a time or two, I'll have a regular four-cornered café," Kit told Sarah as the two of them struggled to raise the two sheets of canvas to form a makeshift tent.

"Pinch and a poke?" Sarah asked. "Poke, as crude as it is, I understand. But what's the pinch?"

"Yup ... the fastest way to do business. Pinch and a poke. Pinch of fifty," Kit told her, demonstrating with her thumb and forefinger as if holding a coin. "A pinch of fifty cents' of gold dust. Pinch and a poke ... pinch and a poke," she sang. "Lift your dress, and there you have a pinch and a poke."

"That fine for you, Kit, but I doubt I will ever need to use such business practices. Don't be thinking ahead of yourself, lady ... I told Niles the same thing this morning," Sarah said, waving off any thought otherwise like there were flies buzzing around her head. "I'm only helping out with the café. None of that pokey stuff," she told Kit, mimicking how Kit had just thrown back her skirt, causing both of them to laugh.

"Is that why you came all this way? To push hard-boiled eggs? Or did you just come along for the ride?" Kit asked. When Sarah didn't answer right away, she added, "If you had nothing better to do this summer, then I guess Deadwood is as good a place as any to do nothing. As long as you can stay alive and your money don't run out."

Sarah looked down the canyon in the direction Niles had taken searching for a photograph. "No. I have to be paid to be in Deadwood. Have to be paid," she repeated.

Kit looked at her, puzzlement wrinkling her forehead. "Don't know what you're talking about, but you must have been paid handsomely. You're here, ain't ya?"

"I'm here, yeah, I'm here." Sarah jerked her attention from the distant canyon and back to the chickens.

Kit returned to her chores, studying Sarah for a hint of what the woman was up to. "Did I ever tell you about my fourth husband?

Now there was a man. He was the only one of my husbands with nerve enough to let me shoot an apple off his head."

"Did you hit the apple or the husband?"

"Neither. Once I got him to say he'd do it, hell, that's all I wanted, anyway, just to see if he'd be man enough to let me do it. I figured right then and there he was a keeper."

"If he was a keeper, where is he now?"

"I don't know."

When it was obvious that Kit was not going to elaborate any further, Sarah said, "If I had to shoot an apple off the head of Niles Dewy, I don't mind admitting this lady might just miss the apple."

Kit gave her another puzzled look. "Wow! What did that man ever do to you?"

"Nothing. Not one darn thing. And that's that."

Kit was busying herself weaving young branches between the pine sapling stakes for her new chicken pen when she watched four men ride up to Eleanor's Backdoor. She figured that they were either stopping for a bath or shave or maybe a midday pipe dream, but when only one of the riders dismounted and went inside the Yellow Doll's tent, Kit stopped her work long enough to take note of the three riders left outside waiting. One looked like a half-breed with long, straight black hair, moccasins on his feet, and beads and ribbons decorating his shirt and leggings. The middle rider was dressed like a Mexican in a short waistcoat and a wide sombrero. And the third was a bald fellow dressed out in buckskins from head to foot. He had a long-handled hatchet stuck in his belt. And there was something about the fellow who had gone into the Yellow Doll's tent that sure looked familiar to Kit. "Probably a wanted poster from the looks of your friends," she said to herself. And then she quickly added, "Talking to yourself again, Kit. Not good. Not good at all."

Kit tossed the branches that she was working with aside, pushed up off the ground, and dusted herself off as she walked into the road. "Hey! Hey, fellows. How about an egg?" she hollered across the road, gesturing for the men to come on over. "Fresh eggs! Bet you ain't had one since you boys left the States. Am I right? Come on, guys. A nickel. You boys look rich enough to spend a nickel for an egg."

But the three men were not in the buying mood; only the bald fellow even made an effort to look her way.

"Come on!" The men ignored her coaxing and did not budge. "What did you have for breakfast, you bastards? Horseshit?" She swore under her breath as she walked back to her camp, glancing every now and then over her shoulder at the riders. The next time she noticed the men was when they had left the Bathhouse and were riding toward the upper end of Main Street, giving Kit a chance to study them as they rode by her place.

She let out a low whistle when she finally got a good look at the fourth rider. "Well, I'll be go to hell, if it ain't the prince of pistoleers himself," she whispered.

Sarah strained to hear what she was saying, finally asking her, "Who's that?"

"Bill Hickok."

Sarah followed the riders as they rode on up the road. "I think the Indian fellow is someone they call California Joe, and the Mexican, I am pretty sure, is Texas Jack. I don't know who the bald one is."

"How in tarnations do you know them?" Kit asked, staring first at the riders and then at Sarah.

"Oh, I don't know, just a lucky guess, probably."

Kit studied her again for quite some time before going back to weaving her branches. "Lady, I think you're going to be my biggest surprise in Deadwood." She then moved her attention to the Bathhouse. "I should be in the bathhouse business," she said, but then after thinking about it, she said, "No, eggs ... a poke every now and then ... that's my business. None of that black-smoke hocus-pocus. Nope. Kit LeRoy's an egg lady. I'll leave that other stuff to you, my friends," she said, bowing toward the Bathhouse. Kit went back to weaving, and then she said under her breath, "Mighty strange who you count as your friends ... China smoke peddlers ... yup, this is a mighty strange place."

"This is a strange place—kind of spooks me, if you know what I mean," Sarah told her.

"Oh, I don't mind telling you, I know exactly what you mean, sister. This place is spooking me big time. And I got me a feeling down in my gut that this place is going to get a heck of a lot stranger," she added. She looked up the road and saw the riders coming back, but this time, there were only three—Hickok, the Mexican, and the third rider was the tall Chinaman called Long Ears. "A lot stranger," she whispered as she watched them ride by.

Rubee stood in front of her tent waiting for the riders. When the came to a stop in front of her, the Chinaman dismounted, leading his horse as he walked over. "You are the Yellow Doll?" Long Ears asked in Chinese.

She bowed, returning the greeting and using the same dialect from the Szechwan region in southern China as he had. She exhibited no greeting toward the Mexican and only met Hickok's stare with a brief glance. Both men were undoubtedly in sight of Niles's rifle scope.

Niles had positioned himself high up the hillside above the Backdoor Bathhouse and the Yellow Doll's tent. His Anthony camera was ready, only needing a glass plate, although Niles doubted that he would get a chance to use it in the day's fading light. The Winchester .44-40 lay across his lap, a cartridge already levered into the firing chamber, and his Sharps .50 with the scope leaned against a pine stump at his side. The scoped Sharps would give him deadly accuracy anywhere along the stretch of Main Street that he could see.

The two worlds of Niles Dewy were once again together. He was a shooter. Guns and cameras had long ago been woven into the fabric of Niles Dewy. He raised the Sharps to his shoulder and watched as the Chinaman dismounted and walked over to Rubee, and then he shifted his aim to the other two riders, Hickok and the Mexican.

The Yellow Doll invited Long Ears to accompany her into her large tent. Offering him a cushion that sat on the floor, she gracefully lowered herself to the one across from him. A cast-iron caldron sat smoldering on the ground between them, and the Yellow Doll's silver pipe lay next to it. Long Ears began, still using their native tongue, welcoming the Yellow Doll to Deadwood Gulch, expressing how good it was to have such a beautiful representative of their country joining him in Deadwood. She thanked him for such a compliment, saying that, coming from such an obviously wealthy man, it was a great honor for her, lowering her eyes to the gold nuggets dangling from his watch chain. Then she fell into silence, affording Long Ears the opportunity to bring up business.

Her wait was brief. She was pleased that Long Ears was not one for wasting time; he immediately began inquiring about the Yellow Doll's opium. "Patna, seventy," she replied, matching his forthrightness with her own, and she could tell with her answer that he immediately knew that she, too, meant serious business.

"That is acceptable," he replied, worthy of him doing business with the Yellow Doll, but please allow him the courtesy of seeing it first, so he could be assured by her that it was the fabled India Patna opium, a poppy resin only harvested from the fields northeast of Bombay, which produced a 70 percent pure grade of the drug.

The Yellow Doll bowed to his request, reaching into her silk embroidered shoulder bag and pulling out one of the parchment-wrapped balls. She said, "You will be able to mix this with much tobacco and still satisfy most customers. Those who want Patna will pay more, obviously," she added as she peeled the leaves of paper away from the ball, revealing the Patna stamp pressed into the resin.

"He is able who is able," he said, reciting a Buddhist proverb familiar to the Yellow Doll. Reaching across, he lifted the ball from the Yellow Doll's hands. He rolled it between his palms, studied the stamp, and held it to his nose, confirming the musty aroma of the high-grade opium. It brought a smile to the man's face, for he knew that there was no mask for the smell of fine opium. Then he pinched a small piece off, rolling it into a tiny sphere between his fingers. The Yellow Doll picked up the pipe, offering it across to him. While he stuffed the tiny ball of the drug into the silver bowl, she lifted the caldron.

"You honor me," Long Ears said as he rested the pipe's bowl in the groove across the top of the caldron. He waited for the embers to heat the drug until it melted, releasing the pungent, earthy, yet sweet aroma that filled the tent. He puffed on the pipe several times, never holding the smoke in his lungs, but just enough to get a taste in his mouth.

He exhaled and let the pipe rest across his lap. "What is the Yellow Doll going to do with such a fine grade of opium in Deadwood? Perhaps start your own smoking den?" he asked her, tilting his head toward George's newly constructed bunk beds.

The Yellow Doll nodded that it indeed was her intention, which he accepted with a gracious bow. "Again, you honor me with your congenial completion," he told her in Chinese. "Would the Yellow Doll honorably sell any of her opium to Long Ears?" he asked.

She once again bowed.

"May I examine?"

Again, the Yellow Doll bowed her assent, laying the silk purse in front of him for his inspection. Long Ears reached into the bag and randomly chose a second ball. He unwrapped it, checked the stamp, and smelled and checked the texture. From a pocket in his frock, he produced a small handheld scale and held it above the caldron for her to see.

"Ninety-eight grams, avoirdupois weight, precisely according to the Calcutta auction house specifications," the Yellow Doll confirmed.

Even so, Long Ears proceeded with his own confirmation, using a set of counterweights with ornately carved elephants that he retrieved from a lacquered wooden box. He placed the opium ball on one tray and added and subtracted a combination of the elephant weights on the other until he had an exact weight. The next ball from the bag proved to be just as accurate, as did the next. Watching him, the Yellow Doll wondered if the man had ever seen this much opium at one time, and if that were the case, could he afford as much as she was going to offer for sale?

Her answer was immediate. Long Ears took out his pocket watch and undid the clasp fastening the chain, holding the span by its ends so that she could see the line of gold nuggets. The Yellow Doll lowered her eyes, appearing to be humbled by the wealth the man carried on a string. She counted seven peanut-sized nuggets. Long Ears placed the chain on the scale's tray and worked to get the right combination of elephants in the other tray to give her an exact weight for the gold.

"The Yellow Doll is aware of the gold price here in the camp?"

"I know the miners are asking twenty dollars an ounce."

Long Ears nodded. "Some transactions have set the price at eighteen dollars, and a few special agreements have agreed to nineteen dollars."

"It is true—a fair price sometimes prevents trouble, and too high a price may breed difficulties," she told him.

"It would please me if the Yellow Doll would accept this as my collateral," he told her, removing the chain from the tray and offering it to her.

"It's $280," she said, laughing.

"This is only a token of my good faith, Yellow Doll—simply my intentions to negotiate a price and amount we both can honorably agree on."

Thirty minutes later, they had come to an agreement. Long Ears would buy seventy pounds of opium at forty-nine dollars a pound, calculated on a gold price of sixteen dollars per ounce. She agreed to sell an additional thirty-five pounds to him at both an opium price and gold rate in one week's time.

One week was about as long as the Yellow Doll planned to stay in Deadwood Gulch. And she was certain that the price they had just negotiated was far more than the price Long Ears had had in mind, probably nothing more than the cost of hiring a killer and a thief.

"At noon tomorrow, deliver the gold to the Yellow Doll, here in my tent."

Long Ears nodded his agreement. "Five o'clock tomorrow afternoon, the opium delivered to my shop on Main Street."

"In front of your shop, not inside," the Yellow Doll insisted, wanting the delivery to take place out in the open, within Niles's rifle sights and to avoid the chance for an ambush inside the butcher shop. With all of the commotion on Main Street, no one would give a second look at the two Chinese or what they were doing.

"As you wish, Yellow Doll. Tomorrow, then, our business will be concluded."

She bowed, knowing that the Yellow Doll and Niles would be safe until the opium was delivered, but after that, they were all that stood between Long Ears and his greed.

The Chinaman rose to leave, but before he ducked through the tent flap, he turned back. "It has been an honor to conduct business with a gracious and beautiful lady." Then he was gone.

Niles watched as Long Ears mounted his horse and rode up the road toward his shop. Hickok and the Mexican rode around the Backdoor Bathhouse and began making their way up the hillside toward him.

Niles was ready to make Hickok's photograph. The last hours of sun washing the gulch with its eastern-cast rays would provide the finest light of the day. Niles would use the side of Sarah's tent as his backdrop, posing Bill on the pine stump being used as one of the tent stakes. Bill would be looking right into the sinking light, and the light would penetrate the dark shadows, wrinkles, and sunken eyes, hopefully allowing Niles to portray him as other that the sullen man he had become. Every other time Niles had made a picture of Hickok, the man had been drunk, and over the years, he had become a very sad man and seemed to be gloomier each time they met. Today's photograph would be the fourth time that Hickok had sat in front of Niles's camera box, and Niles wondered how many more times their secret roads would cross. The photograph was only part of this meeting coming up the hill. Niles's instincts check his firearms, twelve shots in the pair of Smith and Wesson pistols he wore on his hip, another six in the Winchester rifle, six more in the Colt .45 in his shoulder holster. Twenty-four shots might be enough or would at least help to even the odds between himself and Hickok.

When he checked on the progress of his visitors coming up the hill, three more riders joined them. "Twenty-four shots ... five men," he whispered. When the men were close enough, Niles allowed his hands to relax. Hickok was in the lead, and riding just behind him on the left was the Mexican and Texas Jack Omohundro. On Hickok's right, Niles recognized Bill Cody, and he said under her breath, "I'll be go to hell … or else I'm already there." Nobody had said anything about Cody being in Deadwood. The other two men were strangers.

"I see you are still wearing your pistols, Mr. Dewy," Hickok said as he rode into Niles's camp.

"Good guess, Bill. But if you could see this far, you'd see the fat lady standing next to me," Niles answered.

"Don't get personal now. I'm coming into camp with some old friends."

Niles reached up to shake Hickok's hand before he dismounted. "I see. Somebody told me all roads are leading to Deadwood this summer," he said, turning to greet the other riders. "Nice to see you again, Jack. Cody, when did you sneak in?" he asked, extending his hand.

"Last night," Cody explained. "I was scouting for Merritt's Fifth down in Nebraska country along Hat Creek—had some time off, so I decided to check out the gold camp before I die."

Hickok shot a hot stare at Cody. "Cody, you lying sack of shit, you'll outlive me. Hell, you will outlive all of us, you clean-living little weasel!" Hickok shouted. His face was drawn tight with rage, and his eyes seemed helpless to change what they saw. "You don't drink, don't smoke the pipe, don't even screw whores. But you know the only real difference between you and me, Cody?" Hickok's was now screaming, losing more self-control with every word. "I'll tell you the difference between you and me, Cody. You kill buffalo for the army and the railroads." His voice shook, and then he pointed a long, steady finger at Cody's face. "I kill men for the pleasure of my own nightmares," he told him. "Am I right?" he asked, spinning around to look at the other men, and no one was about to suggest anything different.

Cody had not moved. He stood steadily, his eyes locked on Hickok's as the man ranted in his face. Like most of Hickok's friends, he had seen the temper flare, and he knew that the calm would come just as quickly.

Hickok stepped back as if he were not sure how he had gotten so close to Cody, and then he hung his head as if it all had come back to him. "Sorry, guys," he said, almost inaudibly.

"You know you never have anything to apologize for with me, Hickok," Cody assured him.

Niles decided to move everyone along. "Light is wasting, and I want to get a photograph of this notable bunch of outlaws here in Deadwood Gulch. Let's get a move on," he said as he directed them toward the stumps next to Sarah's tent. "You haven't told me who your other two friends are," Niles said, jerking his head toward the two buckskin-clad gentlemen.

"Green." Cody pointed to the fellow tying his horse to a low-hanging pine branch as Cody had done. Then he nodded toward the other fellow. "Gene Overton. We was within spitting distance of the Black Hills, so the three of us made this little side trip just to see what Deadwood is all about before the civilized folks overrun it."

"From what I've seen so far, I don't think Deadwood will ever be civilized," Niles told him as he made his rounds, shaking hands with Cody's companions.

"We'll be heading out in the morning. Got to get back to Fort Robinson before they miss us," Cody told him as he dusted himself off and headed for the tent.

"This is the third time I've had the pleasure of you sitting for me," Niles told Hickok. "And the second time I've had you fellows," he said, pointing to Cody and Texas Jack.

"You'll have to open up a picture gallery, Dewy," Hickok said as he straightened his own attire. "Show off all these photographs ... or are you like Cody here, waiting for me to die before you cash in?"

"At the going rate, a picture of a dead man is worth more than a picture of a live one. You're right about that," Niles agreed. "Now why don't you sit here?" he told Hickok, taking him by the arm and moving him over to the taller of the stumps.

"That means you're going to shoot me ... 'cause if it does, you'll have to take a picture of my back, because that's the only way you'll ever get me. Guarantee you of that, Mr. Dewy. That is the only way anyone will ever kill James Butler Hickok—in the back!"

Suddenly, Niles threw his hands into the air. "Where, pray tell, are my manners? Here you boys come all this way up here, and I haven't so much as offered my guests a beverage," he said, skipping off to one of his cases and quickly returning with a fresh bottle of Tennessee whiskey. "Now, gentlemen, make yourselves comfortable," he instructed, handing the bottle to Hickok, who twisted the cork out, sniffed at it, smiled, and took a sip.

"A true gentleman's whiskey!" Hickok exclaimed, wiping his mouth with his sleeve before obliging himself to another, much longer pull from the bottle.

Niles took hold of Green, setting him down on the shorter stump to Hickok's right. He then moved a couple of cases around, stacking them to Hickok's left, where he sat Cody and Texas Jack, and finally he stood Overton on the end. After studying their positions, Niles switched Cody and Omohundro around, sitting the shorter Mexican on the taller of the stacked cases. That was the photograph he wanted to make.

"Okay, listen up," Niles said, clapping his hands to get everyone's attention. "I want each of you to make yourselves as comfortable as you can. Set yourself however you want," he told them as he moved the lens back and forth until he had the group in focus. "I have to go into the tent for a moment and get the plate. When I come out and get under the hood, I'll tell you to freeze. Do it! Freeze, and don't move a muscle. Don't even blink if you can help it."

While he was inside the wigwam, Niles overheard Hickok joke, "No man alive, 'ceptin' the ol' picture man here, can boast he made Wild Bill stand still once, let alone three times."

"Thrice ... cold as ice," Cody added.

Hickok was drinking from the bottle again when Niles made his dash with the chemically coated plate from the wigwam to the camera. "Put away the bottle—don't want folks to think we was have a party," he ordered while he slid the glass plate into the back of the camera box. Green sat as stiff as a board with his hands together in front of him as if he were about to pray, his rifle rested against his knee, its stock on the ground under Hickok's foot. Bill stashed the bottle behind the stump, grabbed his rifle, and pointed it barrel down between his legs. He had already arranged the knife and pistol in his belt and was staring into the camera. Cody sat straight and proud, fluffed his long, wavy hair with his hands, and rested his rifle in front of him after adjusting the pistol stuck in his belt so that it could be seen. Texas Jack moved his pistol from its hip holster to the cartridge belt around his waist so that it would be in the picture, setting his Winchester between his legs, even though his feet were nowhere near touching the ground. And Overton just kept fidgeting from foot to foot.

"Stand still!" Niles hollered. "*Freeze!*"

As soon as the picture taking was concluded and the bottle was passed around a time or three, there were handshakes for everyone, and then Cody and the other two army scouts mounted up and rode off to explore the gulch. Jack and Bill stayed behind. Niles was more than familiar with Hickok's habit of staying put until the bottle was dry. *Better to have him here with me,* Niles thought to himself, *than down there with the Yellow Doll.* He was sure that dreaming would come later in the evening, but for now, Hickok seemed to want nothing more than to lean against that stump, sitting on a cushion of pine duff and watching whatever his eyes allowed him to see of the sunset.

"Thanks, Dewy," Hickok said, raising the bottle in his direction.

Niles waved him off. "I'll always take your picture, Bill. You should know that by now."

"Not what I'm talking about. Tell him, Jack."

Omohundro turned his head away so that Bill would not see him roll his eyes toward heaven. "No, Bill. It is just all cobwebs in your head, anyway. Just forget about it."

"Tell him," he ordered.

Jack shrugged his shoulders. "Bill thinks this place is where he is going to die. I tell him that nobody knows things like that. Maybe Jesus Christ did," the Mexican explained, making the sign of the cross. "But that was a long time ago and far from here. I tell him he is no Jesus Christ. That I know for sure. *Si,* this is a crazy-feeling place, and I'm going to be a very happy Mexican when I can say we was and we ain't here no more."

Omohundro's words were cut short when the sounds of singing broke through the woods surrounding the campsite. "'Joshua fought the battle of Jericho … Jericho … Jericho. Joshua fought the battle of Jericho, and the wall come tumbling down.'"

Bill took it upon himself to investigate the breach of camp peace caused by the rider making his way up the hill. When he saw that it was a Negro, he straightened and walked right up to the rider, his hand extended in friendship. "What's you name, boy?"

"Joshua Monroe. And your name, sir?"

Niles could not help breaking out in a fit of laughter at George's name change since arriving in the Black Hills. It just seemed funny to him that when everybody else seemed to be trying to hide who they were in this place where they all were considered outlaws by the United States government, George was being as honest as they came. *He probably can't help himself,* Niles thought, starting him laughing all over again. And then his asking Hickok who the heck he was nearly brought tears to Niles's eyes because he was laughing so hard.

"Joshua Monroe, your momma did right by you; that be a good darky name. James Butler Hickok—pleased to make your acquaintance, Mr. Monroe." George reached out, and the two shook hands.

"You're shaking hands with Wild Bill Hickok, boy!" Omohundro shouted.

"Wild Bill at your service, Mr. Monroe," Hickok said, reintroducing himself, this time with a grand flourish of his hat nearly dusting the pine-needle-covered ground, the long strands of his auburn hair falling forward and mingling with his bushy handlebar mustache. "I suppose you have heard nothing good of me. I'm a cold-blooded shootist, a killer of men, even a murderer … I deny it!" he said loudly enough for everyone in the camp to hear. Then, raising his right hand and as if he were placing his left on a Bible, he said, "That I have killed men, I admit. But it was either them or me, and I wasn't about to make my momma a sad woman by getting myself killed. No, sir, it was always in self-defense or in the performance of my official, lawful duty." Bill lowered his hands, turned, and staggered back to his spot against the tree stump.

"So why don't they call you Wild *Jim* Hickok?"

Bill stopped dead in his tracks, turning to face the Negro. "Daddy's name was Bill. The day he died, I left Illinois and took his name with me. That's why," he explained. He studied the Negro for a minute, squinting his eyes and trying to focus. "That's kind of funny, Joshua Monroe. Nobody ever made such an inquiry until you. You just made my daddy proud up there in heaven. I will be forever indebted to you for that. Thank you."

Joshua kicked his heels in the horse's belly, moving toward the camp's picket line. "Why's that, Mr. Hickok?"

Bill waited to answer, taking a few sips from the whiskey bottle while he watched Joshua loosen the saddle cinch before he came over to the campfire. Bill offered him the bottle, but Joshua waved it off. "Smart boy. Whiskey'll make you scared—women will steal you blind," Bill said, stumbling around the ring of stones circling the fire before making a rather clumsy landing against the stump. "Not one of you probably know this," Bill started, waving the bottle at all of them before he took another drink. "My ma and pa moved from Vermont to Illinois to set up a station on the underground railroad so darkies like you could get yourself to Deadwood Gulch a free man. That's when I started up with guns, guarding the backs of niggers moving through my folks' hideaway cellar. By the time I was thirteen, I could shoot off the ears of a bounty hunter from a hundred yards with my rifle, either hand. Saving niggers' asses. Yes, sir, that's what got me started in the murdering business. Bet you didn't know that, did you, Mr. Monroe?"

"Don't be blaming that on us Negroes; they blaming us for enough already. You fixed it upon yourself to be a right powerful shootist. No, you did that all yourself."

"I ain't blaming … simply showing you, boy, that James Butler Hickok's been on the side of right more times in his life than he's stepped over the line. That's all."

"Well, there you go," Niles called out. "Deadwood Gulch proves again that innocent wonder awaits just around the next bend in the creek. Is anyone here traveling under his real name?" he joked.

The Mexican jumped to his feet. "Texas Jack Omohundro ... this is me ... me is me."

"You ain't from Texas," Hickok quickly corrected him.

"*Si*, that is true. I'm from Chihuahua, Mexico, not Texas. But how would it sound if they called me *Chihuahua* Jack? No, I never set foot in Texas. No, they skin Mexicans alive down there. I think a Sioux would be more friendly to this Mexican than a Texan."

Niles was left scratching his head. Teasing, he said, "So let me see if I have this straight. You are called *Texas*, but you hate Texas. Am I getting this right?"

"*Si*. You can look how big I am," Jack said, pointing at himself from head to toe. "A little man like me needs a big name. So I'm Texas," he told them, tugging his big hat a little farther down over his left ear and acting quite satisfied with his explanation.

Bill stirred himself. "Who can write around here?" he asked.

Joshua was the first to shoot his arm up into the air. "I know my letters. I learned myself to write my momma's words down on paper. Yes, sir, I can write. And read the Bible some, too."

"Well, ain't that just fine and dandy. Then sit yourself down here, boy," Bill told him, patting the ground next to his stump. "And write down my words."

Bill dug a pencil and a bit of paper out of his coat pocket, handed them to Joshua, took a deep breath through his nostrils to gather himself for the task at hand, cleared his throat, and then pulled at the ends of his mustache until the right words came to him. "Ready? Dear ... no. Start it, 'Dearest wife—'"

"Hold it!" Niles immediately interrupted, not sure that he had heard correctly. "Wife? Since when?" he asked.

"*Si*. Since the fifth of March," Jack quickly said, adding the all-important detail. "He married Miss Lake in Cheyenne, and Texas Jack stood up for Mr. Hickok."

"That's right. Fine, fine lady, Lady Lake. Dear, dear Agnes," Bill sang, swinging the near-empty bottle in the air.

Omohundro leaned closer to Niles. "She's old enough to be his momma, maybe ten years. She runs Lady Lake's Circus … married him for his name."

Looking up from the paper, Joshua flashed a big, white grin. "Which one? James or Bill?" he whispered, starting to laugh.

"Both are *loco*," he warned, pretending to write on the palm of his hand and urging Joshua to do the same.

"'In my last camp and will never leave this gulch alive …'"

Still leaning toward Niles, Jack told him, "He got thrown out of town for running a soap game."

"What? A soap game?" Joshua asked while Bill was collecting his thoughts.

"Bars of soap, each wrapped. One's got a greenback wrapped inside. You buy a bar of soap, you buy a chance it's the payoff," Niles quickly explained, trying to keep his voice low so that Bill would not hear.

Bill, though, was too caught up in his own words to listen to anyone else's. "'Please understand, my fairest Agnes, I never allowed a man to get the drop on me. But perhaps I may yet die with my boots on—'"

After scribbling Bill's words, Joshua turned back to Jack, asking, "What happened?"

"Miss Lake put him up to it—pretty certain nobody would challenge Wild Bill. She was right. Instead 'vagrant' was what he was called and run out of Cheyenne," the Mexican told them, slapping his knees for punctuation.

"'If such should be we never meet again, while firing my last shot, I will breathe the name of my wife—Agnes—and with best wishes even for my enemies I will make the plunge and try to swim to the other shore.'"

Well after sundown, Sarah made her way up the hill. "I stayed down there long enough waiting for you gentlemen to either move on or pass out," she told them, marching past the campfire. "Seeing that you are not about to do either, I am going to count on your gentlemanly graces to not disturb my sleep."

Bill hurried himself off the ground and was barely able to make a clumsy bow before balancing himself against the stump. "I shall not bother the lady's slumber. I will not stay the night … unless invited," he said, bowing to her wishes before moving to the front of Sarah's tent, where he flung back the flap opening, standing aside to permit her entrance.

Shaking her head in obvious disgust, she said, "You are right about one thing. You are not staying the night. You're not invited!" She swept past him, taking hold of the edge of the canvas flap herself and yanking it from his hand. "You are a whoremonger and a crooked lawman, Mr. Hickok," she said, spitting the words at him through her clenched jaw, adding, "You're more inclined to shoot someone in the back these days, because you're so blind you can't face them eye to eye." She ducked into her tent, snapping the flap closed behind her.

Hickok remained standing next to the tent for a while, and then he broke out laughing. "I take whatever comes along. Ain't never shot a lady yet, and I don't intent to start now." He then began circling the camp, gathering up his belongings—rifle, hat, near-empty whiskey bottle—untying his horse from the picket line, and leading him down the hill toward the Backdoor. Niles was pretty sure that he was not on his way to take a bath, not at this time of night. Niles thought about giving Omohundro a kick to wake him up so that he could follow after his friend, but decided to let Hickok, the Yellow Doll, and the opium be alone. She would be safe; Bill would soon lose the battle he fought within himself, eager to surrender to the mercy of the narcotic.

The Yellow Doll had been entertaining customers since sundown. At one time early in the evening, a line of more than a dozen men stood waiting outside her tent. George's new bunks were all occupied, some accommodating two dream-bound prospectors. The floor was crowded wall-to-wall with bodies, barely leaving enough room for the Yellow Doll to set her tiny slipper-clad feet. Eleanor had even cleared away some of the underbrush behind the Backdoor, and a contingent of smokers was sprawled out there.

Eleanor spent the night collecting the price of admission to the Yellow Doll's tent, always trying to drum up some business for herself at the same time, giving every customer a choice. "Bath, barber ... bath or barber? Does anyone want a bath or a shave? Have it your way," she'd finally say in frustration. "Who wants a puff of China smoke?" Few of the customers would even admit to that, so she had begun simply inquiring of each man, "Do you want to get close and friendly with the Yellow Doll?" Then she would collect payment. "Twenty-five cents for the first look ... ten cents for the second." She accepted coins or pinches of gold dust, which she promptly dropped into the leather pouch she kept secreted in the folds of her ample skirt.

By the time Hickok had made his way down from Niles's camp, Eleanor had already joined the dreamers behind the Backdoor, taking her rest slumped against the Backdoor's lone wall.

Hickok staggered straight into the Yellow Doll's tent. "Mr. Hickok," the Yellow Doll said in greeting. "Always a pleasure to be with you," she told him, bowing as a smile spread her apple-red lips.

"Why don't you ever have chairs in the dang places?" he grumbled, stepping over a couple of the bodies on his way toward the back of the tent.

"The Yellow Doll's customers would fall off." She laughed, which loosened Bill's mood some as he limbered his legs to sit himself down on the ground to the side of the Yellow Doll, facing the tent's opening. He squirmed around searching for a comfortable position, finally having to remove the revolver stuck in his belt so that he could bend over more easily, lying the gun across his lap instead. He absently dusted off his knees and finally sat up straight, setting his eyes on the Yellow Doll with a look of wonder like a boy gazing at a glass jar of candies—so close, yet so untouchable. She bent forward so that, when Bill glanced over to see what she was doing, he stalled for a moment, staring at the slope of her neck. Her hair was pulled back, showing ears as delicate as flower blossoms, and her neck made a long, slender slope like fine porcelain growing out of the top of her silk tunic's high color. He hesitated, wanting to rest his eyes there. Instead, he looked away toward the tent opening.

"Damn!" he whispered. "You being so downright pretty and that silver pipe of yours makes this a hard one."

Bill Hickok was a handsome man and pleasant of face, although his inner torment showed in the dark circles under his eyes and in his tightened brow. But the Yellow Doll had always thought that he possessed a certain softness, and the waves of auburn hair could be disarming. But his deep-set eyes and the overgrown mustache drooping over the corners of his mouth added a sadness that never seemed to go away. But when he turned dead serious, those woeful eyes went vacant like two bottomless holes on either side of his nose. "When Bill Hickok gets serious, it means there is nothing standing between you and him killing you," Niles had told her once.

With a practiced, elegant twist of her wrist, she pinched off a small piece of the opium between her forefinger and thumb and rolled it between her fingertips, forming the sticky resin into a tiny sphere, which she reverently moved the last few inches on its long journey from India into the bowl of her silver pipe, laying it to rest finally. It was the end of its secret road. Laying the pipe to rest across her lap, she lifted the caldron and gently blew on the coals, bringing them to life. She set it on the floor in front of Hickok. Then, with all of the reverence of a sacred ritual, she rested the bowl in the groove atop the caldron, offering the silver mouthpiece to Hickok.

Bill moved his eyes down the stem of the pipe to the bowl, took off his hat, and then, shaking his head, he said, "Been a long time since I last smoked from the Yellow Doll's pipe." But he hesitated, and there was a look in his eyes that, if she didn't know better, she would have thought was from the eyes of a praying man. The Yellow Doll waited, still offering the pipe even as the opium resin began to melt, releasing a dragon's tail of sweet smoke into the air above the bowl.

She had seldom tried to understand why a person sought out the opium dreams. Some, she knew, smoked for the fun of it; it was just another elixir to fuel their celebrating. Others sought the dreams because of the mystery of the unknown. But she knew for many that the dreams hid them from life for a few precious hours. And she also knew that Hickok was one of those who desired never to wake from the opiate's refuge. The Yellow Doll was an opium merchant, smuggling and selling the drug as many in her family had done for generations, passing neither judgment nor concern for the narcotic nightmares it could inflict. "Steel your heart away," she had warned Niles in the beginning. "Our compassion is supplying the drug."

Bill tilted the bottle, pouring the last of the liquor down his throat. His eyes closed, and for a moment, the Yellow Doll thought that he had passed out. Finally, he opened his eyes, looked down at the pipe, and took it from the Yellow Doll's hands. She used her fan to liven the embers as Hickok lowered his head, placed the tip in his mouth, and inhaled a long, slow draw, pulling the smoke deep into his lungs. Almost immediately, she could see the drug's veil descend over his eyes.

His head slumped ever farther until his chin rested on his chest. Then, the Yellow Doll heard the quiet sobs. Tears streamed down his cheeks, and fits of sobbing heaved his chest. "I killed him ... I killed him," he whispered. Finally, the opium freed him, and he cried out, "I killed Williams! I killed him. He was so young, a good man. I killed him. I killed my deputy." Then, as if asking the god of the drug for forgiveness, he said, "I dug his grave with these hands ... buried my badge with him ... I killed him."

The Yellow Doll had heard the stories about the Abilene gunfight—the Texas cowboys and Hickok's accidental killing of Deputy Williams. She gently lifted the pipe from his hands, repacked the bowl, and laid it back in his lap. "This will help," she whispered.

He smoked a second time, but the sobbing grew worse. "Five years ... five years ... I have not taken another life in five years, but the nightmares won't stop. They won't stop!" he cried out. "I don't want to kill in Deadwood. Not again. Don't make me. Please don't make me," he said, sobbing, but his words began to slur, and his painful rocking grew slower and slower until his body slumped to the side. The Yellow Doll carefully removed the pipe from his hands and moved one of the cushions under his head, leaving him to his dreams.

"You will not have to kill. Not here, not in Deadwood," she whispered. "The Yellow Doll promises."

Chapter 13

August 1, 1876

William Clay walked the gold camp's main thoroughfare as the sun broke over the edge of the canyon walls. He had slept the night before about a quarter of mile downstream of Deadwood, the end of a nearly thirty-hour, headstrong dash to the Black Hills. As soon as the Russian freighter had told him that the gang of four had taken off in the middle of the night, followed the next morning by his hired hand, Clay had been on his way. The freighter had warned him that he'd better hurry, because the hired hand was after "the yellow-skinned bitch" and that he "might just kill her first."

As the morning grew older and more and more people congregated along the street, Clay paraded back and forth up one side and down the other, carrying a pot in each hand and waving the merchandise over his head for everyone to see. Of the twenty-four pots he had left, two had been chipped, and one had lost its handle. But already that morning, he had traded one of the chipped ones for a shot of whiskey and glass of warm beer, another chipped one for a cup of hot coffee and a cold flapjack, and the vessel missing its handle had gotten him a cold roasted potato—his first food since trading the freighter for a handful of jerked venison and a couple of hard biscuits.

"Sell ya a pot, mister?" Clay asked, walking up to the man standing in the shade of a Main Street business advertising itself as a butcher shop. Considering most of the folks doing something or other along the busy roadway, this fellow looked to be a bit more prosperous, making him a prime customer to buy one of Clay's chamber pots. "I can tell you have a nice place for a fine porcelain pot like this," he said, holding one of the pots forward. For some time, the customer pulled at his drooping mustache, looking Clay over and making no secret of his attention to Clay's pistol. Finally, he looked at the pot, motioning for Clay to bring it closer.

"You're a bigger man than I, pot salesman."

"How so?" Clay asked. To go with the mustache, the fellow sported long, curly, auburn hair. He wore store-bought clothes, and a black coat concealed the bulge of the two pistols he had snuggly tucked into a sash that he wore around his waist. The shirt appeared to be recently laundered, and his pants had been recently brushed, displaying none of the dust or yellow pine pollen that coated everything in the gulch. Only his boots showed any day-to-day life of Deadwood, covered as they were with Main Street's pavement of mud, dust, and animal waste.

"I, for one, would not be caught dead peddling piss pots. That would take a real shithead to do something like that. Wouldn't you agree?" Two men idling near the fancy dresser laughed, and then each took a step or so away.

"The pilgrim's only trying to work up a stake, Bill," the bold one said.

"Señor Bill, do not make clouds on such a beautiful day," the second fellow added, moving back toward Clay's customer. "If you kill him, we will have to drag him away and pay Madam Mustache to bury him. No, señor, this is not a good way to spend such a fine day." The one pleading Clay's case wore a sombrero and a dark Spanish waistcoat trimmed with a felt collar and cuffs. He carried a rifle almost as long as he was tall, and where a pistol holster would have been on his hip, there was a leather scabbard for a bone-handled Texas bowie knife instead. The man removed his hand and bowed, announcing, "I am Señor Omohundro."

"That's fancy Mexican talk for telling you his name's Texas Jack," the bald man said, snickering.

Ignoring him, the first fellow continued, *"Sí.* Texas Jack Omohundro. And the gentleman who is not going to kill you is Señor Hickok. You know Wild Bill?" he asked.

Looking back and forth between the three men, all that Clay could muster was a nod of his head.

"Well, Mr. Pot Salesman, now you have met Señor Wild Bill. What do you have to say to that?" Jack went on.

Clay sort of bowed in Hickok's direction. "Pleased to make you acquaintance, sir." Then he turned to the bald gentleman. "Is he someone famous?"

"No. He's only Señor Steve. His brother, me, and Señor Bill came together from Cheyenne. Where did you come from?"

"Illinois." That news caught Hickok's attention. "As a matter of fact, Mr. Hickok and I have something in common."

"You don't say," Hickok said, giving the man a second hard look. "Now what would that be?"

"Back in Illinois, I was a sheriff … county deputy sheriff."

"I ain't the law anymore. And seeing that there is no law in Deadwood Gulch, I guess we're both out of work—except you, of course. You're peddling piss pots."

Clay tried unsuccessfully to hide the pots behind his back, saying, "We got something else in common besides the law. I was the deputy in Champaign County, Illinois."

Hickok tilted his head. "I know Champaign County—"

"You should. That's were you was born," Clay interrupted.

"I'll be damned, boys. This here pot salesman was a sheriff in Homer."

"Oak Grove. Changed the name to Oak Grove. Another town named Homer up in the north part of Illinois, so they changed the name to Oak Grove."

"I'll be. Didn't know that. Funny, isn't it? Here in Deadwood Gulch, the beginning of my life shows up. Hope this ain't the end." Hickok's mood turned sour. Sadness overtook his eyes, and his mustache drooped even farther.

Clay quickly tried to redeem himself. "Sorry. Didn't mean to make you sad or anything." Then, pointing at Texas Jack, he added, "Like your friend said, it is too nice a day for that."

"*Si*, too nice a day to be sad."

Hickok seemed to snap out of his slump. "We may not be lawmen anymore, but that don't stop me from supporting a fellow lawman." Waving at Texas Jack, he said, "Buy a pot from my Illinois neighbor." Then he said to Clay, "What's your name? Don't seem right to go around calling you 'pot salesman.'"

"Clay. William Clay."

"Tell you what, William Clay—when you're done peddling your pots, how about if you buy old Bill Hickok a drink? What do you say to that?"

"Sure, that would be fine."

Jack had yet to move. "I told you to buy a pot from this man," Hickok said.

The Mexican walked over to Clay. "I always needed a chamber pot."

"Now all you need is a chamber to put it in," Steve said, laughing.

"How much, señor?"

"Dollar for one," Clay told him, offering one of the pots he was holding. "Two pots for the same buck if I can ask ya a couple of questions."

"Lawman kind of questions?" Hickok asked.

"Nothing like that," Clay assured him. "It's some folks that owe me something. I know they were headed to the Black Hills, and I am here to, shall we say, collect the debt. How about it? Two pots, one buck?"

"Pay him," Hickok encouraged Omohundro. "Who exactly are these friends of yours?" he asked as he watched Clay turn over the pots when Jack gave him a dollar.

"Eastern fellow, a picture man. You know, he make those photographs."

Bill pushed himself away from the wall he had been leaning against. "So tell me, lawman to lawman, what sort of debt could a picture man owe you?"

"Let me just say him and the little gang he's traveling with did this deputy wrong, real wrong. And I'm here to make it right."

"You say this picture man wronged you? Must be some wrong for you to come all this way to collect," Hickok said.

"Oh, it was wrong, all right. The son of a bitch cost me my job. Got me fired!"

Hickok pulled at the ends of his mustache. "Does this picture fellow of yours travel with a Chinaman?"

"That's him. Then you've seen 'em here? He got a blonde gal traveling with him and a nigger boy. Where'd you see 'em?" Clay asked as he looked up and down the main street.

Bill walked over to Clay, stopping right in front of him. "You're sure it was a picture man and a slant-eye?"

"That's them. I been trailing 'em since Illinois."

Bill turned to his two friends. "Have you boys seen a picture man in the gulch?"

Both men hung their heads, scuffing the toes of their boots in the dirt. "Nope, seen nothing like that," Steve said. Jack nodded his agreement.

Clay believed them about as much as he believed that it was going to snow in the gulch that afternoon.

"Put those pots out there," Hickok told the Mexican, pointing him out into the street. The man obliged, dodging around a horse and rider and then a buckboard until he was finally in the middle of the road. He turned around, shrugging his shoulders and asking if this was the spot. Bill motioned with his hand. Omohundro set the pots down and made his way back to the front of the butcher shop.

"You know what, Deputy Sheriff Clay? You and I might have something in common, after all," he said, looking back at him. "Just so happens I have a friend who makes photographs. Now wouldn't it be something if it turned out your friend and my old friend are one in the same? Now wouldn't that just beat all? Imagine—we all meet up here in Deadwood. Can you believe it?" he asked, turning to his friends, who looked in every direction except at Hickok and Clay.

William Clay did not see Hickok's hand move or see the pistol fire, but like everyone else who heard the gunshot, he ducked for cover. Life on Main Street came to a midstride halt. Out in the middle of the street, one of Clay's pots was a pile of enameled shards. Suddenly, the second pot exploded, but not from a pistol shot. Clay had to look twice before he saw the Mexican's bowie knife stuck in the dirt where the pot had been, its pieces laid around it like the petals of a flower.

Bill raised his eyebrows, making sure that Clay was paying attention. "If you see this picture man before I do, please tell our friend that Bill Hickok welcomes him to Deadwood."

Clay took a look at the smashed pots in the middle of the street, tugged on the reins of his Indian pony, and tipped his hat to the gentlemen. "Thanks for everything," he told them, and he moved on. When he was far enough out of earshot, he whispered to himself, "Damn it! I'm still going to get ya. Bill Hickok's friendship can go to hell."

The noise from a night spent on Main Street still rang in Bill Hickok's ears, a ghostly echo competing with the sleepy quiet of the canyon's dawn. He followed the creek instead of using the street to get to the Yellow Doll's tent, hoping that no one would catch him making a predawn visit. He did not want Madam Mustache to see him, either, for the woman would blab his whereabouts from one end of the gulch to the other by noon. And, of course, he had to keep Niles Dewy in mind; he was sure to be lurking in the shadows somewhere, keeping his vigil. No, it would be better all around if he kept their little meeting this morning private.

Outside the Yellow Doll's tent, he stopped to peer through the darkness, making sure that no one was around to see him go in. "Yellow Doll," he whispered. "It's me, Hickok."

"Come in. No one is awake. They are all dreaming," she told him.

Hickok slipped inside. He quickly glanced over both shoulders and behind him; the Yellow Doll had no vacancies. George's three-tiered bunks lined the walls of the tent on either side and across the back. Including the dreamers passed out on the floor, the Yellow Doll had twenty customers enjoying their escapes. He moved farther into the tent, avoiding looking directly at the Yellow Doll, which made her suspect that he had something on his mind besides a smoke—something she undoubtedly would not like to hear.

"I was coming down here just now, feeling kind of bad," he began, still avoiding looking at her. Instead, he checked the dreamers close around him. "Just plain bad. I have a bad taste in my mouth; even this mountain air smells bad. Ever have a time like that when everything just feels bad?" he asked, finally looking at her.

"Yes, when I see an old friend feeling that way."

"I don't want you to feel bad. No, I want you to be … how should I say? … relieved."

She decided that she had better hear him out, so she began to prepare the silver pipe. He watched her pinch of a piece of opium, place it in the bowl of the pipe, and press it down with the tip of her thumb. "You know what's making me feel bad? What made me feel really, really terrible?"

She laid the pipe across her lap, waiting for Hickok to sit down across from her before she set the bowl to smoldering.

"I got myself to thinking today. And I decided to help the Yellow Doll. Help keep her alive."

The Yellow Doll slowly lowered her hand from the pipe to rest on the cushion beside her and the coach gun hidden under it.

"And to do my part in keeping you alive, I am going to have to take all your opium. All of it," he said. His eyes were locked on her face. "The black smoke is worth a hell of a lot more than a bag of gold dust. Hell! Magicians have been trying since the beginning of time to turn water into gold. Well, poof! Opium turns smoke into gold! And the Yellow Doll is going to turn James Butler Hickok into a rich man."

"The Yellow Doll would be happy to compensate you for your protection."

"Shut up! Get this into that China head of yours. I'm not talking about a partnership." He snapped the words at her so loudly that she thought for a moment that he would wake the dreamers. Hickok paced about the tent, studying each of the men sleeping off their night's smoke. Then he moved over to the tent's flap and moved it aside to check outside. He came back to stand over her again. "Let me explain why you can't keep the opium or the gold," he began. He was so close to her now that she could smell the liquor on his breath. "When I heard what you all did to that lawman back in Illinois—"

"Heard? Where did you hear about that?"

"News gets around in a gold camp. Now you hear me out. When I heard what you did, it soured my guts. No matter what people may think of my reputation or me, I have nothing but respect for lawmen. Any and all lawmen." His arms hung at his sides, and his buckskin jacket was open, showing the revolvers stuck in the sash around his waist. She relaxed her hand on the cushion concealing the shotgun.

Outside, Kit's chickens began to greet the early dawn, and inside the Yellow Doll's tent, one of the dreamers woke, groaning as he washed off the night by rubbing his face with his hands. He rolled over on the bunk to look down the barrel of Hickok's pistol. The fellow quickly threw up his arms as best he could. "Gotta pee real bad, mister. Let me pee first, then kill me," he pleaded. Hickok raised the barrel skyward, motioning with his empty hand for the man to get out. He was off the bunk and out of the tent by the time Hickok had started nudging each of the Yellow Doll's customers to life. It took him a few minutes to shove the last of the groggy-eyed men out of the tent, and then they were alone.

His pistol still in hand, he told her, "I'm not going to kill you. No, I'm just going to leave you with nothing—no opium, no gold, nothing—just like you left that Illinois sheriff." He paused, looking her over from head to foot. "I won't take your clothes like you did to that poor slob, although seeing you run out of Deadwood wearing nothing but that yellow skin would be quite a sight for everyone." He raised the pistol and aimed it right at her forehead. "Deadwood's just waiting for people to die."

"If anything happens to the Yellow Doll, you're a dead man, Bill Hickok. Just like you said, you could die very easily in Deadwood."

The pistol's aim relaxed some, but she could still see the desire to pull the trigger flickering in his eyes. "I'll at least get a decent burial. That's more that this camp'll do for a slant-eyed, poppy-pushing whore. I'll take the gold and opium now," he commanded.

Making sure that her hands were always in full view, she slowly reached behind her cushion, lifting the buffalo robe folded there and uncovering two embroidered purses. One contained Long Ears's payment, and the other held the Yellow Doll's opium. Keeping the pistol trained on her, he grabbed the purses out of her hands with his left. "Keep the picture man out of our little business. I like him too much to have to kill him." He backed away from her and ducked out of the tent.

"He likes you, too," she muttered to herself after he was gone.

Hickok left the same way he had come, slipping through the dark behind the tent down to the creek and back up the gulch. He did not notice that there had been one more dreamer lying on the ground behind the tent than when he had arrived.

The runt did not move a muscle, not even daring to breathe until Hickok was well upstream. He had been following him all night in and out of saloons, watching him play poker and even playing a hand of poker with him, losing the last of the money that he had in his pocket. The famous gambler had felt sorry for him and had given him a whole dollar to buy his breakfast with the next morning. But the runt kept following him, figuring eventually that he would lead him to the China woman, and his hunch had been right. Not only did Hickok lead him straight to her, the runt had also overheard every word that Hickok had said. And when Hickok left, out of the corner of his eye, the runt saw the purses that he was carrying.

"I'll kill him. I'll kill Bill Hickok and get your money back," he said as he ducked through the tent's flap.

The runt's surprise entrance found the Yellow Doll right where Hickok had left her, sitting on the cushion with the silver pipe still resting in her lap. She bowed to her new guest as if nothing was wrong. "Welcome to Deadwood, sir. I am pleased to see your prairie crossing was successful."

"Yaw, I made it. And a good thing for you I did," he told her with a bit of a swagger. She saw that he had that old pistol of his stuck in the waist of his pants. His hat looked even worse for the wear than the last time she had seen him, and the hole in the knee of his pants had nearly torn completely around, leaving the pant leg held together by a few threads. All in all, the runt appeared to her to be pretty much the poor soul he was when she had last seen him.

In a matter-of-fact way shared between two old friends, the Yellow Doll asked, "Who are you now? Jack McCall? John Southerland? Or someone new?"

"I'll kill him! Swear I will. I swear Jack McCall will kill him for you."

She bowed and then lifted her head so that her eyes stared right into his. The Yellow Doll was about to declare an opium war in Deadwood Gulch, and she wanted to make sure that the runt got it right, or it could end up getting them all killed. But here was her chance to get the opium and the gold back, and no one would suspect her or Niles Dewy. She pushed herself up, stepping off the cushion and over the smoldering cauldron in front of her. As she moved, she began slowly unbuttoning her tunic with her free hand, revealing with each loosened button more of her bare skin. With the other hand, she offered the silver pipe, her smile inviting Jack McCall to accept.

Chapter 14

August 2, 1876

"Wake up, Mr. Niles. Wake up. It is time to make a picture!"

The shouting outside of the tent pushed Niles's dreams away. His eyes blinked open to confirm where he was and then closed again.

"Wake up!"

Niles rolled out of his bedroll and stuck his head out of the tent's flap. The sky above was clear and bright blue. Not a cloud could be seen hanging between the rims of the gulch.

"Mr. Niles, I have it. I have a picture for you. See the head?" Omohundro stood in front of him, the bloody head of an Indian swinging from a lone braid he held in his hand right in front of Niles's face. "Take my picture," the Mexican insisted.

"Before breakfast? Coffee—"

"*Si*, before whiskey."

"Now you're asking a bit much," Niles told him as he crawled on hands and knees out of the tent.

"This is a picture you have never made before."

"I can swear to that," Niles confirmed as he committed to standing up. Just then, Jack's toe stubbed against a fallen branch, and in an effort to try to maintain his balance, he let go of the head. It rolled across the ground like a lopsided ball. Niles could not look at the grotesque object. The Indian's face was contorted by death, and the butchering had left deep slashes across its cheeks, exposing white bone underneath. The mouth was frozen in a sickly, blue-lip-outlined smile. One of the eyes was stuck open, and the other was only a black, sunken socket.

"Get out of here!" Sarah hollered, quickly coming up behind Niles and furiously waving a pistol back and forth. "Get the hell out of here, and take that with you!" she shouted, pointing the gun at the head lying on the ground. "Go on. You and that awful thing—get out of here!"

Jack scurried over to retrieve his prize and made a mad dash down the hill with Sarah fast on his heels. Finally, she stopped and watched as the Mexican half ran and half stumbled down onto Main Street, where he once again began waving the gory trophy in the air.

"Are you all right?" Niles asked her once she had made her way back up to the campsite.

"Oh, yeah, I'm just fine. Just peachy keen fine! I guess smugglers and gunmen are used to waking up to the sight of death."

"Shh, now just calm down."

"Calm down! Calm down! Let me tell you, mister, I am calm. If I weren't, you would both be dead," she told him, waving the gun. "I guess you just take it for granted … waking up to a dead head in Deadwood." She slumped to the ground next to the cold campfire. "This is no way to start a day. No way any day. Sorry, I didn't mean to lose my temper," she apologized, finally tucking the gun into the waistband of her trousers. Then she used her empty hands to push the hair out of her face and rub the sleep out of her eyes.

"If you had a bed, I'd just chalk it up to you getting out on the wrong side. But seeing you don't, I think you just came out the wrong end of the tent this morning."

"You got that right. But I'm sure you can understand. This whole business of yours caught me off guard. I mean, I knew you were up to something—never did buy that picture man story of yours hook, line, and sinker. But opium? How in the world was I to react when I found out that Mr. Rubee was really Madam Rubee? Come on!

How would you feel if you suddenly found out that I wasn't some innocent, sweet girl … but, say, a government agent sent to break up your opium business and bring the two of you to justice instead? What would you think?"

Her question sent a shiver up Niles's spine. Sarah Culbert a government agent? Was this some kind of backhanded admission? Quickly, he inventoried what he knew about Sarah Culbert.

She had cornered him at the British embassy party, and he had taken her word that she lived in Washington. It was perfectly reasonable for the daughter of a congressman … or federal police officer. But how she knew when to be at the train station had puzzled Niles halfway across the continent.

Money seemed to be no problem for her.

She was comfortable with firearms, having demonstrated that already on several occasions.

Yes, it all added up to a scenario that Niles could imagine. "That would probably explain why you were so eager to crawl into my bed that first night back in Washington."

"Eager! You stuff-assed, pompous bastard. I seem to recall eagerness on your side of the bed that night, not mine!"

Niles gave himself a stiff mental kick in the head. "Don't think there is no government around that would send the likes of you all alone through Indian country after a couple of no-name criminals."

"Don't be so sure. Besides, I would say that, for a couple of no-name criminals, your notoriety seems to be pretty common knowledge to quite a few people in places like this."

Niles went over to the picket line and began saddling his horse. "Seeing that we are playing the imagination game, imagine how much trouble you could get yourself into if you are a federal agent of some kind. If you haven't noticed, there ain't no law around here to protect you," he told here as he tightened the saddle cinch. Hoisting himself into the saddle, he told her, "I'm going down to talk to Rubee. Find a cup of coffee. Some breakfast. And then maybe look around for a picture or two." He twisted the horse away from the picket line and slowly began picking his way down the hill toward the Backdoor Bathhouse. Sarah remained seated, watching him as he swayed back and forth to the rhythm of the horse's gait. She lifted her arms as if holding a rifle and aimed at Niles's back, moving the make-believe gun to match his.

"Bang," she whispered. "I'll shoot my own picture."

By midafternoon, after riding partway down Boulder Canyon and letting his camera eye search unsuccessfully for a photograph, Niles made his way back to Madam Mustache's Bathhouse and the Yellow Doll's tent. He was still more that twenty-five yards away when Madam caught sight of him and began running toward him. "Niles! Niles! Hickok's been killed! He killed Hickok!"

Niles spurred the horse to a trot to close the distance between himself and Eleanor. "What happened?" he shouted.

"Not sure, but I'll tell ya all I've heard so far."

Niles was even with her now. "Where'd it happen?" he asked as the horse circled around the woman.

"Down there at Nuttal's place. You know, on that ol' claim number ten of theirs."

Niles headed the horse at a fast pace toward the Bathhouse with Eleanor trying to keep up beside him. "Rubee all right?' he hollered back to her.

"She's fine, but the feller that kilt him was with her right before it happened. And Hickok had been in to see her before that."

Niles pulled the horse up. "What fellow was in to see her?"

"That crooked-nose runt. You know—the one you all traveled with before you left that Russian freighter. McCall."

"McCall? You mean Sutherland."

"He's claiming his name's McCall now. Jack McCall."

"He was in with Rubee?"

"Yup! Right after Hickok left."

"But she's all right?"

"She's fine. But let me tell ya what I've heard so far, before you go talkin' to her."

In the two hours or so since the killing, Eleanor had scoured Deadwood for information. "There's more rumors buzzin' around this camp than flies around a dead buffalo," she started. "But here's what I know so far. The runt come up behind him and shot him in the back of the head. Bill left here, I guess, and gone down there to Nuttal's and Mann's Saloon to play some afternoon poker. That's where the runt kilt him. Blew the back of his head off."

"Why?"

"That I can't tell ya for sure—not yet, anyways. And the runt's given them a bunch of different stories, but I ain't heard a word even breathed mixin' you or the Yellow Doll in the mess."

"So they caught him?"

"Oh, ya, they caught him, all right. You know that old Mexican friend of Hickok's, Texas Jack? Well, he was up there on Main Street trying to auction off some poor injun's head—"

"I know all about that. That's how I started my day," Niles interrupted her.

"Well, this ol' crowd around the Mexican got the news that Hickok had been killed, and they all took off looking for the killer. Well, it didn't take them long to find him, either. Guess where they found him? Go on, take a guess."

Niles shook his head. "Not here?"

"No, you idiot. They cornered him in the Chinaman's butcher shop."

"Long Ears?"

"You heard me."

"So why'd he do it?"

"Runt says Hickok killed his brother down there in Kansas for stealin' chickens. Runt said he shot Hickok in the back just like he'd kilt his brother."

"I'm pretty sure Bill never shot anybody in the back. He liked looking them in the eyes when he did; that much I know for pretty certain."

"Hey, I'm just tellin' ya what I've heard. And that's about it for now."

"Thanks, Eleanor. Now I got to see Rubee. You get back out there and see what you hear. Then get back here and tell us."

"Watch your back, picture man. You know how these gold camps can be. They're like powder kegs, and they could blow at any minute. You might have to start shootin' for real."

"I hear you," Niles told her as he ducked into the Yellow Doll's tent. Eleanor headed back up Main Street.

"You okay?'

"I'm just fine, Mr. Dewy."

"What happened? Eleanor said Hickok and the runt both were in here. What happened, Rubee?"

As she told him the story of Hickok's robbery and the runt's visit, Niles drew out his revolver, checked the load, and moved toward the tent's flap so that he could watch for any eavesdroppers.

Eleanor came waddling into the tent, out of breath. "They caught the runt with a pocketful of gold. But that ain't all. Apparently, Bill was there in Nuttal's playing cards with three fellers—Mann, Nuttal's partner, an ol' river capt'n goin' by the name Massey, and some gambler Bill apparently knew from Cheyenne. Well, none of them would move from their stumps, and Bill had to sit with his back to the door. And bang, the runt come'd in, walked up behind him, and kilt him."

"What's this about him having a bunch of gold?" Niles asked.

"Yup, says the runt was a rich man when they found him there in Long Ears's joint. Kind of funny, though, 'cause folks is sayin' he'd played poker with Bill yesterday, and Bill supposedly cleaned him out. The runt was broke, and now he's got pocketfuls of gold. Go figure."

Niles shot a knowing glance toward Rubee, who only stared straight ahead. But Eleanor had spied Niles's look. "Hey, what do you two know? Come on, 'fess up."

"Miss Dumont!"

Eleanor's prying was cut short by someone outside the Backdoor yelling her name. A teenage kid soon stuck his head into the Yellow Doll's tent. "Miss Dumont?"

"You found her. Who are you, and why you looking for me? I'm sure you don't want a bath, and you ain't old enough, kid, to need a shave. So what's you want?"

"McClintock's the name—John McClintock. Doc Pierce sent me looking for you. He's got a dead fellow needs burying. So he sent me looking for you."

"Hickok?" she asked him.

"Yes'm."

"Tell Doc I'll be over at his place as soon I gets my diggin' nigger," Eleanor told him. She turned back to Niles and the Yellow Doll and said, "We'll finish this little talk of ours when I get back." She ducked out of the tent. "George! George! It's diggin' time!"

When she was safely out of earshot, Niles turned to Rubee and said, "The runt got our gold."

"And Long Ears got our opium," Rubee added.

"It may be time for me to go to work."

"No, Mr. Dewy. We will go about our business just as if nothing has happened. We will wait. I'll open for business when Eleanor gets back. I'll listen to her news and what my customers have to say. Then, if necessary and prudent, we will act. Until then, you go up to the campsite and keep a sharp eye."

Niles bowed. "As you wish. But the first sign of trouble, I'll be down here."

"I know, Mr. Dewy. I trust you will."

Niles bowed again and ducked out of the tent. He surveyed the immediate vicinity around the Backdoor, gathered up his horse, and rode up the hill to their campsite, where he settled in to wait as Rubee had instructed.

The wait was short lived, coming to an abrupt end when gunfire erupted on Main Street and seemed to Niles to be moving in their direction.

The sound of gunshots was common in the gulch. As long as it wasn't close by or directed at them, most folks just ignored it as if it were a screech from one of the hawks that seemed to continuously circle the gold camp. But when the sound of the gun battle seemed to move closer and closer to Kit's place, she fell to the ground, one of her own pistols in hand. A spray of dirt exploded in the middle of the road not more than twenty yards away from her chickens. They sent up a clamor of clucking and wing flapping in protest.

But Kit's attention did not stay long on her chickens when she saw George running out into the road from between two makeshift buildings along the banks of Whitewood Creek. He dodged around unsuspecting pedestrians and riders as fast as his legs would propel him. She watched him take temporary refuge behind a barrel, and then he moved along to a stack of crates ... and then over to a pile of lumber ... and he finally slid himself under a buckboard parked in front of one of the businesses.

That was when Kit finally caught sight of the man chasing him.

Clay tried to hold onto a blue porcelain chamber pot in one hand while aiming and firing his rifle with the other. Two shots went wide, and his next hit the back of the buckboard wagon under which the Negro hid. The wagon's team, spooked by the shot, reared up, twisting in their harnesses and breaking free of their tether, leaving George lying on the side of the road unprotected. Clay raised his rifle, resting it across his other arm and letting the pot dangle under the rifle barrel. There was no place for George to hide, and when he heard the shot, he covered his head with his arms, expecting at any second for the bullet to rip into his body.

Instead, Clay let a spine-chilling howl as shards of pottery showered to the ground around him, many of them sticking point first into the roadbed like little darts. Clay danced around in circles clutching the hand that had held the pot, trying to live with the pain that felt like a hammer had just whacked his hand. George didn't wait around to offer his sympathies. Instead, he took the opportunity to take off running. "You owe me a pot, nigger boy! You owe me!" Clay yelled after him. When Clay was able to live with the throbbing hand, he retrieved his rifle and searched up and down the road, but his prey had disappeared. Men up and down the street went about their business once again. The carpenters started banging away, and Kit stood up, dusting herself off and tucking the pistol back in her waistband. Before going back to her chores, she squinted against the bright August sunlight filling the canyon. Looking up the hillside above the Backdoor Bathhouse, she saw Niles sitting against a tree, his eye still pressed against the rifle scope as he continued to guard

Main Street. "Dark angel," she whispered. "You owe the picture man one, too, Mr. Monroe," she added before going over to her chickens to calm them down.

"Sell ya a pot, lady? Fancy pot for a fancy lady." Making the offer was the man who had been chasing George, and now he was standing right in front of Kit's Egg Emporium trying to sell her one of his chamber pots.

"Did I miss something, mister? 'Cause I didn't know it was open season on nigger boys—unarmed nigger boys, no less," she said, not even breaking stride as she crossed right in front of him to check her boiling water.

Clay stared at her for a moment. "Seems someone's the boy's protector," he said, giving his stung hand a wave toward the road. "Do you want to do business or not? Two eggs for a pot."

"Two eggs, two pots!" Kit bartered.

"Deal. I'll go get my horse and bring you back your pots. I like my eggs a little runny so I got something to dip my biscuit in," he told her, touching the brim of his hat before heading back up the street. Kit gave the man's back a piercing glare and then dropped two eggs into the boiling water, giving them a stir with the pine branch she had shaved of its bark and fashioned in a Y-shaped fork that was ideal for fishing eggs out of the boiling water.

Clay came back, making good on their barter, and he settled down on Kit's quilt.

"Where's a pot salesman like you from?" Kit asked.

"Illinois."

"Where in Illinois?"

Clay made no effort to answer her. Kit shrugged. "Guess you're too hungry to talk," she said as she ladled out the eggs, rolling them in a rag to dry them off. "You know, talking and eating make the digestion work better," she tried again, but Clay remained silent. "Talking goes good with just about anything. Eating. Walking. Even poking. You ever had a poke and never said a word? Not even a please and thank you?"

"That an offer?"

"No, it ain't. I got my standards," Kit told him, clamping her hands on her waist so that he would have no doubts about her resolve.

"I heard a fellow sayin' there's a bathhouse somewhere around here. Said it's run by a slant-eyed whore."

"There, see? That weren't so hard, now, was it? I figured you could shoot off that mouth of yours as well as you shoot that rifle. Now ain't that better for your eatin' enjoyment?"

"What about the bathhouse?"

"You don't strike me as the sort looking for a bath. Might be wrong—wouldn't be the first time. Maybe everyone should take a bath after a little gunplay. You know, cleanse the body and the soul."

Clay stared at her, pushed up off the quilt, and stepped around her. With a swift kick, he smashed one of the pots. "If you weren't such a stupid bitch, you'd have two pots," he said, and then turned and walked way.

"Why, you bastard! You're the right shithead to be sellin' chamber pots—got that right!" she yelled at his back, and then she shrugged and went back about her chores. She rescued her remaining pot, admiring it briefly, and then she set it near the edge of her canvas shelter well out of the way of any other flying boot heels. She grabbed the corners of the quilt and gave it a quick shake, smoothing it out again on the bed of pine needles, all fresh and clean for her next customer. She kept an eye on the pot salesman, watching him wander across the road toward Eleanor's Backdoor Bathhouse.

She spent the next hour strengthening her chicken pen. "Just in case some critter—two legged or four legged—tries kicking around Kit LeRoy's golden hens, ladies," she said, checking the street for any sign of the pot salesman, but he was nowhere to be seen. She then gathered up a few freshly laid eggs and carefully put them in the porcelain pot atop a cushion of pine duff for safekeeping.

Steve Utter, Hickok's friend Charlie's younger brother, used the pot salesman's shooting on Main Street to cover his approach to the Yellow Doll's tent, keeping Dewy in sight and waiting for him to look through his rifle scope away from the Backdoor. As soon as

Niles shot the pot out of the salesman's hand, Steve stepped around to the front of the tent and through the flap opening, all in plenty of time before the Sharps's cloud of black powder smoke had a chance to drift clear of the scope.

The Yellow Doll bowed a greeting, pleased to have her first dreamer of the day. She noted that the man was new, maybe part Indian judging from the buckskins and from the straight black hair worn long and loose. He was armed only with a tomahawk tucked under the belt around his waist. "Welcome, sir. Perhaps you are in search of a smoke?" she asked. It was her practice with first-time customers who were usually ill at ease about how to go about conducting business. She motioned for the gentleman to join her on a floor cushion across from her opposite the smoldering caldron. While he was obliging her invitation, the Yellow Doll focused on filling the silver pipe's bowl with a tiny ball of opium. "Twenty-five cents for your first bowl, sir. Fifty cents for your second," she explained as she held the bowl over the caldron's coals.

She noticed that he reached behind his back, presumably to get his coin pouch, and then with the other, he quickly grabbed her hand. From behind his back, his other hand came up gripping the hatchet, which he swung down, chopping off the Yellow Doll's arm in one mighty swing. Before the pain even had a chance to force a scream from her throat, he swung a second time, this time burying the hatchet's honed edge into the top of her head. The Yellow Doll slumped to the side, red blood pulsing from both wounds and staining the silk tunic as well as the floor cushions. Then he grabbed the other arm and sliced it off, and finally, he pinned her legs, chopping each one off above the knees.

Niles had not recognized the man chasing after George, and he had not recognized him again when he was at Miss Kit's place, but when he saw the fellow nosing around the Backdoor Bathhouse, recognition smothered him like a wet blanket; it was that damn Illinois sheriff. Rubee's guess was right; somehow, the fellow had followed them all the way to the Black Hills, and in a strange twist, he had gotten tangled up with Hickok. But Hickok was now dead, so what was this fellow doing around the Yellow Doll's tent? Niles was still trying to figure that out, trading the Sharps for the Winchester before making his way down the hill to find an answer.

Clay had slipped into the bath tent when Hickok's friend had ducked into the Yellow Doll's, but even in there, he could hear the horrible sounds coming from the other tent. The place was deserted, so he settled down on the buffalo robe-covered step next to the bathtub to wait out whatever was happening. The horrid noise soon ceased. He waited a bit longer and finally chanced a peek outside. Assured that no one was around, he stepped out, making his way rifle first toward the other tent. With the barrel of the rifle, he moved the flap aside and slowly entered. He had all that he could do to not vomit right then and there when he saw the body parts strewn about the far end of the tent, but he managed to gag away the sick feeling, and he snatched up the first thing he saw—a silk purse. A quick look inside revealed a treasure of gold dust, nuggets, and coins, so he tucked it inside his shirt and made a quick exit. Once outside, he took a deep breath, trying to settle his stomach.

"Where you going in such a hurry?"

The question had come from behind him. Clay spun around, greeted by the barrel of a .44 aimed right at his head. "Well, well, well, if it ain't Blondie. And it be none of your business where I'm going."

"I think this pistol aimed at that empty head of yours sure enough makes it my business," Sarah told him.

"Don't kill him, Miss Sarah!" George hollered, coming around the side of the tent. He carried the pistol she had bought for him back at Fort Pierre. As soon as Clay saw the Negro, his revenge ignored his current situation. He spun around, aiming the rifle toward George. The sound of the gunshot and the hole under Clay's left eye seemed to happen in the same instant. Clay stood motionless for a moment as if nothing had happened, but then blood began running down his cheek and down the front of his shirt. More blood trickled from the corners of his mouth. He tried to take a step toward George, but his eyes drifted upward, his knees buckled, and he collapsed, falling onto the ground at Sarah's feet. She kept her pistol aimed at his head, waiting for any movement inviting a second shot.

George stood motionless, mouth gaping open, his eyes as big as they could get. Finally, he found his voice. "I ain't never seen a lady shoot a man b'fore," he kind of whispered. "Lord Almighty, I ain't seen nobody ever shoot nobody. Lord, I hope I never sees it again," he prayed.

"Amen, amen," Sarah whispered. She reached down and tugged at the corner of the purse sticking out of Clay's shirt. "He didn't get far with this."

"What is it, Miss Sarah?"

She looked inside and pulled out Long Ears's gold nugget watch chain, letting it dangle over the dead body and twirling it around so that the nuggets' shine reflected the late afternoon sun. She walked over to George, took hold of his empty hand, and piled the chain in his palm. "Got yourself some Black Hills gold, Mr. Monroe. Spend it wisely. It may just be your ticket out of here while you're still alive."

The gunshot sent Niles racing the last twenty yards or so down the hill toward the Backdoor. He ran around the corner of the Yellow Doll's tent out of breath, a pistol drawn in one hand and the other clutching the Winchester.

"Rubee?" he asked. Neither Sarah nor George answered.

Late that night, on the banks of Whitewood Creek just east of Deadwood, Niles stood vigil over a bonfire that painted the canyon walls with its dancing light. Sparks floated into the sky as if they were giving birth to hundreds of new stars. Rubee would have enjoyed the blazing spectacle, sitting beside him watching the life and death of the fire. But Niles sat alone. Come the first hint of gray morning, the fire was little more than a mound of smoldering embers.

Rubee was gone.

Only the embers remained, their lingering glow only a temporary mask before their eternal cold.

The Yellow Doll was a memory best left for eternity in the Black Hills of Dakota.

Niles finally rose from the spot where he had been planted all night and began the walk back. Death was still stalking Deadwood Gulch. He could feel it in his heart.

Chapter 15

August 3, 1876

Niles took a last look around their camp, seeing nothing that he would miss leaving behind. The camera cases were loaded on one of the mules, the only one he was leading out of the gulch. Sarah had commandeered one of the other ones when she had left the camp, moving down to Kit's, and he had given the two remaining mules to George. Eleanor and the boy could divide up everything else.

"You ain't comin' back, is ya, Mr. Dewy?"

"No, George. I have one more picture to make in Deadwood. After that, I'm gone. Like I was never here."

"Thanks, Mr. Dewy," George said, offering his hand. "For everything." Niles leaned over the saddle horn and took hold of the strong, black hand, holding on as tightly as he could for the longest time.

"You're an honest man, George Joshua Monroe," he finally said with a nod of approval. "Proud I know you."

"I'll always remember you and—"

"Get that out of your head right now," Niles snapped, letting go of the hand. "We were never here. Never," he said, letting his eyes wander down to the creek bank to where strands of smoke still lingered over the bonfire ashes. "We just died here, that's all. No more secret roads. They all come to an end right here in this dead-end gulch. That's all you know, George. Deal with it." Niles jabbed the mare's sides with the heels of his boots, yanked on the pack mule's lead rope, and followed the trail they had worn down the hillside toward the Backdoor. He twisted around in the saddle a couple of times, each time finding George still watching his departure, waving his hat slowly over his head. Niles felt a sad lump rise in his throat.

Eleanor bounced around the Backdoor, busying herself to cover her unease. "I ain't got time for no long good-byes. Only time for makin' money. Y'all have set Madam Mustache up quite handsome, and if you ever find yourself in some two-bit gold camp again, be sure and stop by, and Madam'll give ya a free shave and a bath. You ain't going to hear that comin' from me very often, picture man."

"Fresh water?" Niles asked, half joking. He knew that if he made it out of Deadwood alive, he would never collect on her offer.

Eleanor stroked the hair on her upper lip, not sure. Finally, she told him, "Everybody pays extra for fresh water and my special back scrub. Yes, sir, every dirty soul pays extra for that! Seeing you've been such a good friend, though, I won't charge you for the fresh water. Towel will cost ya extra." She moved up closer to him, planting her stubby hands on her hips and looking up at him. "One thing you can always count on, picture man ... Eleanor Dumont'll bury you free, no charge."

"Not to worry, Miss Eleanor. You won't lose any money burying Niles Dewy. He'll bury himself ... far sooner than you might expect."

She looked up at him kind of cock-eyed. "What the heck you talking about? You can't go off buryin' yourself. If folks did that, Madam would be out of the buryin' business. Hells bells, mister, diggin' a grave ... diggin' for gold—both makes ya rich. Yesterday was a slow-killin' day for Deadwood, and I still buried two dearly departed souls."

The McClintock Kid had visited Niles's camp just after sunup that morning, delivering a message from the Utters saying that they wanted to have their picture made at Hickok's fresh grave. The kid did not say it, but Niles was pretty sure that they were figuring on this being the last photograph Niles made in Deadwood—or anywhere else, for that matter. Niles always looked forward to every new photograph, and this one was proving no different. The Yellow Doll's assassin, the end of Hickok's road, and the end of Niles Dewy—this was a picture of the end ... the end of all those many secret roads.

The Utters were waiting for Niles on the narrow plateau just above the south end of Main Street, a place Eleanor Dumont had named Ingleside since she had started burying Deadwood's unlucky souls there after the spring thaw. As he followed the trail up the hillside, Niles could plainly see the two fresh graves that Eleanor and George had placed there yesterday. One dirt-and-rock-covered mound was the final resting place for the Illinois sheriff, and the other—the one being watched over by the Utters—was Hickok's. A newly painted marker stuck out of the ground at the head of Hickok's grave. There was no cover to speak of for him to hide behind once the shooting began. The only ally Niles would have would be the sun, which would be shining right into the Utters' eyes when he made the photograph.

When he was close enough to hear, Bill's friend Charlie pointed at the grave marker. "Had it painted up last night," he explained. Niles did not say anything; he simply dismounted and walked over to the grave, took his hat off, and just stood there looking over Hickok's eternal home. The marker was a plain pine plank bordered in black paint, and it bore a prayer that Charlie had spoken over the grave the day before.

Pard we will meet again in the happy hunting ground to part no more. Good Bye.

"Fine words," he said, replacing his hat. He turned away from the grave and walked back to the mule. "Let's get this picture set up," he said, loosening the ropes holding the camera cases to the pack frame.

"I guess you knew Bill longer than most?" Charlie asked.

"Made his picture quite a few times. Don't know if that means I knew him."

"Looks like you're an regular walking army, all them guns you're totin'," the younger brother Steve said, shielding his eyes with the back of his hand against the early sunlight breaking over the rim of the gulch. Niles did not even acknowledge the remark; he just kept on working with the ropes and cases. Kitty LeRoy was certain that it had been the long-haired brother, Steve, she had seen standing in the middle of Whitewood Creek yesterday afternoon, blood-tainted water washing downstream from him.

Charlie stepped between his brother and Niles. "Everyone's just a little skittish this morning. All the killing went on here in the last couple of days—"

His words dropped off when he saw Niles's hand move closer to one of the holstered Smith & Wesson's. "We got nothing with you, picture man. We just want to make this picture and be done with each other. Deal?"

"Deal." Niles had little to say; he just wanted the photograph etching the brothers and Hickok's grave into the fabric of Deadwood's history over with, and talking only wasted time. They would be done with him, no doubt, as soon as the picture was taken. "I'll set up over there." He pointed to the right of the grave. "You two situate yourselves up there." He directed them to the head of the grave.

While the brothers did some last-minute grooming to themselves and the grave mound, Niles set the developing box up and selected a glass plate. Like a blind man feeling his way, he prepared the glass inside the black box. When it was ready, he hollered, "Set yourselves!" He pulled the plate out of the box, turned to the camera, and quickly slid it into the back of the camera, ducking under the hood and pulling off the lens cap. Charlie stood to the right of the marker and held his hat over the top of the board, his rifle resting on the edge of the grave. Brother Steve was kneeling on the other side of the grave, sitting on his heels. His body seemed taut like a mountain lion about to spring. Both men's eyes were lowered as if in prayer. *A nice touch for the picture,* Niles thought to himself. It was a practice that he doubted had ever been comfortable to either fellow.

"One … two … three … four …"

He knew that he had until the count of thirty and then the few minutes his hands were locked inside the black box developing the plate before they would make a move against him. "Thirty. You can breathe now!" he hollered at the men. He pulled the glass free and returned to the box sitting on the ground just a few feet away from the camera's tripod. He unlatched the top, quickly put in the plate, closed the lid, and then fit his hands into the box's pair of gloves to coat the exposed glass. The magic of photography was protecting Niles Dewy as long as it could. He was sure that as soon as he pulled a hand out of the box, the brothers would start shooting.

The men watched in silence as Niles wiggled around on his haunches, getting himself set. In doing so, he had moved the box enough so that it sat on the ground between him and the brothers. Niles aimed the Remington two-shot pocket pistol hidden inside the box in the direction of the Yellow Doll's killer.

The aim was blind, but Niles was confident that the pistol's barrel and right arm were in a direct line with the middle of Steve's chest. Every muscle in his body was governing his movements, reaching for the Smith & Wesson with his left hand while his right killed. His ears went pin-drop silent, and his eyes only saw the middle of the man's breast where the Remington's bullets would hit. There was no face, and there were no arms or legs. He seemed to look at the scene through the camera in his mind's eye. He saw Niles Dewy poised over the developing box moments before he would kill Rubee's murderer. It was a picture that would be frozen in his mind like an autumn leaf trapped in winter ice.

His finger measured the pressure against the trigger.

Now!

The box, masking the two quick shots, muffled the revolver's pop. Steve was immediately pushed backward like he had been hit by a boxer's one-two punch. He flipped headfirst over a wooden railing around the grave behind Hickok's, landing facedown on top of the stone-covered mound of dirt.

Charlie's confusion lasted long enough for Niles to free his left hand and draw the pistol. Charlie quickly came to his senses, but when he turned back to Niles, he was confronted by his pistol's aim. "Got no argument with you, Charlie," Niles told him. Charlie hesitated. Niles could see that he was figuring his chances to draw against him.

"Don't even think it, mister. We got you coming and going."

Niles let his eyes move just briefly off Charlie, long enough to look where the voice had come from. Just below the slope of the graveyard, he saw Sarah. She held her pistol with both hands and leveled it at Charlie's back.

Charlie raced his eyes from Niles to Sarah and then back to Niles. Slowly, he raised his hands above his head, took a look at his brother sprawled on the neighboring grave, and took his first step backward, withdrawing from the scene. "Smart man, Charlie Utter ... probably why Hickok befriended you," Sarah told him as her aim followed him down the hillside.

Niles had not shifted his aim, but since Charlie had moved out of the line of fire, he was pointing the Smith & Wesson right at Sarah. She slowly moved her pistol from the direction of Charlie's departure back at Niles. For a moment, Rubee's question echoed in his head. "Will you kill her?" He still did not know the answer. They remained like that, their guns trained on the other, until Niles broke the standoff, raising the barrel of his revolver skyward and gently releasing the hammer back to safety.

Stillness had settled over the cemetery and seeped into Niles's very soul. He heard Whitewood Creek gushing down the bottom of the gulch and the wind's hollow whistling through the pines. Somewhere, a hammer landed blows; an ax was attacking another ponderosa. But the still of the place itched at his very insides, and he suspected that it would not go away until he was out of these Black Hills. Sarah finally lowered her aim, and without a word, she turned and walked down the hillside. Niles lost sight of her, but he heard her horse kicking stones and breaking deadfall as they made their way down the mountainside.

Niles ignored the deadly scene as he packed up the camera gear. One last stop before leaving Deadwood Gulch.

The clock already erected on Deadwood's main street reported that it was just before noon when Niles rode up the middle of the roadway, leading the mule through the jam of animals, people, wagons, and confusion. No one seemed to pay any more attention to him than they did the hawks circling above the canyon. He reined his mare aside to move around a wagonload of rocks only to have to wait for an ox train to roll past. Finally, he kneed her toward the front of the Emperor's Meat Market, waiting there while he scouted up and down the street, making sure that he had not missed somebody more interested in Long Ears's well-being than his own. On the corner, about fifty yards up the street, a crowd had gathered around a fellow ringing a bell in one hand and a book in the other. "Preacher man," Niles whispered to the horse as he carefully dismounted. He wrapped the reins around a post supporting a porch roof over the front of the shop. After one more look up and down Main Street, he walked through open door of the shop, leaving it open behind him and allowing the ringing of the preacher's bell to follow him inside.

Clang!
Clang!

The shop was empty as Niles slowly walked toward the back counter, his attention focused on the market's back door. The sound of Niles's boots against the plank flooring brought Long Ears's into the room, ducking to clear his head under the frame of the low doorway.

Clang!
Clang!

Niles lifted his right hand, reached across his chest, and pulled the Colt out of its shoulder holster. Before either of them could take another breath, the revolver was aimed at Long Ears's head, freezing the smile he was wearing.

"Be just and justify the sinner that believeth ..."

The preacher's soapbox sermon drifted into the store between each ringing of his bell.

Clang!
Clang!

"I see men before me in a state of spiritual death ..."

Clang!

The bell seemed to tick away time that had frozen inside the market.

"I see mankind ruined by sin and depravity ..."

Clang!

The Colt's trigger pressed against his finger's pressure.

Clang!

The Colt's shot was covered by the bell's sharp chime.

Clang!

"Regain the favor of God, the Almighty Savior ..."

Clang!

As the Chinaman slumped, sunlight streamed into the dimly lit room through the roof planks that Niles's bullet had splintered after exiting through the top of Long Ears's head.

Clang!

Clang!

"God's law comes in fire ..."

Clang!

Clang!

The bell seemed to move closer as if the preacher were parading his soul saving down Main Street toward the meat market. Niles lowered his eyes from the crack of blue sky peeking through the splintered boards to find Sarah standing in the back doorway again, holding her pistol in two hands and again aiming at Niles. For the second time that morning, he let his pistol drop to his side. He turned and walked out of the shop.

Outside, in front of the Emperor's Meat Market, everything had suddenly gotten very quiet. No bell ringing. No preaching. Everyone who had suspected that they might have heard a gunshot gawked curiously up and down the street, trying to catch a glimpse of the confrontation, but all they found was Niles loosening the mare's reins before he pulled himself up into the saddle.

The momentary lull on the street was an open invitation for the preacher, who moved his sermon down the street in search of more converts.

Clang!
Clang!
"The soul that sins shall die! That's our Lord's glorious justice."
Clang!
The preacher now had Niles in his religious sights. "Go ye into the world."
Clang!
Clang!
"Justice demands the blood of the sinner ..."
Clang!
The preacher then saw Sarah walk out of the butcher shop, and he renewed his bell ringing with greater vigor. "Mother of Jesus, save your soul sister. Leave sin behind."
Clang!
Clang!
Clang!
"Shame! Shame on you, sinner!"
Clang!
Clang!
Clang!
"The bells of heaven ring. They toll for your poor souls."
Clang!
Sarah calmly stood her ground in front of the meat shop, watching the preacher move even closer to her.

Finally, she pushed her pistol into her pants pocket, and as she walked by him, she looked him square in the eyes. "Gold is God in Deadwood, preacher man, and blood is its only forgiveness," she said before moving on.

Sarah caught up with Niles just on the other side of the Crook City mining camp, following the Cheyenne Crossing trail out of the canyon. The powder-blue sky had yielded to low-hanging gray clouds that rested on the very tops of the ridgeline, and before long, they were riding in a steady drizzle that stayed with them the rest of the afternoon. The fog of the steady mist painted the pine forest even darker than normal, turning the canyon into a black gorge, a place and time that Niles was anxious to put behind him.

At Cheyenne Crossing over Spearfish Creek, they continued south, following the winding stream through the canyon. Going through the canyon in the misty fog was like traveling in a giant cemetery, the towering tombstones of granite and limestone disappearing in the low clouds above them. The ponderosas were thick along the water's narrow shore, their branches bent low from the weight of wet moss that hung like gnarled and snagged strands of hair, causing downpours to cascade on the riders whenever they rode too close. Well after nightfall, when it was too hard to guide the horses any farther along the treacherous trail, they finally made it to Cold Springs Creek on the downside of the Black Hills western slope. There, they spent a miserable, wet, fireless night. Not only was it a wet, cold, and hungry camp, it was dead silent; neither Sarah nor Niles were in much of a talking mood. It was just too hard for either of them to start up a conversation; there was little to say. It was not only the weather; five killings in two days had taken the talk right out of them.

At first gray light, they started out again. The rain had stopped, but the low fog still rested along the tops of the ridgelines. But by the time they were on the Wyoming Flats, on the west side of the Black Hills, the sky had widened, white towering clouds dancing a slow waltz from horizon to horizon.

Maybe it was the break in the overcast, but Niles decided that it was time. He reined the mare around in a tight circle and came to a stop right in front of Sarah. "Are you the law?" he asked, hoping that the answer would be as forthright as the question. She remained silent, staring over the prairie. "There is no congressman father, is there? And I suppose Sarah Culbert—"

"A stage name," she interrupted. "I knew everything I needed to know about you before we left Washington—before we had even left the British embassy. I knew everything except where you were going."

"And what were you supposed to do with all this knowledge?"

"As the law … one smuggler is dead, Long Ears is dead, you've lost your ill-gotten gains, you've lost most of your contraband, and all there is left to do is either arrest you …" she looked at him long and hard. Finally, she added, "Or kill you, Mr. Dewy." She then spun her horse around and trotted off as if she were purposefully exposing her back to him as a challenge to decide if her story were true or false.

Niles's mare shied away from the departing horse and rider and spun around several times, but when Niles had control again, he rode off after Sarah. When he was close enough, he shouted, "I probably don't want to know the answer to this question, but at this point, I don't think it will make any difference! Was part of your assignment to seduce me?"

Sarah pulled back on the reins, allowing Niles to catch up to her. "Spending the night with you on your parlor sofa was just part of my job … undercover work, I guess you might call it. Think about it, Mr. Dewy." She waited as her smile grew. "Become a smuggler's girlfriend … what better way to find out about your illegal enterprise?"

"Hired killer … hooker … the law, that's a deadly combination."

"A profitable one in our nation's capital," she told him, showing off her big grin again.

"I'm sure you find all sorts of ways to make a profit wherever you happen to land."

"Oh, let's just say I can make a living most anywhere, Mr. Dewy."

Niles turned his horse away from her, saying, "How about Wyoming Territory?"

They rode in silence for about a quarter of a mile when Niles decided to pry a little further. "If you are supposed to kill me in the name of justice, why am I still alive? Did you get religion? Or did you figure that I wasn't worth it? Or, heaven forbid, might you feel bad if I weren't around? Hell, woman, maybe the weather didn't suit you. How do I know?"

Sarah twisted around in the saddle. "It's too nice a day to kill you, Mr. Dewy," she told him, her smile still firmly in place. She slowed down, waiting for Niles to catch up. "Got a proposition for you. How about a deal, Mr. Dewy?"

"A deal made in heaven or hell?"

"An agreement of sorts, just between the two of us—Sarah Culbert and Niles Dewy," she said, pointing a finger at herself and then at him.

"Now there's a deal between a couple of nobodies," Niles joked.

"I'm not joking. Just hear me out. Rubee is gone, right? So no one will ever know, or care, if you are alive or dead. Right?"

"Not even you?"

Sarah gave him a frustrated look. "Now hear me out. As far as the law is concerned, you don't see a jailhouse around here, do you?"

"Not until we get to Fort Laramie; that's probably the closest."

She ignored his information. "All we have to do is come to an understanding."

"A crooked lawman's kind of understanding? A whore's? Or the understanding of a murderer? Which kind of understanding did you have in mind?"

"Our understanding!"

"And that would be?"

"All we have to do is not kill each other."

"That's all!"

"My deal is your life."

"Doesn't that make our little deal a deal for your life, too?"

"It does. But you won't kill a woman. Not this woman."

"What makes you so sure about Niles Dewy?"

"I didn't say Niles Dewy would never kill a woman. I said you would never kill *this* woman."

Niles rode alongside her for a ways. "Why do you say that?"

Sarah slowed, reining her horse to a stop. "Because I am a woman, that's why … a woman who happens to know something about the heart of a certain man. Regardless of what name he goes by, the heart remains the same. And I think I know what is in that heart of yours. I didn't fail to notice there was some reason you haven't killed me before now. Lord knows you have had plenty of opportunities. But you didn't. And you know why you didn't?"

Niles just shook his head.

"Leave it up to a thick-headed man not to have a clue. Because you care, you nitwit! You ended up caring for me."

Again, Niles remained silent, studying the distant horizon instead of looking at her.

"And because of that, I'll throw in a bonus …"

Niles turned to her, half expecting a seductive offer.

"No, not that. You can just forget that," she told him, recognizing the look on his face.

"So what's this big bonus?"

"Go anywhere you want. You and your camera equipment." She waved an arm toward the pack mule he was leading. "That's your Black Hills gold. Go anywhere you want with it and make as many pictures as you want when you get there. You'll be surprised how quickly this whole Deadwood business is forgotten."

"And Niles Dewy along with it."

She nodded in agreement. "Niles Dewy died in Deadwood, along with the Yellow Doll. Both will soon be forgotten. Bill Hickok will be remembered as a pitiful opium addict driven to the crooked side of the law, finally getting himself killed in Deadwood's opium war. Opium has a way of leaving death in its wake. The Yellow Doll, Long Ears, Hickok, Steve Utter—all casualties of a war. A war over drugs. All of it will long be forgotten like the last puff of smoke from the Yellow Doll's opium pipe. Poof—gone!"

Niles rested his arms across the saddle horn, still studying the far-off horizon.

"Or should we keep fighting Deadwood's opium war? We're the only ones left standing. You know it as well as I do. Deadwood's a hellhole now and always will be, probably. It ain't worth dying over. Get yourself a brand-new you, Mr. Dewy."

He was listening, but Niles Dewy was looking for a photograph.

The sun was still low enough to light a shelf of white chalk cliffs paralleling the western edge of the Cheyenne-Deadwood Trail. The lonely monoliths were long, wide slabs of stone layered one on top of the other with the precision of a master stonemason. The sunlight carved shadows into the cracks between them like it was some kind of mortar fixing them in place. Dark forests of cedar, juniper, and spruce surrounded the base of the bluffs and really did nothing more than remind Niles of just how barren eastern Wyoming Territory really was.

"Okay," Niles finally told her.

"You agree, then?"

"I agree. Let's do it."

Sarah watched him for a brief moment, searching the country surrounding them, and she made her decision. "All right. Then this is where we part company. I guess this looks like as good a place as any to get yourself lost in."

Niles followed her search, but his eyes finally settled on her. They looked at each other for some time, unable to find any appropriate words to say. Finally, Niles broke off his stare and dismounted. "You go on. I'm going to make a picture. Go on, get out of here! And stay out of my camera sights."

Sarah did not hesitate. She nudged her horse forward and started following the vague trail to the south toward Mule Creek somewhere over the horizon. Not more than twenty yards down the trail, she pulled up and turned the horse so that she could see Niles. "I latched onto you, and I have to say that you gave this lady one hell of a ride to the end of the road. A lady shouldn't expect more than that. For that, I thank you, Mr. Niles Dewy. I thank you." She reined the horse back down the trail but turned in the saddle to watch Niles. "I'll never forget you," she told him, and then she tipped the brim of her hat in his direction, turned, and rode off, leaving Niles standing by the side of the pack mule.

"And I'll never forget you, Miss Sarah," he said to himself. He lifted his own hat high into the air and waved it back and forth at her, but she never turned around to see his last gesture.

It did not take him long to get his camera set up and the developing box ready. He had kept an eye on her progress the whole time, waiting for her to reach a rise on the prairie's horizon where she would be a lone silhouette against the vast, empty sky. When she neared the spot he had selected, he prepared the plate, pushed it into place in the back of the Anthony, and waited. She was there. The chalk cliffs were the photo's right border, and the prairie spilled off the left edge of the frame. The sky was empty. The prairie was empty. And right in the middle of all that nothing was Sarah.

He removed the leather lens cap. "One … two … three … four … five … six …"

Niles almost lost track of his count as he stared off toward the horizon where Sarah was riding. He caught himself just in time. "Twenty-seven … twenty-eight … twenty-nine … thirty."

He pulled the plate out of the camera, carried it over to the developing box, and locked it inside. Using the gloves, he applied the dry gel to secure the image. He left it in the box, walked over to the horse, and pulled the Sharps rifle out of the saddle scabbard. He raised the scope to his eye and found Sarah, bringing her back to him as if she were only a few feet away from his eye. She had halted her horse and turned her head as if she knew that he was watching her. He could see her smile and a slight nod of her head, and suddenly, she was gone. She had moved her horse over the edge of the horizon and was no longer in the Sharps's scope. Niles lowered the rifle, staring at the empty horizon for some time. Then returned the Sharps to its scabbard.

THE END

Thank you my reader, my friend.

Epilogue

The juice of the poppy seed, for centuries cultivated in the "raja poppy" states of India, was bought at auction from the opium warehouses in Bombay, India, once a year, three to six weeks after the harvest and processing. A chest of top-grade Patna, a 70 percent pure opium, sold for anywhere from $500 to $700 a chest, each chest containing 140 pounds of the narcotic resin rolled into forty three-and-a-half-pound balls. Auction house receipts, meticulously recorded and cataloged, set the average price in the mid-1870s at about $4.90 a pound in Bombay. The same pound in an American opium den, parceled out a few grains at a time, could fetch as much as $3,000. Smuggling of the drug into the United States in the nineteenth century was done by ship, concealed in clothing, shipping crates, food, or any other type of merchandise that could mask the clandestine cargo. United States Customs' records indicate frequent confiscations of the drug both on the West Coast, mainly in San Francisco, and on the East Coast, most frequently in the port at Bladensburg, Maryland, just outside the federal district of Washington. Once across America's coastline, the drug secretly traveled far and wide, its presence documented over and over in mining camps, boomtowns, railheads, construction camps, veterans' hospitals, brothels, and even in civilized society. There is no lack of evidence that those caught smuggling the drug were dealt with swiftly and often severely, both by the legal authorities and by vigilante "good citizen committees," never weak in their efforts to stamp out the dreaded "China smoke." Such groups ran the dens out of town, burning them out when they had to, and, if that did not work, they humiliated the operators in public. In the worst of situations, they resorted to murder and lynching to clean out their town's undesirables. The narcotic was usually sold to its addicts for fifty cents a pipe, never more than one to three grains of the sticky resin at a time, valuing an ounce of opium, depending on the scruples of the smuggler, from $80 to $240—as much as an 80 percent profit over the price paid half a world away in India and a far cry from the $18 an ounce for gold in Deadwood Gulch in the summer of 1876.

There are still tunnels under Deadwood's main street, where the smoking dens were concealed for many years. Some are six feet wide and seven feet high, the longest running parallel up to the corner of Lee Street. Tourists now wander these dark, wet caverns, often posing for a photograph lying on one of the wooden bunk beds or pallets once used by Deadwood's pipe dreamers. Less than six years after the murders of Bill Hickok, Steve Utter, the Yellow Doll, Texas Jack, Long Ears, and William Clay in what some storytellers of the time referred to as Deadwood's opium war, an editorial headlined Poppy Smoking in the *Black Hills Pioneer* on February 11, 1882, indicated that the practice was still quite active in the gulch.

> The attention of city authorities is called to the opium joints now being conducted wide open in that portion of the city known as the "badlands." Where white people, and black ones too, hit the pipes as often as they can raise 50 cents ... where can be seen at almost anytime of the day or night, forms of men and women stretched out perfectly unconscious of their surroundings, reveling in the pleasant dreams that the devilish narcotic brings them for a brief one hour.

As recently as the 1960s, agents of the South Dakota Office of the Attorney General and officers of the South Dakota State Police made several arrests in Galena, an old mining camp outside of Deadwood, for possession of opium and for operating an ongoing illegal enterprise—an opium den.

Miss Kitty "Chicken Lady" LeRoy became the proprietress of the Mint, a saloon and brothel on Deadwood's main street. In one of the rooms above the bar in 1879, she was killed in a gunfight with Dave Curry, her fifth husband, who then turned the pistol on himself, committing suicide. She was twenty-eight years old.

Sarah Culbert's pony and mule wandered into Wyoming's Fort Laramie on the Platte River on the sixth of August with no rider and with the saddle and packs twisted. After a lengthy search conducted by the US Cavalry, no trace of the woman was ever found.

John S. McClintock, "the McClintock Kid," was a veteran of many of the early 1870s Montana gold camps. He came to Deadwood in the spring of 1876, arriving shortly before Bill Hickok and the Utter brothers. He lived in Deadwood well into his nineties, having operated a successful stagecoach line between Deadwood and Spearfish for thirty years and having gathered many real estate holdings in Deadwood, including the present-day Franklin Hotel. In the 1930s, he wrote his memoir recording many of the events that took place in Deadwood Gulch during the days of 1876.

Joshua "George" Monroe turned the two mules left to him by Niles Dewy into a prosperous stable and corral located in the Badlands of Deadwood's main street, collecting a handsome pinch of gold dust from customers frequenting the nearby gambling parlors, saloons, and brothels. In 1880, he made a trip back to the federal city on the Potomac River on word of his momma's passing, returning to Deadwood several months later with a bride. They raised a family of two sons, Niles and Bill, and one daughter, Ruby, in Deadwood. He retired from his blacksmith business in 1911, dying from natural causes two years later. His body was returned to Washington DC by his family and laid to rest through eternity next to his momma.

Eleanor "Madam Mustache" Dumont operated the Backdoor Bathhouse through the fall of 1876. Word on Main Street at the time was that she was also operating an opium-smoking parlor, but no evidence of such has ever been uncovered. Come the spring of 1877, she was keeper of the faro bank at Jim Persate's Wide West Saloon. Later in 1877, she up and left Deadwood without a word and bounced her way back to Nevada, setting herself up in a bawdy house in the mining camp of Eureka. In 1879, a brief dispatch found in the *Sacramento Union* reported: "A woman named Eleanor Dumont was found dead today about one mile out of town, having committed suicide."

After his capture in Long Ears's butcher shop, Jack "the Runt" McCall, a.k.a. John Sutherland, was brought to justice before a miner's court that convened in Deadwood the following morning. The jury acquitted him. "A man's moral right to take … a life for a life," said the jury's foreman, Charles Whitehead, when he read the verdict, clearly accepting defense attorney Judge Joseph Miller's argument that Hickok had been killed in revenge for the murder of McCall's brother in Kansas several years prior. Proof of such an accusation has never been uncovered, and there are no public records identifying such a sibling. A free man five or six days after Hickok's murder, the runt left Deadwood and was finally arrested in the Wyoming Territory by federal authorities, who took him to Yankton in Dakota Territory. A new trial convicted him for the murder of James Butler Hickok, and he hanged for the crime on March 1, 1877, identifying himself to the executioner as "Crooked Nose."

Bosh Brodovich's body and burned-out wagons were discovered in the summer of 1877, east of Peno Springs on the Dakota prairie, the apparent victim of an Indian attack. The big Slovenian's team of twenty oxen was never found.

Texas Jack Omohundro was killed in Deadwood Gulch near Central City two days after Bill Hickok's murder, apparently the result of an argument over the ownership of a severed Indian head. Reports at the time said that the body of a Mexican called Tex, along with the Indian head, were burned in a bonfire later the same day "to snuff out the foul stench of death."

The Yellow Doll was in Deadwood Gulch during the summer of 1876. Several eyewitness accounts pay tribute to her beauty and generosity. Her involvement in an opium-smoking den has never been corroborated, and her role in the capture of Jack McCall is, at best, clouded by the legends and myth surrounding the murder of Wild Bill Hickok on August 2, 1876. The Yellow Doll did meet a gruesome end, hacked to death with a hatchet within days of Hickok's assassination. No one was ever brought to justice for her killing, and there was never a grave found marking her final destination. But the memory of her brief appearance in Deadwood's history is honored every year when the city's Days of '76 celebration's annual parade is led by the Yellow Doll, a Chinese-costumed local young lady reigning along Main Street from the seat of her rickshaw.

Charlie Utter operated a stage and freighting business in Deadwood Gulch, eventually leaving the area and moving to Central America, where it was reported that he passed himself off as a medical doctor, often prescribing coca and opium to his patients. His date of death and place of burial is unknown.

James Butler "Wild Bill" Hickok was born in Homer, Illinois, later changed to Oak Grove. In March 1876, he married Agnes Thatcher in Cheyenne, Wyoming, after a more than four-year courtship. Later that spring, Hickok was thrown out of Cheyenne by the authorities for vagrancy and intoxication as a public nuisance. He arrived in Deadwood Gulch on a wagon train organized by Charlie and Steve Utter in late June 1876. He was murdered in Nuttal & Mann's Saloon, located on the tenth mining claim from first gold in Deadwood's Badlands on the afternoon of August 2, 1876, while he was playing poker with Charlie Rich, Carl Mann, and Captain William Massey.

The "dead man's hand" he was holding at the time of his death was a pair of black aces, a pair of black eights, and the nine of diamonds. He was buried the next day wearing a pair of Smith & Wesson pistols and a Sharps rifle at his side by Eleanor Dumont and Joshua Monroe in Ingleside Cemetery. The original hand-painted, wooden grave marker was supplied by Charlie and Steve Utter. In 1879, his remains were moved to Deadwood's Mount Moriah Cemetery. Hickok claimed that he had killed thirty-nine men, the last being his deputy in an Abilene, Kansas, gun battle in October 1871. He was thirty-nine years old when he was assassinated.

In 1871, one of the two photographers on Dr. Ferdinand Hayden's survey expedition to the Yellowstone Country in the Wyoming Territory vanished. According to the Hayden Survey recording, he was from Baltimore, Maryland, and had been an apprentice to Mathew Brady after the war. That is all. When the old Grand Pacific Hotel in Bismarck, North Dakota, was going through renovations during 1970s, one of the hotel's eighth-floor suites was opened to discover that it had been the home, apparently for quite some time, of a photographer, judging from the collection of pictures and old exposed, glass-wet plates found cluttering the suite's rooms. They were photos of early Bismarck and Fort Abraham Lincoln in its declining years, as well as hundreds of landscapes depicting the Missouri River breaks and sandbars, ancient Indian mounds, and the vast grasslands still untouched by steel plow or overgrazing of the upper Great Plains. Also discovered among the room's possessions was an 1870s-model Anthony View camera and finely crafted, polished wooden cases to carry it, as well as all of the other photographic equipment needed to make picture a century earlier. Found in one beat-up tin box were fifteen exposed glass plates and a neatly folded piece of stationary with the words *"Deadwood, '76"* written on it. The last glass in the box was the image of a lone horse and rider, which looked like they were swimming in a vast sea of prairie grass with the only shoreline being a stack of white cliffs seen along the right border of the photo. Other than the folded paper, the only identification found in the dusty suite of rooms was a solitary gentleman's calling card that read D. C. SMITH, and, below the name, the word *Photographer*.

Henry Weston "Preacher" Smith, Deadwood's first churchman, followed his faith to the Black Hills in March 1876 from Cheyenne in Wyoming Territory. On Sunday morning, August 20, 1876, he tacked a note to his cabin door: "Gone to Crook City, back at 2 P.M." Later that day, his body was discovered along the Crook City trail, supposedly the victim of Indians, but there were no reports of Indians in the vicinity of Deadwood Gulch that Sunday, and the body was not scalped, the usual Sioux practice during the summer of 1876. This created speculation that a white man may have committed the crime. Eleanor Dumont and Joshua "George" Monroe arranged a Christian burial, with the graveside service conducted by Mr. C. E. Hawley and attended by dozens of miners and prospectors from up and down the canyon who were familiar with the preacher's Main Street sermons. But that did not save him from the overcrowding in the gulch's first graveyard, having to share his final resting place—a plot located not far from Bill Hickok's—with a fellow by the name of Charles Mason, another unfortunate killed the same day in Whitewood Valley. The death of the forty-nine-year-old preacher orphaned three children and widowed Lydia Ann Smith, who returned the family to her home in Worcester, Massachusetts, in 1885. While preparing the body for burial, E. T. "Doc" Pierce discovered a scrap of paper in the pocket of preacher's coat. On the paper scrap was scribbled the verse of a poem he was writing to his wife:

And when I sit on Zion's hill,
No more in need of gold.
And sing with those who love me still
The songs that ne'er grow old,

Perhaps I'll look on this sad eve,
Beneath this stormy sky,
And think that this was long ago,
And wonder was it I?

CPSIA information can be obtained
at www.ICGtesting.com
Printed in the USA
FFOW02n2042011215
19156FF